ECHO ONE

PRAISE FOR MERCEDES LACKEY

"*The project feels like a throwback to the glorious days of Stan Lee and Jack Kirby, when creativity was king, and having inspired ideas was more important than how famous you were.*"

—SF Site Nathan Brazil

"*[C]omes together seamlessly ... an awesome and lightning-paced story: read it on a day when you will not have to put it down.*"

—San Francisco Book Review

"*With [Mercedes Lackey], suspense never lags ...*"

—Kliatt

ECHO ONE

Stories from the Secret World Chronicles

MERCEDES LACKEY   **CODY MARTIN**   **DENNIS K. LEE**
VERONICA GIGUERE

WFP
WORDFIRE PRESS

Cover design by Larry Dixon and Janet McDonald
Cover artwork images by Larry Dixon
Kevin J. Anderson, Art Director

Published by
WordFire Press, LLC
PO Box 1840
Monument CO 80132
Kevin J. Anderson & Rebecca Moesta, Publishers

Printed in the USA
Join our WordFire Press Readers Group for
sneak previews, updates, new projects, and giveaways.
Sign up at wordfirepress.com

CONTENTS

PREFACE

The "Secret World Chronicles" is a five book superhero series. It's set in the present day, and begins with an invasion of alien Nazis delivered by express mail trucks ... but if you are reading this anthology you probably already know that.

But we've been doing backstory and bits and pieces of in between things that never made it into the books, on and off for the entire time the series has been in production.

The backstory is that super-powered heroes and villains began appearing during the early years of World War II. And we wrote about a few of them. Here they are. Including the first, never before seen, of what was really going on inside the Secret World in 1935.

RISE

MERCEDES LACKEY

JANUARY 5, 1935

The primitive world known to its inhabitants as "Earth" was exactly what the Masters were looking for. Its technology level was just barely pre-Atomic, and it was ass-deep in a global conflict. Yet it had nothing that could detect even the craft roaming its skies, much less the Masters' World-Ship.

So it settled into the deep waters far off the coast of the "United States," and once it was settled, it unfolded, and when their stealth technology fully deployed, it would literally take bumping into it for any of these creatures to become aware that it was there.

And before any of the "humans" got that close, the Masters would have them. Whatever craft bumbled into their waters would be seized in tractor beams and hauled in to be captured. The radio, if any, would be silenced and they would become subjects of experiment. Said craft would become just another missing mystery of the ocean.

After deployment, a few specimens were taken at random from remote areas of the coast, and a few lunar cycles later, drones deployed to spread the Masters' nanotech mutagen far and wide over the planet. This atomized powder was designed to trigger metapowers in each species the Masters' machines encountered. Humans had been a bit trickier than most—the genetics for metahuman powers involved transposons, the so-called "jumping genes," DNA sequences that moved from one location on the genome to another, and not simple mutations. But the Masters' machines were clever, and with few exceptions, they could almost always find ways to trigger metapowers. They had only failed with their current servant-race, the Klathans— but those had been easy to conquer, and easier still for the legacy printing chambers to copy and program. That had been fortuitous rather than otherwise. Really, they were the best servants the Masters had ever had, all things considered.

The Masters were going to pay a little extra-special attention to the part of the world known as "Germany." That particular country had some interesting attitudes that should make the triggering of metahumans *there* particularly delightful.

With the drones away, all the Masters had to do was deploy viewing equipment and wait for the entertainment to begin. It might take a little longer for metapowers to trigger with this species, but anticipation and uncertainty added to the entertainment value.

SEPTEMBER 9, 1940

Lt. Commander Nigel Patterson of the RAF was having a very bad day.

Then again, everyone in the RAF was having a bad day—and every day had been bad since the beginning of July. The bloody Huns were throwing every damn plane they had at Britain in the hopes of breaking the back of the Allies, and he and his mates were the only thing standing between Old Blighty and Nazi flags over Buckingham Palace.

And it didn't help that besides some of the best planes and pilots Nige had ever seen, the bloody Huns had—Them. "Metahumans," the science-johnnies were calling 'em. Bloody damned supers with superpowers like in the Yank comic books.

Predictably, the Nazis called them "*Übermenschen.*" *Vaterland* and *Hitlerjugend* had been the first, and truth to tell, Nige hadn't been impressed when he'd seen them in the newsreels and winning every Gold Medal in the Berlin Olympics. He'd figured they were some sort of freaks or cheats.

Then the fighting had started. And those two mowed down Frenchies like a couple of Yank harvesters rolling across fields of wheat.

But worse than that, *more* of the blighters started showing up. *Valkyria. Übermensch* himself. The *Panzer*-triplets. And ...

Nigel cursed and put his Spitfire into a diving roll, and avoided being cut down out of the sky by mere inches.

... the Black Baron.

Nige's coveralls clung to him, drenched in sweat; every muscle cried out in protest, as punished as his Spitfire was. The stick shuddered in his hand, and the plane shuddered around him, and he would have sworn he could hear rivets popping. He pulled up out of a suicidal dive, clenching his entire body to keep from blacking out, and did a wingover just as she was about to stall, dropping into another dive.

The Black Baron had inhuman reflexes, bullets literally bounced off him, and he scarcely needed a plane at all, just a frame with an excuse for a skin, a whacking big engine, a couple of wings, and a tail. Oh, and guns. Two of them. And both of them were stitching the sky behind Nige. He pulled up again, this time making a tight right-hand turn, then a left, then another right. Bullets traced the sky in front of him and he dove again.

Almost radio silence in his ears, but he stayed off the frequency. No point in begging for help; help wasn't coming. The Black Baron had Nige in his sights, and the best he could do right now was to try and keep the bastard engaged for as many minutes as he could and allow his squad-mates to try and take some of the Baron's fighter-bombers out of the sky before they could unload their deadly cargoes. If he was lucky—unlikely, but it was possible—he'd be able to bail out before he augered in. And then he'd have to hope the damned Huns didn't shoot him as he dangled helplessly from his 'chute.

He probably should have been making his peace with God.

Instead ... he was in a red rage, his eyes hazing over, and not just with the g-forces he was pushing. *I'd give bloody anything, anything, to take this bastard on one-on—*

And that was when he felt the screaming bullets finally stitch their way across his fuselage. And hit his fuel tank. Fire erupted all around him, although, strangely, he felt nothing yet. But he would. It would be terrible. And flaming red rage was still all he felt, knowing he was about to die.

Except ... he didn't.

The plane exploded, and he was on fire. Literally on fire. In vain he looked to the sky, strained for it, flames all around him, reached for it the way a drowning man reaches for air he'll never breathe again.

But—he wasn't falling....

With a jolt of shock he realized he was *flying!* Still afire, still feeling nothing but, perhaps, a tingling, as if his skin was electrified. Climbing straight up into the sky, out of the flaming, falling wreckage of his plane, himself still on fire like a bloody phoenix! How?

Dunno. Don't care. If this was a dying hallucination, so be it. He was going to enjoy it and act as if it wasn't. There was a Stuka in his path, and he was going to do something about it.

The "something" was to stretch out his body, fists forward, and punch a hole through the right wing, flip in midair like a falcon, and come back down through the left wing. Then for good measure, come back up again and rip the top of the tail clean off.

As that plane heeled over and headed for the ground, he hovered in midair a moment, flames wreathing around him, caught sight of a second, and went for it.

He'd managed to punch his way through every plane in the formation when the Black Baron finished off another of his mates, looked around, and realized what he'd just done. And what he was sharing the sky with.

And the blackguard made a run for it.

Oh, now there's another super-man to tangle with you, you aren't so brave, are you, tosser?

Setting the air on fire with his curses, Nige went after him.

He caught the bastard just above the Dover coast after a tail-chase that had him painting flames across the sky of London. He managed to land on the airframe, and without even thinking, crawled his way hand over hand to the cockpit, his eyes so fogged with red that he barely saw the Baron's terrified face before he punched the man's nose halfway back into his head.

Then he reached down, ripped out the control cables with his bare hands, and stepped off the falling plane, and watched it drop out of the sky and hit the ground at full speed.

Leisurely—but still on fire, he followed it down.

There wasn't much left of it. Just a blackened crater in the earth. And while the Baron survived bullets, it was clear that he hadn't been able to survive that kind of impact.

He looked up at the sky. His mates were tail-chasing the Huns home. And as the fires surrounding him slowly died away, his ability to think beyond the next blow returned.

And it came to him with a sense of wonder and awe what he'd just done. What he'd just *become*.

Guess I'd better pick a name for myself, he thought, as he heard the engines of motorcars racing towards him across the green meadow where he and the Baron's plane had ended up. *Before they pick something for me....*

He looked up again at his mates, disappearing little dots in the clouds.

Spitfire ...

$$\triangle$$

The Masters were exceedingly pleased. Finally, in the presence of death and his metahuman counterpart, the first of the metahumans of the "Allies" had triggered. While it had been amusing to watch the Axis metas trample the air and ground unimpeded for a while, such one-sided combat grew boring quickly.

Now things were going to proceed on an even basis.

Let the Games begin.

SGIAN DUBH

MERCEDES LACKEY

Not for the first time, Roddy MacSgian wished he hadn't been born a bloody metahuman.

It wasn't that he was unhappy with being dragooned into MI6 ... the good gods knew that every man jack and plenty of woman jills were needed in this war. The bloody damned Nazis had run over everything in their path and had eaten most of France by now. About the time they took all of the Netherlands, they had started bombing the hell out of London ... not just the damned *Luftwaffe* but the *Luftwaffe Übermenschen* too. The "Superior Men," like Eisenfaust and his squad. *Blitzkrieg*, they called it, and it looked like a lightning storm every night. Not that Roddy had seen it when it first started; no, he'd been where the Auld Woman said he belonged, right on the farm, tending the shaggy, sleepy-eyed cattle, like his father, and his father's father, and so on back to the first of his line to hold that particular piece of Highland land. Not that he wouldn't have volunteered if the Auld Woman hadn't strictly forbidden it, on account of his being the only male left of his clan, the oddly named clan "Son of the Knife." But even so, they wouldn't have taken him. Not on account of being the only male left of his clan, but on account of his size. He knew jockeys that were taller than he was. The Auld Woman said it was the Pharisee blood in him; once he'd gotten his marching orders, the learned fellows at MI6 looked interested and said that it might well be he was almost pure Pictish. Whatever the case was, it was a fact that Roddy topped out at four feet tall, and they didn't make uniforms in his size, nor boots, nor rifles that weren't taller than he was.

So when the whole bleeding War started, and the Nazis began wrapping up other countries and taking them home, and Tommies started joining the Frogs at the border of Lorraine, well, the Auld Woman wanted him to stay. He saw no reason not to; the Army had no bleeding use for him.

That was true through the months and weeks that followed, right up to the point where three things happened. The Blitz began, and Spitfire, and then the rest of Wing Alpha suddenly proved that the Nazis weren't the only ones that could spawn what the authorities decided primly to call "metahumans." The Yanks didn't sit around on their hands the way some people had predicted, as newsreel footage of the *Übermenschen* in action was enough to convince even a pacifist that the Germans weren't going to stop at the Channel.

And he, Roderick MacSgian, woke up to find himself in a bed that was not his own.

The lady already in the bed, Deidre of the grass-green eyes and flaming hair, of the tiny foot and the winsome smile, of the breasts of a goddess and skin like newly skimmed cream, who he had in fact been dreaming about before he woke up, was not anyone he'd have had a ghost of a chance with by all rights. She proved it by screaming her fiery head off when she too awoke and found him beside her.

And Roddy, panicked, did ... something.

And found himself back in his own bedroom, though he missed his bed by about a foot and landed on his arse on the cold stone floor.

It was that bruising that convinced him he hadn't been dreaming.

Now, even the Auld Woman would admit that Roddy had a knack for thinking quickly, especially when things went badly wrong, and the first thing that flashed into his head was that he had better be able to prove he was in his cottage and not in Deidre MacFarland's bed ten miles away, which meant he'd better get himself one or more sober witnesses to this at some point in the next five minutes.

He pulled on a pair of pants with naught on beneath, because he slept with naught on, shoved his feet into boots, and ran out into the street. "Didja hear that?" he shouted to his neighbor, who was just feeding his hutch of rabbits, doing his best to look wild-eyed.

"Roddy, ye wee bastard, I heerd nowt!" the neighbor laughed. "Ye bin dreamin' again."

Then the neighbor sobered, for it was known that the Old Blood was thick in the MacSgian family, and although the Auld Woman swore that not a bit of the magic had made its way into him, there was always the chance it was late in coming. The neighbor knew this, because it was his wife that stood for the East in the Auld Woman's monthly Gathers. "It wasna that sort of dream, now?"

Roddy shook his head, rubbed the back of his neck, and looked sheepish. "Och, nay," he said, and forbore to say what kind of a dream it was.

Now Deidre MacFarland was a canny lass, and before she went accusing a man of being where no man should have been at six in the morning, and especially not a man she did not know, and did not care to know, she made certain inquiries in that man's neighborhood. And not wanting to be made a fool of, when she found witnesses that he'd been standing in his own back garden at six-oh-one, she kept her mouth tight shut.

And being no fool, and a month later, sober reflection on Roddy's ability to keep his own mouth shut, and a good memory telling her that not everything about Roddy MacSgian was less than a proper man's size, when a general, no less, came and took him up by special draft, Miss Deidre MacFarland gave him a proper patriotic farewell which bade fair to match that dream. And even at this moment, his ability to be ten miles (or more) awa' in seconds was known only to her, him, and MI6.

By the time the general came for him, the village and most of the district knew of his other talent, for it had manifested in front of most of them.

Roddy could turn invisible.

He'd done it in full view, in a young host of people, in the middle of market-day, when he was in the public house, when he was *supposed* to be making rabbit hutches for the Auld Woman.

Now the way that came about was this. The Auld Woman was as tightfisted as any six Scots put together, which is saying a fair bit, and the wood and nails she had given Roddy to build those hutches with were all scavenged from every scrap of an abandoned structure that the Auld Woman's sturdy boots could carry her to. Before he could even use the nails, he had to straighten them, and after having banged his fingers and thumbs to flinders doing so, he reckoned he needed a dram or two or three to take the ache out. As to why the Auld Woman wanted rabbit hutches, well, she and every other person in the village remembered the Great War, and the meat all going to the soldiers, as well it should. That was rationing, and it was understood as something that had to be done. There was War again, and the young men marching off, and there was no doubt the little fellow that looked like Charlie Chaplin and sounded like a madman needed to be put down. Even the Auld Woman, though she would not let Roddy go, said that Hitler was doing some wicked bad things and needed to be put down. But it was a hard thing to be sending the cattle off and getting no meat for yourself.

Ah, but there were plenty alive who remembered the last dustup. And remembered rabbits now ... the last time the rabbits had been poached, mostly, but you needed a more reliable system than poaching for a war that looked as black as the inside of a widow's hat. The last time, no one had been making tinned rabbit, and the chances of rabbit-rationing were pretty slim. So hutches were being put up all over the village, and rabbits, after all, could be fed on hay and grass and cabbage leaves and such-like that was easily come by in the country.

So the Auld Woman was to have her hutches too, and no shilly-shallying about the work, for all that she had given him shite to build with. And he was just lifting his second dram to his lips when he heard someone sitting at the window of the pub exclaim, "Ach! 'Tis the Auld Woman a coomin' this way!"

And the men that had been standing shoulder to shoulder with him at the bar cursed, and looked through him, no more did the Auld Woman see him when she poked her head in through the door.

When he went visible again, there was a great old to-do, the Auld Woman boxed his ears and checked him for magic and still found none, and he wasn't at all surprised when the general turned up looking for him. Likely so, and rightly done. With talents like his, there was a lot even a little fellow could do.

By then, of course, the Auld Woman had cast his Weird, and had summoned him, and looked at him in the way that made him go hot and cold together, and told him soberly that though he hadn't a smidge of the Old Magic in him, he had something else, and he had best go to use it for to save a great many lives.

So that was why he was in a tiny little fisherman's smack on the English Channel, one among hundreds, maybe thousands even, of more tiny little boats and not so tiny boats and great huge troopships and all manner of craft, all rushing towards a place called Dunkirk. *They* were going to evacuate troops off the beaches, the troops of the Allies that had been trapped there by German troops and a tank division, and three Übermenschen—Panzer-Wolf, Panzer-Loewe, and Panzer-Tiger. *He* was going to save, if he could, the pride of the USA, the first two metahumans to come from the United States to fight at the side of the British and French—Dixie Belle and Yankee Doodle.

And here he was, one lone, little man, crouched in the bottom of one lone, little boat, trying not to be sick, with the weight of the Alliance on his back and the blessing of the Auld Woman on his head. Not Young Roddy anymore. Now he was something else entirely. He was, by fiat of MI6, Sgian Dubh, the "little black knife," the last, hidden, and most desperate of the weapons of a Scot.

△

In the chaos that was the evacuation of the Allied forces from the beachheads up and down the coast of France on either side of the seacoast town of Dunkirk, it was easy for one small man, going the wrong way, to make himself lost without ever going invisible. In fact, going invisible was probably ill-advised; he'd have been trampled.

It was unbelievable, probably horrible, and Roddy was right glad that the darkness hid most of it from him. The fear was so thick you could cut it. The smell of exploding shells and gunsmoke and woodsmoke mingled with the smell of blood and death and the smell of the sea. The men crowded onto the beaches were in despair, seeing escape from the meat grinder that was the Nazi *Blitzkrieg*, and yet fearing that they would be cut down before reaching safety. The noise was incredible. The beaches were being shelled, and the edges of the evacuation harried by Nazi storm troopers. If there was a hell on earth, this was it.

And yet it was not as bad as it could have been, and he knew why. The tank division had halted far short of here. The commanders on the ground expected it to arrive at any moment and were harrying their men into the hundreds of tiny shallow-drafted boats coming right up to the sand that would take the evacuees out to the larger ships.

The tank division was not going to come. In fact, it would not arrive until the beaches were deserted and every last man that could be got off, had been.

That was the Auld Woman's doing, her and her Gathering, and Gatherings and Moots and Meets wherever they had been alerted as to the need for a Great Work tonight. Roddy was entirely vague as to what they were doing, but he had no question as to how it was being done.

Magic.

Magic that ran in Roddy's ancestry, but that he did not share. Not that he was terribly unhappy about this. There were all manner of rules about using magic, and he was pretty sure he would run afoul of them. And the wizards and witches and sorcerers and what all generally seemed to always be having some sort of quarrel with each other, which made it all the more rare that they ever could get together long enough for a Great Work, like chasing off the Spanish Armada or stopping a German Panzer division.

But the men here didn't know that was happening, and wouldn't believe him if he told them, so they were vibrating between panic and apathy, though they tried to show neither. And Roddy couldn't blame them, seeing as he was steadily making his way *towards* the enemy lines rather than away.

In an hour, he had cleared the jam-up. That was when he went invisible.

Immediately he felt a rush of relief. Every moment since he'd waded ashore, he'd felt terrified. It had all sounded so simple, back in that briefing room. Get onto the beach, under cover of the evacuation; ghost his way to his contact, find out where Dixie Belle and Yankee Doodle were being held, free them, or more likely, help them to free themselves. They were infinitely more powerful than he was. Both of them could fly without needing an airplane; Yankee Doodle shot some sort of energy blasts from his eyes and Dixie Belle was unbelievably strong. He'd seen footage of Belle punching holes in airplanes and picking up cars. Freeing them seemed almost trivial; two people like that, probably all he had to do was go invisible, meet his contact, go invisibly to wherever they were being kept, unlock a door or some such, and they would do the rest.

But of course, he hadn't been able to take on his invisibility at first to avoid being run right over, and he had felt as if there was a target painted on his back the whole time he had been scrambling through that mess—short as he was, he stood out as something unusual, and the Nazis *knew* the Alliance had its own metahumans now, and why would there be someone as short as he was on that beach unless he had something to make up for what he lacked in size?

But now, now in the safety of a copse of shattered trees, he faded into nothingness and drew a deep, relieved breath. Now he had only to get through the enemy lines and find his contact. From here on in it should be smooth sailing.

△

Roddy was coming to the conclusion that nothing was ever as simple as it seemed. He had found his contact easily enough, and the first complication set in right there. His contact was a woman—a girl really—and one who carried a rifle on her back as casually as Deidre MacFarland carried a fine straw hat.

They huddled just outside the high brick wall—with broken glass or other nastiness atop it, no doubt—where she said Belle and Yank were being kept. "Eet ees some sort of laboratory," she had explained. "It was so before zee *Boche* came, and zay took it ovair. So, you *poof* yourself within, *mon ami,* free zem and—"

"Ah, it doesna worrrk that way, lassie," he whispered apologetically. "I canna go where I havena been before, or at least—" he amended hastily "—where I know some'un that's there." He flushed, thinking of Miss Deidre. The Auld Woman would have been scandalized to know how little she slept in ...

"*Nom du nom! Sacré merde ...*" The young woman swore vehemently under her breath. "You can at least *poof* out again, no?"

He thought about that, and flushed again. "Ah ... I dinna think so," he admitted. "I canna see where we are, ye ken. It bein' dark an' all. I mean, I could likely go *home,* but not out here. It'll haveta be the harrrd way."

The woman tossed her head, and unslung her rifle. "It is not to be helped, then," she said with resignation. "I will to remain here. Someone must report if you do not succeed."

For a moment he felt a surge of resentment, but in the next moment he realized she was right. "Right," he said with resignation. "I'm off."

He might be invisible but that did not mean he was undetectable. Dogs would smell him, for instance. He could leave footprints. People could bump into him and he could bump into things. In fact, he had to be twice as careful in tight quarters, as he couldn't see where his feet and arms were.

So the first step was to get past the dogs. Prowling carefully about downwind told him that there were two with their handlers at the gate, and at least two more patrolling the area between the walls and the building. He considered this carefully. He couldn't slip past the ones at the gate; there wasn't enough room between them, and they would surely smell him. He could go over the wall, perhaps, but then he would still have to contend with the dogs and handlers inside.

On the other hand ... he looked up at the top of the wall. If he could get up there, and didn't get slashed up on whatever was up there ...

He prowled around the outside until he found a section in shadow. The wall itself was no challenge for a lad who had been scampering about the Highlands most of his life. It was the glass and added razor wire atop it that made it a challenge, and if he got too cut up, he'd bleed, and a trail of blood was not invisible.

Finally he balanced precariously atop the support and peered at the roof of the building itself. This was going to be very tricky —because he couldn't teleport himself and stay invisible at the same time.

Oh, oh, let there be no lads with sharp eyes at those windows.

He waited until the dog and handler were out of sight. Waited until everything seemed quiet. Fixed his eyes on a shadowed nook where the chimney met the slippery slate roof, took a deep breath and—

—found himself sliding momentarily down the slates until he lodged against the chimney, cast frantically about himself to make sure he hadn't been seen, made the little twist of his mind that made him invisible again and—

—clung to the tiles and tried to catch his breath. No turning back now.

It took careful climbing and hunting, spread-eagled on the roof-pitch, to find the entrance to the roof that he knew must be there. A building like this one, with over a dozen chimney pots and three or four times as many fireplaces, would have needed the attentions of a chimney sweep regularly, and people who put walls with glass atop them around their buildings did not want sweeps leaning ladders against their walls, so there had to be a roof access. By now, of course, the fireplaces were disused and possibly boarded up, but the roof access was still there.

He paused and listened with every fiber, but heard nothing. Cautiously, he tried the hatch.

It was locked, but he could tell it was a simple slip-catch. A bit of knife-work, and it wasn't locked anymore. It opened up on complete blackness. There was no way of telling if the attic was clear or crammed with rubbish, or full of snoring soldiers.

Well maybe not the latter, not unless they could sleep without breathing. He glanced up; he didn't dare risk a match. Not with the air above full of the drone of planes.

Breathing a prayer, he lowered himself down until he was hanging on by his fingertips, then let go.

It was just about a four-foot drop; he hit as "softly" as he could, and remained crouched in place, frozen, listening. Had anyone heard him? Was anyone coming?

Nothing. Feeling his way inch by inch, he moved away from the open hatch and took a chance with a match.

Except for some crates piled up in half the attic, the low-ceilinged room was empty. And there was another hatch in the floor. He let the match burn almost down to his fingers, memorizing the room, then blew it out.

Once again, he listened with everything he had at the hatch, and heard nothing. If luck was with him, this building, now labs, had once been a stately old home, and this hatch gave out into the little rooms that had once been the servants' quarters. Provided they hadn't been gutted to make more lab space.

He raised the hatch open a hair.

There was light, but it was dim, and seemed to come from

some distant point. There was no one he could see immediately. He raised it a little more and took a better look. It looked like the hall of servants' quarters. They were probably used for storage, being more convenient than the attic. Moving as quickly as he could and still be quiet, he slid through the hatch and let it down.

Again, he sighed. *Now* he was safer. The soldiers would notice doors and hatches opening and shutting, but they could not see him, and the dogs were all outside.

Halfway down the hallway, he heard the tramp of boots on stairs and the sound of voices speaking what he assumed was German. For a moment, he froze—then slipped quickly to the end of the hall and the blacked-out window there. He squeezed himself in next to it as four soldiers, smelling slightly of wine and sausages, clumped their way past him and separated, two to a room. So the guards on duty here were using these rooms as their quarters ... so much for using the roof as an escape route if he was spotted and pursued.

Pressing his back to the wall, he inched his way down the stairs to the second floor.

This one was lit, much better, and he realized that now he had another problem.

He didn't know where, exactly, Belle and Yank were being held. Which essentially meant that he was going to have to check every room—wouldn't he?

It was a big building. Why, there must be twenty rooms on this floor alone!

His moment of hesitation was cut through by the sound of a child screaming.

The sound sent a rush of electricity fueled by fury across his nerves. As the child continued to cry out, screams fading into a pitiful whimpering that was worse than the screams, he raced down the hallway, following his ears. And he was just about to break down the door that the cries led him to when his good sense kicked in, and instead of crashing through it, he placed his hand on the knob and opened it just a crack. Just enough to see inside.

He saw the back of someone dressed in a surgeon's gown, as pristine and white as bleach and scrubbing could make such a garment. The man leaned over something or someone, utterly preoccupied, muttering to himself. Silently, Roddy slipped inside, closing and locking the door behind him.

At this point the contents of the room were in full view. There were four beds here, if you could call something with straps and harnesses like a torture device a "bed." Only one was occupied, by a frail looking girl who could not have been more than thirteen or fourteen years old, dark-skinned, black-haired; without thinking twice about it, Roddy knew what she was. A gypsy—one of the Travelers.

The man turned away from the little table he had been fussing with, and back to the girl strapped down to the bed. There was a wicked sharp scalpel in his hand, and at the sight of it, the girl's whimpers turned to screams again.

Less than a second later, the man was on the floor, with his own scalpel sticking out of his eye. He was quite dead. Roddy was no stranger to killing, although this was the first human being he had killed. Then again, anyone that would do what that man had been doing to that poor little girl—her body was a mass of scars, healing wounds, and fresh ones. Even as he fought with the straps to get her undone, one of the fresh wounds began to heal before his eyes. It was pretty clear what had been happening here; the wee thing was a metahuman too, one that could heal herself, and this butcher had been cutting on her, trying to find out how she was doing it.

Now, she watched him silently, looking remarkably calm for someone who had just been rescued from torture by a man who had been invisible. But when he got her right hand free, the first thing she did was to reach for him, and rest her fingers lightly on his forehead.

He froze, as a picture formed in his mind, which pretty much confirmed what he had guessed. The Auld Woman had quite a bit to do with the Travelers, or the Romany, as they liked to call themselves. There was a lot of magic in some of their bloodlines, and when one magician entered the territory of another, it was only polite to come calling, unless you planned on open warfare. And no one in his right mind would go to war against the Auld Woman. So he knew a bit of the lingo, and he struggled to make himself plain. *"I didn't come here to fetch you, but I'll get you out anyway, lass."*

Her eyes widened and filled with tears, and another picture came into his mind ...

It fair made him sick to his stomach and infused him with an energy he hadn't known he had. Fired by it, he gathered the girl in his arms and—

—landed heavily on the painfully clean stone floor of the Auld Woman's cottage. As he knew she would be, the Auld Woman and her Gathering were convened in their Circle, one small cog in the Great Work going on that was keeping the worst of the German menace from falling on the heads of the evacuation at Dunkirk. And because they were only one small cog, it did no harm for the Auld Woman to rise from her place and take the fainting girl out of Roddy's arms.

"Her people be dead, I got no time. Take care of her!" he said, the first time he had ever issued an order to the Auld Woman. He barely had time to register her nod before he gathered himself again and—

—landed back on the corridor, outside the door to the room of horror.

He made himself invisible again, then knelt where he had landed, exhausted, and unable to move. That was the longest he had ever jumped before. He wasn't sure he could ever do it again.

...

Fortunately, it seemed that the sick bastard that had been torturing the girl was not exactly popular with the rest of his lot. The rest of the floor was empty, and there was not even so much as a single soldier guarding the area. Roddy was left undisturbed while he waited for the weakness to pass.

And it was while he was kneeling there with his head down that he realized that, no, he was *not* going to have to hunt through every room in the building to find the American metahumans.

He was only going to have to look for the room with all the guards on it.

△

The room with all the guards on it was on the ground floor, and whatever its purpose had been when this was a house, it had been heavily reinforced with a bank-like vault door. The purpose of such a thing puzzled Roddy for a moment, as did the symbol on a sign beside the door, a small red dot with five red lightning bolts radiating outwards from it. Whatever it was that the former owners of this place thought needed such protection, it must have been dangerous.

But not nearly so dangerous—at least to the Nazis—as what was in there now, judging by all the guards.

But Germans were nothing if not precise. And that very precision made it possible for Roddy, moving slowly and carefully, to ease his way past them and into the room beyond just in time to hear a resonant voice say in heavily accented English—

"... I think that there is no more need for a mask to hide behind, little white dove—*Gott im Himmel! Du bist ein Schwarze!*" He jumped back, giving Roddy a clear view of the female captive, her arms and legs encased in what looked like layer upon layer of anchor chains.

"Watch who you're calling *white,* you Ku Klux Klan reject!" spat Dixie Belle, her dark, handsome face contorted with contempt as she looked up at the chiseled features of Eisenfaust. Roddy recognized both of them from photographs, although he was probably the only person outside of the select circle of enlisted metahumans that knew Dixie Belle was not, in fact, the blond-haired, blue-eyed girl on the American recruitment posters. Then again, the ongoing romance she had with Yankee Doodle—assuming there really was a romance and not that it too was a complete fabrication—was illegal in several states. Or so this had been explained to him as the reason why the rescue had to be kept secret.

"Dieses ist unmöglich," the German muttered, the back of his neck going red. Then he straightened. "I was going to offer you the opportunity to join us," he said, his voice so cold as to freeze the very air in the room. "But—"

"Oh, don't I fit in with your Master Race?" Belle replied, the sweet sarcasm in her voice as palpable as the ice.

"I guess you don't, sugar," said a second voice. "Not that we would have accepted, of course. Beer gives me gas, and that tin-pot despot of yours gives me worse gas."

Eisenfaust pulled back and slapped Yank with the back of his hand so hard that the *crack* sounded like a gunshot. Belle screamed an obscenity and Eisenfaust raised his hand to slap her too—then thought better of it.

"I will not contaminate my flesh with touching you," he said contemptuously. "Contemplate your fates. When Herr Doktor Herbsten is finished with his subject upstairs, he will come to study you. Most of his subjects have not lived too long. Perhaps you will be the exception."

With that, Eisenfaust turned abruptly and marched out the door, which swung ponderously shut behind him.

Now Roddy could see that, like Belle, Yankee Doodle was tied hand and foot to a chair that had been bolted to the floor. But the top half of his head was encased in a kind of helmet with an opaque visor. That visor, Roddy realized immediately, must be mirrored on the inside, so that anything Yank tried would just get shot back into his own face.

But the important thing was not what their captors had

intended to do to them. The important thing was that he and the prisoners had the entire room to themselves.

He allowed himself to become visible; Belle reacted with a startled, smothered squeak.

"Marie? Baby?" Yank reacted with alarm, turning his head blindly from side to side. "What is it? What—"

"'Tis all right, laddie," Roddy assured him as he stepped forward to take the helmet from Yank's head. "I'm Sgian Dubh of MI6, and I'm here t' help."

△

With a little puff of displaced air, the Scotsman landed beside his French Resistance guide, falling wearily to the ground as she bit back a scream that turned only into a swift intake of breath. "*Sacré merde!*" she whispered harshly. "Do not—what happened? Were zey not zere? Could you not free zem? What—"

Roddy tiredly held up one hand for silence, forgetting that in the dark she couldn't see it. But it hardly mattered as in the next moment the old stone mansion literally erupted with the sound of the pride of the USA metahuman forces as they began the grimly joyful task of kicking and blasting their way out of imprisonment. Holes began to appear in the slate roof as Yankee Doodle's energy blasts reached for the heavens.

Under cover of the ruckus, Roddy and his contact slipped away. He looked back only once, just in time to see the two figures, illuminated by the flames licking up from the ravaged building beneath them, shooting off into the sky.

Roddy smiled. The Auld Woman couldn't have done it better herself.

WHITE BIRD

MERCEDES LACKEY

Jeanne Blanchette guided her Spitfire through the low-hanging winter clouds, ducking below the ceiling only now and again to confirm her heading. This was no kind of weather to be flying in, but the Armée de l'Air needed their planes, and as soon as one was fit to fly, one of the ferry pilots would be called from the barracks to take it out to its destination. British Spitfires and some P-51s were replacing the Dewoitine D.520s, despite much anguish on the part of the French pilots. Still, it could not be denied that the Spitfire was, in every way, superior to her French counterpart. Jeanne loved the way they handled, and whenever she had to turn her charge over at the end of a flight, a part of her mourned at giving it up. They called to her soul, these lovely creatures of war. They called to her heart.

They told her that it was she who should be guiding them against the filthy *Boche*, and not ... whoever would get them.

It wasn't as if she wanted to be a ferry pilot. She was as good as the best of the Frenchmen flying now, and better than most. She had thousands of hours in air races under her belt, and she knew this countryside from the air as most folk knew the roads and lanes around their little villages. Most of the poor boys in these airplanes hadn't a fraction of her air-time. She had been racing over this land since she had been old enough to beg, bribe, and browbeat those around her into letting her into a cockpit. Most little girls were horse-mad, and grew out of it. Jeanne was airplane-mad and never would. Unlike the vast majority of those horse-mad little girls, Jeanne had the wherewithal to satisfy her craving, and the stubborn temper to persist in the face of the most adamant opposition.

She dropped below the clouds again, just verifying that she was where she thought she should be. The war-torn landscape was a hell of shattered trees, shattered villages, and cratered fields, but the wretched *Boche* tried to refrain from shelling the village churches directly. Not because they were any kind of religious; the opposite in fact, since they went out of their way to defile the places and murder and torment priests and nuns. No, it was because the tall steeples gave them landmarks to fly by too, as well as marking points to shell or bomb.

She spotted the tipsy little shell of Saint Marie au Fleur below her, and corrected her course a trifle, then eased back up into the shelter of the clouds.

No, she did not want to be here, in a plane she must give over into the hands of some clumsy recruit, a plane with six empty guns, an easy target for Eisenfaust's Messerschmitts. She wanted to be fighting. How not? She was raised in Orléans, she was named Jeanne, and like every little French girl, she was fed the tales of Saint Jeanne d'Arc the way American children were fed the tales of Mickey Mouse.

A broadside wind buffeted the little plane, and again, she dropped below the cloud cover to check her bearings. The storm was worsening. She remembered another day, another storm.

△

Jeanette played in the opulent nursery of her parents' chateau outside Orléans, with her birthday presents. Or, to be precise, with one of her birthday presents, the only thing she had specifically requested that she had gotten. The lovely dolls, porcelain beauties all, sat on a shelf with the rest of her dolls, pristine and untouched. The beautiful dollhouse, a miniature of the chateau itself, served only one purpose; to house the wood and paper, the glue and thread that she used to make her air fleet. And now she played quietly with the pride of her air fleet, an exact model of a real plane. But she did not play with it as another child would, soaring it over her own head as she ran, and making it do all the aerobatics she had seen the stunting pilots and fairs and shows do. No, she was studying it, so that she might make more. Only her grand-mère, who understood her, had given her the model airplane she had asked for.

Her papa should have understood her. Her papa was mad for

motorcars, for speed, and raced as often as he could escape from the business of his wine and vineyards. But he did not. Perhaps because he seldom saw her, and then, never looked at her. She knew why. He did not want to see her, he wanted to see the boy that she should have been; instead, she was the disappointing girl who had cost her maman her life. She understood all these things dimly, for eventually Grand-mère had explained them patiently to her. Still, too many times, she retreated to her room in abject misery, after facing his cold rejection of even a simple greeting. Papa was Grand-mère's son, and it made her sad to see how he neglected Jeanne, so it was Grand-mère who tried to take the place of both Maman and Papa.

And it was Grand-mère who was there when, with a clap of thunder that seemed to herald the end of the world, the doors to the chateau burst open, and the building erupted with screams and wailing; Grand-mère who held her and tried to comfort her, when the body of the chateau's master, killed by the speed he worshipped, was carried in on the raging wings of the storm.

Jeanne might have been like a hundred other rich little girls, if it had not been for Grand-mère. But Grand-mère would not let her give up her need to fly. It was Grand-mère to whom she told the dreams she had, of soaring, arms outstretched, through blue skies and stormy, without need for a plane. It was Grand-mère who bought her books on aviation, took her unfailingly to aviation displays and shows. It was Grand-mère who persuaded a pilot who gave lessons that teaching the little girl could do no harm, for after all, what would she do with the lessons? Everyone knew that girls did not fly. Of course, the fat wad of francs did a great deal of persuasion too.

But girls did fly, were flying, in increasing numbers. Jeanne got her lessons. Then Jeanne got her airstrip where the unused tennis courts had been. Then Jeanne got her racing plane. And

before she died, Grand-mère got to see Jeanne win her first race.
She did not weep at Grand-mère's funeral. People whispered, she
knew. But she had had a dream that night, of flying free beside a
startlingly youthful Grand-mère, who told her "The sky is your
home, and your lover, chérie. Never let anyone make you give
it up."

"But what about you?" she asked, crying then, as she had not
at the funeral.

"Ah, my home is the stars now!" Grand-mère had said, with a
brilliant smile. "I am going on such a journey!"

And with that, she had shot ahead of Jeanne, soaring into the
night sky, until Jeanne lost sight of her altogether and she was
gone.

The wind buffeted the plane again, slewing it sideways. Jeanne
did not fight the controls, she caressed them, eased them over,
making the plane fly with the storm and not against it. No one
really understood how she was able to feel so at one with
machinery. Not even Henri, who lovingly worked on these beauties, who crooned to them and talked to them and coaxed them
back to life after grievous injuries.

It was hard for a woman like Jeanne to find a lover. Fellow
pilots did not hold the women in great esteem. Some regarded
them with anger, as interlopers. Some regarded them as an
affront to nature. Some laughed at them, as if this need that they
shared was something in a female that was nothing more than a
childish whim, soon grown out of. And last of all, some men
regarded them as something to be conquered and cured of their
affliction, so that they could display their trophy before all the
other men as proof of their prowess.

But Henri Dubois, engineer and mechanic, shared her love of
the planes without sharing the love of flying. He did not understand it, but he did understand how it was an all-consuming

passion. He of all the men she had ever met was willing to share her with that passion. He had given her the nickname of "White Bird," a pun on her name of Blanchette.

But perhaps even that would not have happened had the war not come. The war, and the *Boche*, and their hideous supermen ... which she must, at all costs, avoid, every time she delivered an airplane to the airfields of Belgium.

She dropped below the clouds again, into lashing curtains of rain. And a tiny, tiny thread of alarm thrilled along her nerves.

This storm was stronger than it should have been. Much. Not only had there been no prediction of such a storm, but it felt wrong. Jeanne had always had a kind of sixth sense for the weather, as she did for her planes. And this storm felt *wrong*.

There was one of Eisenfaust's hellish squadron who was said to fly in on storms like this one.

Valkyria—

—that sixth sense was all that saved Jeanne at that moment, when the clouds tore open, and lightning slashed through on either side of the golden Messerschmitt with its distinctive snarling-horse nose painting. As bullets from the Messerschmitt's guns tore through the place where she had been, Jeanne had sideslipped the Spitfire out of the way, and sent her into a steep, diving turn.

The forces of gravity and centripetal force shoved her back and sideways into the seat; she felt the skin of her cheeks stretching back over her bared teeth. She squeezed her insides as hard as she could to keep from blacking out and felt the telltale juddering in her hands wrapped around the stick, as the Spitfire warned her that she was reaching the limit of what the plane could take.

At the last possible moment, she pulled up, mere feet from the churned-up earth of the field below her. The Spitfire soared, and she glanced down and sideways, hoping without much hope to see the smoke and crater where Valkyria's own craft had plowed into the ground.

Instead, she felt, as if in her own body, the bullets stitching across her right wing.

She had no weapons of her own. All she could do was try to outfly the German bitch. And Valkyria was one of the super-humans. She could take more g-stress, she had better, faster reactions—and should Jeanne somehow make her crash, she would walk away from it.

No! thought Jeanne, as she did a wingover that turned into a hammer-fall. *I will not let you take my sky!*

They did not fight their way across the sky, with lightning arcing all around them, even striking the planes themselves. There was no fight here, for Jeanne could not fight. She could only try to run, tiny silvery-white falcon pursued by the cruel golden eagle, losing a little more ground with every line of bullets that stitched across some part of the plane.

And then, Jeanne felt it. Felt the moment when the damage reached the critical level. Felt the weakened wings start to part from the body, the tail-empennage bending and about to snap under the stress of the turn. And felt, rather than saw, the massive bolt of lightning that enveloped plane and Jeanne and all in a moment of searing whiteness and a mental shriek of outrage and denial.

There was a single moment of unbelievable pain, as if her entire body was taken apart on an instant, and instantly reformed in a whole new shape.

And then—

She was flying.

She was not in the plane. She *was* the plane. Wings were at her back, her arms stretched out beneath them, both swept back like a V. She felt—something—something strange and alien. It felt like a second set of lungs, except it was above her, and it sucked in air and squirted it out so that she was propelled as she had once seen a squid propelled. She vaguely remembered something Henri had been obsessed with. Something—a rocket? A jet?

She felt the armor, a part of her, a silver-white metal skin covering every part of her, but especially heavy on her visored head.

Visor?

Yes, she had a visor, a glass visor, protecting her eyes. And she sensed the inches-thick plating on her hands, and her head. And she saw Valkyria's plane below her, and she knew what it was she had to do.

She would knock that Teutonic bitch out of her sky.

She went into a steep dive, and only the German's own sixth sense and lightning reflexes saved her. Now the shoe was on the other foot. She was faster than the Messerschmitt, and more maneuverable. But that speed was her undoing, for she overshot Valkyria time and time again, and had to turn and make up the distance before she could try to close.

And finally, she was defeated in her attempt to get to the German by the only weapon Valkyria could bring to bear to cover her retreat.

The storm.

Suddenly, Jeanne herself was all but knocked out of the sky by the torrent of rain that poured out of the clouds. She couldn't see. She could barely stay aloft. She certainly could not find the German.

It was over in a moment; not even a supernatural storm could sustain itself at that level for long. But when the rain subsided, Valkyria was gone.

And now, too weary to think, Jeanne only turned herself towards the distant airfield that she had flown out of. Home. She wanted to go home ...

△

It was a shock to the airfield command to hear Jeanne's voice on the radio reporting an encounter with Valkyria.

It was a greater shock to see what landed. A strange

construction, some Frankensteinian creation, as if pulled from a science fiction serial, half woman, half silvery-white airplane. It was not much larger than a woman, if that woman could bear carrying swept-back metal wings on her back, and enough armor to make a medieval knight go to his knees.

They only heard snatches of the encounter out there on the tarmac, between what had been Jeanne Blanchette and the engineer they all knew had been her lover, Henri Dubois. Mostly it was drowned in the static on the radio, static that sounded like electricity weeping. "... it does not come off.... but ... I cannot ... *it was not my fault! Would you rather I had died?*"

But they did hear Henri's shouted reply to that question, which rang across the airfield like the bullet from an executioner's rifle.

"*Yes!*"

The man made a gesture in which horror and revulsion were equally mixed, turned, and walked away without looking back, as the terrible static sobbed over the airwaves and the men in the control tower fell utterly silent.

They sensed that, had the rigid skin allowed it, the strange figure on the runway would have sagged in despair.

And then, as the static faded and the silence stretched as tight as an over-wound violin string, the figure raised her head, and—from the posture—looked into the sky.

"Clear the runway," said the voice, like Jeanne's but with a hardness in it they had never heard before. "There are *Boche* in my sky. When I am finished with my patrol, there will be fewer of them."

"But Jeanne—" someone ventured.

"Jeanne Blanchette is dead," the voice replied, hard and dead. "I am La Faucon Blanc, and the skies are mine."

VALSE TRISTE

MERCEDES LACKEY

My name is Triste Steinmann. I am fifteen years old. I have been a prisoner for two years, three days, and six hours. I have been an orphan for two years, three days, and twelve hours.

Triste always began her journal entries with the record of her imprisonment. It amused Gruppenführer Bruenner when he read it. And he did read it. She had to leave her journal in a drawer in a little desk in his big office, and she had to write in it every day. She had thought he would be angry the first time, but he laughed uproariously. He would never say why, but by this point she knew. Gruppenführer Bruenner was a sadist, like all of the SS, and a narcissist like many of them. She knew what both of these things were, because she had read about them in the works of Herr Doktor Sigmund Freud, which were in French translation in the library of this stolen mansion. Gruppenführer Bruenner did not know this, because he never bothered to read anything that was not related to the war, much less anything in French. His lover did not bother to read at all. As for Frau Gruppenführer Bruenner, well, she was back in Munich, with the half-dozen little Bruenners, so Triste did not know what she did, other than produce babies nine months after der Gruppenführer made a visit.

Today I began the piano works of Schumann. Gruppenführer Bruenner wishes me to particularly learn the Lieder, *since the Über-mensch—though perhaps that should be* Überfräulein—*Brunnhilde is to perform a concert here tonight. There was a piece of Jan Sibelius mixed in with the others, a "Valse Triste," and I learned it quite by accident. I think I will play it when the Gruppenführer requires music for his guests to mingle by. It ... speaks to me.*

Triste closed her journal and put it in the drawer of the desk where, of course, the Gruppenführer would find it and laugh. There was a little time before the party, a few hours. She would go upstairs to her room, eat when food was brought to her, and wait until she was told to put on the black gown and come down

to entertain. She would not need to look at the scores she had
studied today. They were in her head, in her fingers, already.

As soon as Triste had been old enough to walk, she had
played—first on the little toy piano, to her parents' bewildered
astonishment, then on the piano in her teacher's studio, where
she could not even reach the pedals. As soon as she had
connected the black notes on the page with the keys on the
keyboard, she had only to read a score through once, and it was
in her fingers. At first, she had been a mere prodigy, a freak, a
kind of player-piano in child form. It had been her teacher who
had taught her to make her music sing. Her teacher, who was
now dead, or in a concentration camp, along with the other Jews
of the Lorraine.

Triste had escaped that fate, because of Gruppenführer
Bruenner. Not because he was kind. Not because he particularly
cared for music, even. But because the music of the German
Reich was displayed at every occasion, like draping a beautiful
pall over a rotting corpse, and it was easy and cheap to keep her
about. She did not argue, did not disobey, was fundamentally
invisible, she was nearly as good as a music-playing robot, and
rather better than a gramophone. She would be relatively safe,
she hoped, as long as she was amusing and useful. She really did
not want to die.

She reached her little attic room, which had once been the
provenance of one of the housemaids. There was a bed with
many worn blankets and a bright white coverlet, a white-painted
wardrobe, a white-painted washstand. Her gown for the evening
hung on the back of the door, newly cleaned and perfumed with
lavender. It was plain and black, made of heavy, dull satin, with
the yellow *Magen David* discreetly embroidered like a brooch on
the left side. She did not touch it. She went instead to the white-
painted, wooden wardrobe, and made sure her coat was still
there, still untouched. She ran her hands over the inside. The
tough little packets of franc notes were still there, sewn into the
false lining she had hung between the wool outside and the real

lining. The hair she had tied across the front of the coat, from button to button, was intact. No one had touched her coat. She, and it, were still safe from discovery.

Whenever she got a chance, she stole money from Didi, Bruenner's lover. Didi had been a nude at the Folies Bergère. Didi never kept track of the money the Gruppenführer gave her; she tipped lavishly, bought whatever she cared to, sent money accidentally down in the clothing to be laundered, and when she ran out of money, the Gruppenführer gave her more. Triste was often in Didi's rooms, especially when she was tipsy; that was part of her job too, to amuse Didi, playing popular tunes, sentimental German songs, and pieces from operettas, while Didi drank or danced or sang to them. All she had to do was play and tell Didi how beautiful she was. This was easy. Didi did not have a bad temper, even when drunk. Didi had a magnificent body, long, wavy hair that was really, truly golden blond without any help, and the face of a goddess. The Gruppenführer never allowed Didi out except to shop with one of his men, and Didi was exceptionally stupid as well as exceptionally beautiful; she didn't know what else to do with her time but drink and dance alone, and sing. When Didi finally slept, Triste would prowl briefly about the room, steal money, and slip back to her own room to sew another packet into oilcloth, and then into the lining of her coat. She prayed nightly that God would send her a chance to escape—perhaps when the Gruppenführer was away, or perhaps the English would even bomb Paris.

She knew where she would go. She could see it from her window. Montmartre, the artists' quarter. There had been musicians from there who had visited with her before the war and made a pet of her. If any of them were still alive, and still there, perhaps for enough money they could help her escape France altogether. Triste no longer believed in the kindness of people— but money, especially now, when the only place you could get anything good was on the black market, meant you didn't have to trust to anyone's kindness or lack of it.

She sat back in the little window seat, her fingers moving restlessly against the sill as she gazed out at the Basilique du Sacré-Coeur on the top of the hill. Her fingers played the notes she had learned today, and she let them move without thinking about it. They always did this; it was as if her hands had a mind of their own. When she was not doing something with her hands, they played, and played and played. Unless she clasped them, they played on top of the bedcovers at night. Sometimes she wondered if they would keep playing when she was dead. She hoped this idea never occurred to Gruppenführer Bruenner. He might try the experiment. He would find it terribly amusing to have a couple of disembodied, piano-playing hands he could keep in a box. But of course, without her head, they could never learn anything new, so perhaps that would not be as amusing as he would like.

Then, suddenly, her hands paused. This was unusual enough that she broke out of her reverie to look at them. It was as if they were waiting for her to look at them; they lifted gently off the sill, and the fingers came down, slowly, and she knew what they were playing.

The piece by Sibelius. It had had her name. And it had spoken to her in a way no other piece of music had until this moment. It had called to her. There had been a power in it—she had almost run to the piano to *hear* it, but fear and caution had kept her at her task. Brunnhilde would decide what *lieder* to sing on the spur of the moment, and Triste had been told in no uncertain terms that she must learn them all.

But she had never seen a piece that she had desired to hear more, never in her entire life. It had been so strong that she had studied the entire score, hungry to know more. Luckily, there had been notes on the score, telling what it was about.

"It is night. The son, who has been watching beside the bedside of his sick mother, has fallen asleep from sheer weariness, Gradually a ruddy light is diffused through the room: there is a sound of distant music: the glow and the music steal nearer until the strains of a valse melody float

distantly to our ears. The sleeping mother awakens, rises from her bed and, in her long white garment, which takes the semblance of a ball dress, begins to move silently and slowly to and fro. She waves her hands and beckons in time to the music, as though she were summoning a crowd of invisible guests. And now they appear, these strange visionary couples, turning and gliding to an unearthly valse rhythm. The dying woman mingles with the dancers; she strives to make them look into her eyes, but the shadowy guests one and all avoid her glance. Then she seems to sink exhausted on her bed and the music breaks off. Presently she gathers all her strength and invokes the dance once more, with more energetic gestures than before. Back come the shadowy dancers, gyrating in a wild, mad rhythm. The weird gaiety reaches a climax; there is a knock at the door, which flies wide open; the mother utters a despairing cry; the spectral guests vanish; the music dies away. Death stands on the threshold."[1]

She had almost cried, had crumpled the music in her hand, reminded so sharply of her own dying mother. Her mother had not risen from her sickbed to dance with spectral visitors, but she had kept asking for Triste to play so often in her last illness that Triste had sometimes fallen asleep at the piano.

Triste, her mother had named her. "Sorrow." An odd name for a child, but her mother had insisted. Sometimes Triste wondered if her mother had somehow known what was coming, the war, the SS, the camps. Triste knew all about the camps, although they were still a secret to many, if not most. Bruenner made sure she knew about them. The woman with the cruel eyes had shown her pictures and a film before she'd brought Triste to Bruenner, properly schooled and obedient. *"You will obey. You will do everything the Gruppenführer wishes. Or you will go here."* Sometimes those scenes of horror played behind her eyes at night, while her fingers danced on the bedclothes.

Now Triste was glad that her mother had died when she had, for two months later the *boches* had come marching in, and two months after that, they had come for the Jews. The last she had seen of her father, as Gruppenführer Bruenner's men carried her screaming away, was his body sprawled in front of the door in a pool of too much blood, his eyes staring sightlessly, his head caved in by the butt of a rifle. That was when she came to be part of Gruppenführer Bruenner's household, and that two-week session with the cold woman with evil eyes convinced her to do and be everything the Gruppenführer wanted of her. It had not taken much. She was a timid child by nature. And despite all that had happened, she wanted very much to live.

There was a tap at the door. Triste opened it and accepted the tray from the maid. The servants here were contemptuous of her; she was always polite to them, and never gave them a reason to torment her. The Gruppenführer saw to it that the servants kept her fed; he wanted his music machine healthy. Tonight it was fish, with a little salad, vegetables, some fruit, bread. Coffee, to make sure she stayed awake. She ate it methodically, and put the tray outside the door. She went back to the window, to watch the sun set on the Basilique, and waited. She watched as the cloudless sky behind the Basilique turned a deep and translucent blue, and the white building became pink, then rose, then red. This was her favorite time of the day, and her favorite sight. Her fingers danced on the windowsill, the Basilique turned to ashes of roses, then a ghost floating over the city, against a sky spangled with stars. There were no lights, of course, nothing but what the stars and moon provided. No lights to guide the bombs of the English, for which she prayed nightly.

She was not provided a light in this room. It was not thought that she needed one.

Finally came the tap at her door, the brusque order "Get ready." She left the seat at the window, took off her plain dress, slipped on the black dress, brushed her hair and bound it at the back of her neck by touch, pulled on the satin slippers that went with the dress, and went downstairs.

By the servants' stairs, of course. She must be unobtrusive, go like a shadow to the ballroom, slip into place at the piano and begin to play in such a way that no one would notice her coming. It was not hard; the piano stood at one end, in a kind of bulge in the room with windows all around it, and since she needed no light, no light was provided there. All the windows had been covered with thick, blue velvet drapes, and blackout covers behind them. The cover had already been lifted from the keys; she took her place at the bench and began to play, a mere whisper of sound, gradually increasing it as more and more people came into the room. Outside her bubble of shadow, the ballroom was brilliantly lit, the parquet floor shining, the chandeliers glowing with light and sparkling with crystal. There was a fountain of wine on a table, and white-gloved waiters with crystal goblets waiting to serve it. There was fruit, cheese, bonbons, little crystal plates and linen napkins on another table. On a third, waiters with boxes of cigarettes, cigars, and lighters. More and more people arrived, most of the men in the uniforms of the occupying army, the women like exotic birds in form-fitting gowns, spangled with beadwork, jewels at throat and ears. None—or very few—of these women were wives, of course. No respectable wife would be seen at a soirée presided over by a mistress, especially not one who had been a Folies Bergère nude.

Though Didi did make a very good hostess. She had an instinct for when to laugh, when to smile, and when to be silent and merely look attentive. Triste watched them all, as her hands played inconsequential, tinkling music, mostly Bach exercises that would disturb no one, or lullabies, or popular song. They moved about the floor like elegant, dangerous beasts on their best behavior at the waterhole. They were sated now, and had the luxury of being playful with one another.

The servants began to bring in chairs, and she knew the concert was about to begin. Two of Bruenner's men brought in a pair of electric spotlights on tall poles, focusing their light on a spot in front of Triste's alcove. The crowd began to take seats.

She had wondered which of the guests was Brunnhilde, but she should have realized that someone like the Überfräulein would not be inclined to mingle, at least not before the concert. The servants dimmed the lights, and lit up the electric spotlights. The guests took the hint and the few who were still standing took the remaining seats. Then the diva made her entrance from the rear, the two servants manning the spotlights illuminating her as she paused in the door. Everyone began to clap as she made her way to the front of the gathering.

She looked—well, she looked like a very Germanic version of Didi. Taller, built more squarely and robustly, extremely blond, she wore a gown made entirely of silver beads that looked as if it had been molded to her body. A silver belt clasped her waist, with a long piece hanging down in the front, almost to the floor. There was a heavy silver collar around her neck, and a silver diadem around her head. She did not look at Triste, but Triste did not expect her to. She only looked at the audience. When they stopped applauding, she nodded her head graciously, and said, "*Zwielicht.*" Triste obediently began to play.

She had to admit Brunnhilde's voice was glorious, full and rich. She had an enormous range, too, from contralto all the way to coloratura, with no break-point. If Brunnhilde had expected to catch her out, she was to be disappointed; Triste had done her job well, and there was no song that Brunnhilde asked for that she could not play.

Finally the Gruppenführer stepped up into the spotlight as servants began to raise silver balls on ropes to the ceiling. Triste wondered what on earth they could be doing, and why.

"Our gracious and beloved guest has agreed to display for us tonight a little of the power that makes her one of the Führer's chosen Übermenschen," said Bruenner, with a little smirk. "I know that you will be impressed; I know you will be even more impressed when I tell you that this little display will require no more than a fraction of the power she possesses." He bowed to Brunnhilde, who bowed back, then glanced into the shadows where Triste sat at the piano. "Ride of the Valkyries," he ordered.

Triste began.

For the first part of the aria, the spotlights remained on Brunnhilde, but there was something about the tone of her singing that was giving Triste uneasy shivers and making her stomach knot. Then as she reached the thundering conclusion, and the final "to-yo, to-ho" calls, the spotlights swiveled up to illuminate those silver metal balls.

And that was when Brunnhilde showed her power.

With each "to-yo to-ho!" she somehow directed her voice *at* one of the balls, and the ball literally shredded into a silver metal flower. You could see from where Triste sat that these were no flimsy little foil balls, either; the metal plating was a good quarter-inch thick, and it just peeled back the way a child would peel the foil from a chocolate. In her mind's eye, Triste could almost see this happening to the front of a tank ... of an airplane ... to a man ... and her insides twisted with horror. Her hands continued to do their job, however, and brought the aria to its thunderous conclusion.

All the guests leapt to their feet, applauding wildly, as Brunnhilde smirked and took bow after bow after bow.

△

Finally the party began again, with Brunnhilde now circulating among the guests, taking their congratulations. Triste feared that Didi might sulk, but her instincts must have warned her against any such thing; she stood back and smiled, and nodded, and said nothing at all. Finally the chairs were all cleared away, the tables moved back, and Triste knew this was the signal that she was to begin dance music.

Dance music must always begin with a few Strauss waltzes; the Gruppenführer led Brunnhilde out for the first one. Brunnhilde was a competent dancer, and Bruenner was good, if mechanical; there were no mishaps. Meanwhile, Triste played in a sort of daze, still numb with the horror of what this blond creature could do, what a terrible weapon she was. Why, she could be anything from a weapon on the battlefield to an assassin! Who would suspect that music could kill until it was too late?

But there was nothing she could do about it ...

Her hands began to play the fourth waltz, and her attention snapped back to the keyboard. Those soft little notes ... that sad melody ... this was not Strauss.

This was the *Valse Triste*. The Sibelius.

No one seemed to notice. They were all still vying for the attention of Brunnhilde. But the music woke Triste out of her horror, and carried her straight into grief.

She had not wept since her mother died. Not for her father, not for all the people she knew had, must have, gone to the camps, and who were probably dead by now. Not for herself. Her tears seemed to have dried and gone until this moment. But now, as her hands played, the floodgates opened, and the tears flowed, silently; she sobbed silently, weeping for her mother, her father, the sweet, sweet pair of men who loved each other and had unfailingly brought her chocolates, for her teacher ... their sad, gray spirits rose up before her and she wept for them and for all the others she did not even know. Her grief poured out of her in a torrent—

And out on the dance floor, a strange mist began to rise.

The dancers did not notice it at first, and when one or two did, they must have thought it was some clever effect that the Gruppenführer had arranged. It rose to their knees ... and then to their waists ... and then it was too late.

The mist seized them, caught them as the Wilis of legend would catch unwary young men who dared their graves after dark. It caught them; Triste looked up, something telling her that there was something different out there, and saw the moment it caught them, saw the moment the mist formed into human shapes, separated the dancing partners until each of them had a partner made of mist, and whirled them off into a dance of terror. Brunnhilde spun past, her mouth in a soundless "O" of fear. The Gruppenführer, his pupils dilated. Even the servants.

And Triste's hands played on, driving them into the frenzied conclusion of the *Valse,* their faces, their eyes now contorted with horror.

And then, as she brought her hands down on the keys in the final crashing chords, the mist rose up over each dancer like a wave, and engulfed them.

Then there was only silence. The mist vanished, leaving behind a room strewn with the dead.

Triste could not think, but her body, it seemed, had already decided what to do. She got up from the piano, and went to the body of one of the servant girls who was sprawled beside a table. Her hands stripped the girl of her maid's uniform, and re-dressed her in Triste's gown. Now wearing only her underwear and bare-foot, Triste found herself going back upstairs. She left the maid's uniform in one of the rooms, took armfuls of clothing, and the maid's papers. When her arms were full, she took everything to her room. She went down to Didi's room, and took a suitcase from a closet, and the pair of expensive and hard to get rubber-soled shoes Didi wore to go shopping. When she was done, she dressed in some of what she had taken, put on the rubber-soled shoes and her coat full of money, picked up the suitcase, and went back down into the silent house.

The mist was gathering again, following along behind her. But rather than feeling threatened by it, she felt comforted, as if it was protecting her.

At the music room she stopped. Her senses were coming back to her, it seemed; she found herself able to think again. She looked back at the billows of mist.

"I could escape to England," she said, tentatively.

The shadows in the mist seemed to agree. But sadly. As if she were obscurely disappointing them.

"But ... maybe I can ... do something ..." she continued, groping her way through unfamiliar territory. Was this what courage felt like? "If I stay. If you help me. Will you help me?"

There was no doubt. She felt the surge of fierce assent.

She made up her mind. She would stay. And she would need an instrument....

She knew exactly what to get. The music room was full of instruments the Gruppenführer had confiscated, but there was one her hands would know what to do with, that was easy and portable to take—and would not be missed. She dashed inside and came out with the concertina in its case. Now she would have her disguise—a means of moving around Montmartre almost invisibly—and her weapon.

"Now we go," she told the shadows, and headed for the door, and freedom. It would be a long walk to Montmartre, but her shoes would make no sound, and she could hide in shadows with the mist's help when patrols came by. She had the maid's papers, and no one would be looking for *her* now. She would find a little garret or basement room, begin playing in the cafes, and eventually, she knew, she would find the Resistance. And then her real work would begin.

She hurried out of the mansion driveway, into the streets of Paris, with the shadows gathering behind her like dark wings.

NOTES

1. "Valse Triste – Sibelius," MusicWithEase.com, last modified September 30, 2011, https://www.musicwithease.com/sibelius-valse-triste.html.

RETRIEVAL

VERONICA GIGUERE

Crewmen loaded rations and munitions in a steady supply line, crates passing from hand to hand. From the end of the pier, a decorated officer watched with a mixture of pride and satisfaction. His crew, a shining example of the power of the Third Reich, had completed another mission against Britain's feeble fleet. Their return to port unscathed marked four hundred and seventeen successful sinkings, a record matched only by the most experienced captains and crews. Such a reputation marked them as privileged, tasked with a greater mission. The captain clasped his hands behind his back and breathed deeply; in the backyard of the Americans, he and his crew would seal their fate as the most feared sons of Germany's glorious empire.

Next to him, the executive officer seemed to share his pride as the supply line finished loading the last crates on board. The XO gave a shrill whistle, his orders answered with crisp salutes as the men prepared to set sail.

A young sailor, smartly dressed and eager to please, brought a message to the CO. Visitors from the capital had arrived and they had asked to see the captain before he embarked on his journey. Leaving the XO to oversee the final preparations, the captain entered the office and immediately sneered at the pair.

"This is unexpected," he said. "You are aware that we depart this evening, Lieutenant." The other visitor stood behind the lieutenant, trying to hide from the captain's scorn. With her exotic features and swarthy complexion, she was out of place in a uniform of the German forces. She kept her head bowed as the captain spat at her feet. "I have no time for this."

The officer presented the captain with a sealed envelope, ignoring the man's sneer. "I have been instructed to sail with you, Captain. Part of your mission against the Americans involves the use of a new weapon." He motioned to the woman, who cringed at the sudden attention. "You'll see that the orders are legitimate, Captain."

"A woman on board," he snorted. "What nonsense. And a half-breed at that," he said with a grunt.

"An added bonus," the officer added, "is that she speaks very little German. You can be certain that she will not understand you or your crew. And, properly tended, even dogs grow to be extremely loyal to their masters."

The captain folded the paper while circling the woman. As she shied away, he reached forward to tilt the young woman's chin up as if he were inspecting a Shepherd bitch for good breeding. Her trembling brought a smirk to his face. "Excellent, Lieutenant. We set sail within the hour."

△

The expression on the supervising shipyarder's face meant one of two things; either someone was in trouble or someone was about to be in trouble. He held a hushed conference with the two burly men who had come to see him, the detail drowned out by the hiss of welding torches and the clatter of tools on the deck. Every so often, he would raise his head and look in the direction of a team working near the waterline. After a few minutes more consultation, the supervisor motioned for one of the crew to come over.

"Sir?" The young man couldn't have been more than thirteen or fourteen years old, and his voice squeaked as he realized that the men accompanying his boss were honest-to-goodness US Navy officers. In the summer of 1942, it was difficult for any teenager to not be awed by the presence of a decorated military man. He fumbled a messy salute and stood a little straighter. "Yessir?"

"These two men come looking for Mister Gordie," he said. "You seen him, Oliver?" The kid nodded and motioned towards one of the smaller storage shacks and saluted again.

"All right, Oliver," he said. "Back ta work." He waved the kid off and pointed towards the shack. "If ya follow me, sirs, we'll find your man." They walked between the crowds, avoiding the sparks from torches and the jagged pieces of metal scattered about. The USS Shangri-La cast a shadow over the constant activity, but the shade did little to cool the yard in the oppressive July sun. Considering the time of day and the way the summer heat hung heavy over this part of yard, it only made sense that Gordie was trying to find a cool spot to rest.

They found Gordie in the back, a wet towel over his thick neck as he wheezed and snorted. Both shirts he wore had been soaked through with sweat, and more perspiration dripped from his shaven head. In spite of the heat, he wore a pair of thick welding gloves and heavy boots. He raised his head and squinted at the three men, struggling to stand as he recognized the uniforms.

"Sit down, Gordie," he said. "These men come looking for you. Say they need you for some special sort of job." He removed his hat and rubbed his forehead, watching his man with an air of concern. "You want me to have them wait outside until you cool off more?" he asked.

The larger man shook his head, his broad shoulders slumping forward. "Not going to cool off much more, Cap. Besides, these gentlemen look like they came a ways for something." He coughed and mopped his face with a damp kerchief. "Wouldn't want to waste the time of a military man," he said.

One of the uniformed men escorted the supervisor to the door, going so far as to place his ear to the panel until the coast was clear. He gave a signal to his partner, who pulled up a chair next to the heavyset man.

"Gordon Wendell," he began. "Word is that you're a pretty talented man around these parts," he said carefully. "Something of a legend when it comes to finding things."

"I do what I can do with what I got, sir," Gordie replied with a wheeze. "Help where I'm needed, do what I'm asked, all in an honest day's work." He took a gulp of air and managed to lift his head. Thick folds of skin masked the presence of a neck, the stubble about his cheeks and chin white and coarse. His nose appeared to have been broken multiple times, the bridge flattened to the width of a grown man's thumb. His leathery complexion broke into a neat white smile that softened his otherwise rough features. "Not nearly what our boys are facing overseas, but we all work the best we can to help them, right?" he asked.

The man in the chair did not return the smile; instead, he bent to pick up a large wrench that someone had left on the ground. He weighed the heavy tool in his hand, finally letting it drop with a thud. "Say that young pup out there drops this over the side," he said. "You the sort of man to go and get it?"

Gordie shrugged, the sniff he had intended becoming more of a whuffle and snort. "I think it's only right t'help out someone who's still a little wet behind the ears, sir," he answered, turning his head enough to check the man at the door. "Something wrong with good manners and helping out a fellow in need?"

The man at the door ignored Gordie's question. "Mr. Wendell," he said in a brusque voice, "I'll have to ask that you remove your gloves before we go any further."

Gordie scowled and struggled to stand. He took a labored breath and drew himself up to all six feet and seven inches that he possessed. Gloved hands clenched to heavy fists, he dropped his voice to an irritated bass. "I don't know what this is supposed to be," he rumbled, "but I worked too long and fought too hard to make a dollar, just to become part of some big government witch hunt." One step forward, and he towered over the seated military man. "I work out here to help our boys fight them Nazi sons of bitches because I can't do it myself, and I'll be damned if I'm going to see someone disgrace that uniform by acting like one." Gordie's last words came in a snarl as he threw the handkerchief down and waited for an answer.

The man at the door answered Gordie's tirade with a professional chuckle. "Mister Wendell, to make a long story short, those Nazi sons of bitches are making a mess of our front yard."

He watched as the big man's expression went from furious to confused before continuing. "And considering all that we've heard about you," he said, motioning to his partner, "we think that you're the perfect man to help us clean things up."

△

From what she could tell, the man who had brought her on the submarine held some degree of authority. He kept the other crewmen from coming too close, ensured that she had enough to eat, and made certain she stayed in quarters that earned her envious stares from many of the other men. When she did sleep, the memory of the "showers" filled her dreams.

She had survived, burned by the gasses and haunted by the screams of the elderly, the young, and the infirm. Thought to be too weak by the Germans, she had been slated as another casualty. But when they had come to retrieve the bodies, they had regarded her with an air of fascination. How a supposedly weak creature had withstood the horrors of the gas chamber had mystified the doctors at the facility. They tried a second time, watching through the glass as she held her breath while the cells filled with the noxious air. A third time, they tried to drown her, but she remained alive under the water for the better part of an hour. So, they studied her, a pet to show to the visiting officers and a fascinating specimen for their scientists.

They had brought her to see him after the last demonstration. He was rail thin, eyes sunken, and his thick dark hair shaven. The way his eyes lit up, she could tell he was both grateful and envious, for she had been fed and groomed to appeal to the German visitors. Five minutes in strict silence passed quickly, but it had been enough for the Nazis' purpose.

That evening, she had met the officer who had brought her onboard. He spoke her language with a faint accent, and he made her an offer. Serve their cause with her gift, and they would treat her husband well as a household servant. Refuse their offer, and she would join him in the gas chambers, condemned to watch him die before her breath gave out and she succumbed to the same awful fate. To die meant nothing to one whose nightmares haunted her, but to watch the man she loved suffer because of her own selfish choice ...

They both lived, and she followed orders so that he was treated well. When she did see him, he appeared healthy, almost happy. To have him believe that she was not the same would have made him miserable. So, for him, she smiled and continued the pretty lie that kept them alive.

The door opened, the man who had brought her onboard followed by one she had not seen before. She noted his uniform; someone in authority, but not so high as the men who ran the ship. He scowled at her as he continued his disgruntled conversation with her "handler." Once the grumbling man left, the officer sat next to her, his manners almost brotherly since they had arrived on the ship.

"That was one of the engineers," he said. "It would appear that there is a problem with the ship." His expression became grave, his voice low. "They must do repairs, but if the enemy discovers us, then we will not reach the shore for our mission. If we fail, and they believe you to be dead, well ..." He trailed off, watching her eyes as she realized the severity of the situation. If she failed, then there was no reason for her beloved to be treated well. Her promise would have been for naught.

The officer placed a warm hand over hers. "Would you assist? The engineer, he told me what could be done, but they lack your gift," he said. His smile widened as she nodded fervently, and he clasped her small hand in a grateful gesture. "I will tell him myself," he said, standing. "Rest. We will have much work to do soon enough."

The door to the compartment closed softly once more. Both the head engineer and the XO waited, their expressions skeptical. "Well?" the XO asked. "Will she be able to lay the mines? Untethered?"

"You underestimate our *Aufatmen*," the officer said with a wolfish grin. "Of course. That is the strength of having a woman in your service. The bonds to her family are far stronger than any rope we could provide."

At Little Creek, they had clocked Gordie at thirty-five minutes for a thirty-foot dive. The resident doc figured that Gordie could probably go as deep as a hundred and thirty-five feet and not suffer for it. Still, they had reminded him as he had boarded the seaplane, the depth of the water was the least of his worries.

"Mr. Wendell, sir? We're nearly here," the kid yelled over the roar of the plane. "You doing okay?"

Gordie managed a nod despite the amount of sweat pouring down his face and the feeling that his stomach was ready to leap out of his throat. "Doing just fine," he rasped. "Guess they build your types with guts of steel these days, huh?"

"Naw, sir. We lose our breakfast plenty out here. That's why you don't see any fat flyboys." The kid laughed at his own joke before yanking the door open. Below, the water shimmered in the July sun, the serene surface concealing a wealth of trouble beneath. Before Gordie could protest, the kid unfastened his shoulder harness and held his upper arm with surprising strength.

"Straight into the water, sir," he instructed. "We give you twenty minutes to find the target. You mark her, come straight up." He motioned towards a cutter and support boats in the distance. "Crew will pick you up once you surface in the given window," he said. "No later."

Gordie nodded, too queasy to speak. Instead, he flashed a smile at the kid and moved towards the door. With a deep breath, the man crossed his arms over his chest, said a quick prayer, and jumped.

The rush of cool water jarred Gordie out of the nauseous

semi-conscious state he had endured on the plane. He kicked to the surface for a deeper breath of air, then disappeared under the waves. Within seconds, the film covering his eyes cleared, his vision ideal for the task at hand. The water pressed against him as he dove deeper, sinking more than swimming into the darker and colder waters of the Atlantic coast. At twenty feet, the water was pleasant and refreshing, the colors vibrant and diverse. At forty feet, the temperature began to drop, the brighter hues began to fade, and Gordie felt the water begin to close about him. Sixty feet became eighty feet, and the environment darkened to a deceptively calm blur of deep green and cool blue. His nostrils and ears closed tight against the saltwater, Gordie continued to swim deeper and deeper. A shadow flickered along the bottom, an odd clicking noise carrying through the water. He froze, blinked to clear his vision, and listened.

Two years ago, they had all assumed the worst. An accident at the yard had sent him into the water, pinned by a piece of anchor chain as thick as a man's arm. Stuck in the frigid November waters, Gordie had struggled until his vision faded, and his pulse thudded in his ears. His mother had called it a miracle that he had survived. The doctors had called it remarkable and spent weeks interviewing him while he fought off a mild case of pneumonia. Gordie had merely called it luck and asked when he could go back to work running tools and supplies at the yard. In spite of it all, Gordie never shied away from the water. When the newer kids dropped precious tools overboard, someone would find him and ask for a favor. He never let them pay him, but someone always brought him a cup of coffee or a homemade something from a thankful wife or mother. No one had ever told the higher-ups, but somehow, they had found out. And now, he was here.

The shadow flickered beneath him again, the rush of bubbles and metallic *thunk* proof enough that something—and someone—was down there. Gordie swam back and down another ten feet, watching the shadow dart back and forth along the sea floor. An immense shape loomed in front of him, the markings familiar to anyone who read the papers; a U-boat, from what he could tell, and certainly the largest that he had seen. He had seen the pictures at the military briefings, but it didn't compare to seeing one this close. Gordie moved closer, careful to stay well above the propeller shaft. The numbers and insignia matched what he had been told to expect, but the fact that he was here, able to lay a hand against a Nazi submarine, prompted him to pause and shake his head. As long as he kept clear of a periscope's view and listened for critters, he could scope out the area. Perhaps they hadn't tried to lay any of the mines yet.

A thin arm wrapped around his neck, spindly hands clawing at his face. Caught off guard, Gordie jabbed back with a meaty elbow and was rewarded with a bite to his shoulder. The thin skinsuit did little to keep teeth from sinking into his skin. Gordie grimaced at the pain, knowing better than to cry out. If there was even a mediocre set of ears in the Nazi rust bucket sub, they would hear him for certain. He reached back clumsily for something to grab, but his assailant was too quick. He thrashed as teeth sank into his ear, groping blindly as a hand raked across his back. Another came across his face as if to rip off a diver's mask, and the fingers paused for a brief moment as they touched skin and nothing more.

The slow and steady groan of a Coast Guard cutter carried through the water, and the clawing at his eyes abruptly ceased, even as he closed a webbed hand around the thin forearm. Gordie whipped his attacker around, staring into the masked face with a mixture of shock and surprise. Like Gordie, the Nazi diver wore no helmet or tether, but while the Navy's own seal needed no goggles, this diver wore a thick facemask to see through the water.

The face and the mask that covered it came down hard on the bridge of Gordie's nose, and he was unable to contain the yelp as he brought both hands to his face. The Nazi diver darted back to the U-boat, disappearing into what appeared to be a modified torpedo chute. Rather than follow her, Gordie quickly rose to the surface of the water and began to swim for the cutter as blood streamed from his broken nose. Time was of the essence; now, it was only a matter of who would be able to fire first.

△

They had heard the ships in the distance before she returned, bruised and bleeding around her mask. The men in the torpedo room did not concern themselves with her safety, throwing her aside like so much garbage to ready the attack. The officer who had brought her on board found her moments later, and he hauled her to a standing position and shook her violently.

"Did you set them? Did you put them out there before they came?" He tightened his grip, his expression darkening as she shook her head from side to side. Before she could offer some explanation, he threw her against the wall. The back of his hand cracked across her face, the blow drawing blood. She staggered back, only to be shoved forward by someone else in uniform. He snapped at the officer, who shoved her ahead of him towards the control room.

The explosion threw them both forward, the alarms drowning out the groan of metal and the frantic barking of orders from every compartment. The craft heaved to starboard, the outer hull scraping against the seafloor. She clung to a pipe, fingernails scraping the inside as she fought to stay upright. Behind her, a rush of water overtook the screams of the crewmen in the torpedo room. She shared a frightened look with the officer, who quickly moved towards the compartment door and struggled to open it. From the other side, she could hear the officers in their crisp German, the words unfamiliar but the urgency unmistakable. Water pooled about her feet, the level rising quickly as the seal to the torpedo room weakened. Within minutes, the compartment would be filled, and the rest of the submarine would be little more than a tomb awaiting the deaths of the condemned.

She moved towards the broken door, her handler still trying to persuade the others to open the hatch to drier and safer compartments. With an almost serene smile, she put her hand to the latch and yanked. Water and fuel rushed past her, and she quickly ducked beneath the surface. Debris spilled in, and she caught a broken piece of pipe in one hand. With grim determination, she swam to the bulkhead where her handler banged on the hatch. While they could not survive in the water, she could use her curse to solicit aid from the enemy. She swung the piece of pipe wildly, missing her mark but still catching him off guard. He whirled around, surprised and frightened as the water continued to pour in from the torpedo room. She swung again, catching him between the eyes this time. He slipped beneath the rising water, unable to stand as the rush grew stronger. She brought the pipe down a third time with surprising ferocity, crushing his windpipe with the force of the blow. With the water rising past her shoulders, she took a breath and ducked beneath the surface.

Perhaps she would survive to find the other breath-holder that the Allies possessed.

As the Coast Guard cutter stood watch, a crew of divers worked to attach cable and canisters to the sunken submarine. Gordie kept a constant path from the boat to the underwater team. As the last cable was pulled tight, the rest of the crew began a slow ascent along the lead cable. Come up too fast, and they would be plagued with the bends. Some watched Gordie with envy as he swam to the surface for another breath and disappeared beneath the surface for one last check.

He could feel the blood pounding slow and heavy in his ears. Gordie squinted through the murky water. Not thirty seconds

later, he froze as a sharp sound cracked through the water with
surprising volume. It came again, followed by a heavy metallic
groan that shook the entire area. Gordie winced, nostrils flat-
tening as he dove deeper. A rush of bubbles shot past him and he
looked down at the crippled beast on the seafloor. He swam the
length of the craft twice. Aft of center along the port side, the
hull had suffered a massive breach. Experience at the yard told
Gordie that it had been a torpedo hit, and an insufficient one at
that. Most of the submarines that got hit were never so lucky as
to be so intact after a fight. No wonder the Navy boys wanted
him to find it ...

Another shot cracked through the relative stillness, followed
by several more. They came from the inside, which meant two
things: one, someone was alive in there and two, they wanted to
ensure that others would be dead. Gordie pulled his hand back
from the hull and began to swim to each of the canisters. Whatever had fired those shots had to be on the inside of the submarine, and Gordie had no desire to wait to see what might appear.
Bubbles streamed from the top hatch as the wheel inched
around, the seal to the inner compartment giving way as something inside attempted to escape. Placing himself on top of the
hatch, Gordie gripped the wheel to keep it from turning, and to
keep whatever it was inside from escaping.

Gordon Wendell was a big man. A half-inch thick layer of
skin and fat covered a muscular frame and at nearly three
hundred pounds, his weight set firmly atop the hatch made
anyone's escape nearly impossible. It did not, however, keep the
person on the other side from trying to turn the wheel. Gordie
braced himself against the rail and pushed against the efforts of
whoever was on the other side. For a moment, there was no
resistance, but through the water and the hull, he could hear the
muted sounds of a struggle on the inside. A gunshot—he was
close enough to be certain of the sound—rang through the
compartment before the wheel began to turn in his hands again.

The water rushed past him as the canisters popped, air filling the balloons as the cables assisted the submarine's rise to the surface. Gordie fought the pull of the water and the still-desperate attempt of the person on the other side of the hatch. He groaned as the water broke over his back, the submarine heaving topside like some great ill leviathan. Within minutes, a half-dozen men had their sidearms trained on the hatch, the officer in charge of the operation calling for Gordie to step back and let the wheel turn freely.

With nothing to keep the hatch closed, Gordie watched as the only entry to the submarine flipped open and a thin woman in a German uniform scrambled out of the compartment. Wild-eyed, she looked to the sailors, babbling in a language that Gordie couldn't quite understand while frantically rolling up the left sleeve of her jacket.

"Hands up, Miss!" one of the officers barked. "Now!" He repeated the order in broken German, which had the desired effect. Slowly, she brought both hands above her head, the sleeve of one arm falling far enough to reveal a series of numbers and symbols tattooed on the inside of her forearm.

Her voice shook as she tried to speak, her own German heavily accented. "*Aufatmen*," she struggled to say. "*Ich bin Aufatmen*." She searched the faces of the assembled sailors for some sign of understanding, repeating the first word more slowly. For a brief moment, her eyes met Gordie's, and she gave an apologetic nod when she saw his broken nose.

A series of shots rang out from below deck, bullets hitting the end of the hatch and the rail. The young woman crumpled to the deck with a cry of surprise and the assembled sailors opened fire into the submarine. As two of them dragged the woman's body away, the officer in charge slammed the hatch and motioned for a crewman to seal it shut.

"Cut the line," the officer called to the deck of the cutter. "Drop charges and sink that piece of junk. The only Nazis coming out of that can better be the dead ones that float to the top."

△

On the quarterdeck, Gordie watched with a mixture of shock and guilt as they carried the woman's body past him. The officer who had spoken to her in German came up next to Gordie and offered him a cigarette.

"A woman," he said in honest disbelief. He pocketed the pack at Gordie's polite refusal. "Never told us nothing about a woman being there. Guess those scum have no decency." He and Gordie watched in silence as the soldiers placed the body in a canvas bag. "Guess you didn't know either," he said.

Gordie thought about the fight with the creature in the deep water, the bite marks on his ear and the scratches on his face. He hadn't known it was a woman, not with her in the suit and how thin she had appeared. "No, sir. I heard someone trying to get out when I found it first. If I'd known ..." The words trailed off as Gordie shook his head.

The commanding officer of the ship approached the pair, the other man saluting his superior while Gordie did his best to respectfully mimic the greeting. The CO nodded, dismissing the other man and pulling Gordie to the side.

"Son," the man began, even though he couldn't have been more than ten years older than the shipyard worker. "We all have jobs asked of us, and when we perform them to the best of our ability, that's all we can do." He spoke the words with an air of detachment, as if the Navy prescribed them for this very situation. "You did the right thing," he finally added, reaching up to pat Gordie on the shoulder. "Done your country proud."

The sea heaved and shook as the depth charges ensured the final resting place of the German submarine. With his task complete and the parcel retrieved, the Navy's Seal leaned heavily against the railing and anxiously awaited their return to port.

△

Once WWII was over, metahumans organized under the auspices of ECHO, the Extrahuman Coalition for Humanitarian Operations, under the command of the son of Nikola Tesla, Yankee Doodle, and Dixie Belle.

But there is another secret world at work in the world of SWC, as I showed in "Sgian Dubh," and that is the force of magic.

Under the threat of the Cold War, a very few magicians emerged in the US to aid law enforcement and ECHO, posing as metahumans. Two of those were the werewolf, Alexander Nagy, and his witch wife, who I modeled a little on Poul Anderson's characters from his novel Operation Chaos. *These are the parents of Vix Victrix.*

I've said many times that Victoria Victrix Nagy is my favorite of my SWC characters. That's probably why I wrote (and am still writing) so many prequel stories about her, before she became the mentally and physically scarred creature she was at the beginning of Invasion.

EXEMPLAR

MERCEDES LACKEY

Vickie Nagy hefted the backpack up onto her shoulders, and winced. It was freaking heavy. Why couldn't magic books be light? You'd think that *someone* would think of adding a little lifting spell to the spines, or something, when they were bound. But no.

Teachers prolly just want us reminded of how "weighty" our studies are, she thought with resignation, as she faced what looked like the blank cinder block wall of the basement. Mom and Dad had already gone to work; she had locked up the house completely behind them, Locks and Wards as well as physical locks. She'd locked herself in, of course; she wouldn't be leaving the house by a door.

Not a conventional door, anyway.

She closed her eyes and envisioned the mathemagical formulas for the Apporting spell (*"remember, a spell is a process and not a thing"*) then ran through them as her hands sketched the glyph-components in the air in front of herself. Then, with her eyes still closed, she walked confidently to, and through the wall.

There was the expected moment of disorientation, and the burst of nausea caused by every Apporting spell. When it passed, she opened her eyes.

She was no longer in the basement of a little bungalow in Quantico, Virginia. She was somewhere—and only a handful of people knew *where*—in upstate New York. She stood in the Center Courtyard of St. Rhiannon's School for Exceptional Students, in the exact center of a Magical Circle carefully inlaid in the granite of the paving, under a blinding blue, warm September sky.

The Magical Circle was a construction built of several Circles, actually; this was one of the most complex permanent Circles she'd ever seen. Literally a Master Piece, it had been put together by the Founders as one of the first constructions of this School, so there would never be a road leading to it. She had to presume that all of the material used to construct the School had been Apported here directly. It must have been a massive undertaking.

The school buildings were some of the oldest in North America, had been built on the pattern of Merlin College in Oxford, and the Founders had left no safety factor unconsidered when creating the "landing pad" for their institution. Well, *she* called it a "landing pad." The people who spelled magic with a "k" on the end referred to it as a lot of other things, most of them sounding like the terms came straight out of a D & D book. The location of St. Rhia's was so secret not even Vickie's parents could get there by anything but Apport. Probably the Dean and a couple of other senior Professors who literally never left the place knew where it really was, but no one else. Somehow, some way, they were even keeping the school screened from satellite and other aerial cameras. You couldn't see it from an airplane, and nothing led to it.

It sometimes seemed ridiculous to Vickie that in an age where metahumans saved the day with their superhuman powers so often their stories only ended up on Page Three of the newspaper, her fellow magicians should be so paranoid about keeping their existence ultra-secret from most. But ... *well, maybe not. It's true that the majority of metahumans have secret identities. And I've never heard of any schools for super-teens either. Maybe all of us are better off hiding in plain sight.*

There were four smaller primary Circles within the larger one, one at each of the cardinal points, and a slightly bigger one in the middle. Vickie was in the North, the Earth point. She quickly moved off it and onto clear pavement. As long as she stood there, whoever was next and was Earth couldn't come in. Simple physics; two bodies cannot occupy the same space at the same time. Of course, the Founders had never thought of it as physics, but they had understood the principle.

The central courtyard was paved with what looked like granite, and the four buildings around her were likewise built of stone, and looked positively ancient, although they were equipped with modern things like central heating and electricity and all that inside. Thank the gods. Otherwise going to school here would be like torture, especially in the winter. Or like living in a Dickens novel, an experience she would really rather pass on.

The buildings looked a lot like many of the buildings at Oxford University in the UK, actually; Gothic, but in the pretty way, not the morbid way. Stone made graceful. More of the "dreaming spires" that poets talked about. It was hard not to feel a little awe.

North and South were the classrooms, East was the dorms for the live-in students, and West was home to the teachers' apartments, theater, gym, library ... all the other things that weren't classrooms or dorms. The place was set in the middle of an extensive garden. Outside the garden were thick woods that looked really, really old, and impenetrable, although Vickie knew for a fact that the students were actually encouraged to explore them.

Most students lived here; there were only a few that were "day pupils," like Vickie. There were a lot of reasons for that, but the chiefest were that most students didn't have the benefit of having parents as magically apt as Vickie's—or even had parents that actually believed in magic. And those parents who *were* magicians were busy making sure everyone around them thought they were mundies. That made it hard to cover up for your budding Magikal Childe. Very few kids understood as young as Vickie had that making fireworks and drawing attention to the fact that you were very different was dangerous.

She'd had a full day of Orientation already, though thanks to working unofficially with her parents for a couple of years now, she thought of it as a "briefing." So she set out confidently for North Quad, knowing exactly where her first class was.

Maybe other kids came here with mingled dread and anxiety; all she could feel was relief. Finally, she was going to go to a school where she didn't have to hide what she was. Finally, she *wasn't* going to be spending every waking hour in *some* kind of lesson or other—because for as long as she could remember, she had been going to normal schools like every other kid, then coming home and plunging straight into magic lessons. She generally hadn't been finished with homework and magic-work until an hour before bedtime, and freshman year at Chafee High School had darn near finished her.

After seeing her shorting herself on sleep and running herself ragged, to the point where she had permanent dark circles under her eyes and the teachers at Chafee High School were calling her folks for conferences and asking pointed questions about drugs, Alexander and Moira Nagy had decided enough was enough. They'd wanted her to have a "normal" life—but this was anything *but* normal. They pulled her from Chafee after Spring Break and arranged for her to come here.

All that the State of Virginia cared about was that you were in *a* school until you were old enough to quit. The authorities didn't really care which school. St. Rhia's was no different from any other private school so far as they were concerned.

So far as the parents of about half of the students here were concerned, this was some sort of correctional school supported by eccentric benefactors, and as long as they saw their offspring as little as possible and there were no obvious signs of abuse, the lack of parental access bothered them not at all. Budding mages born into normal families tended to get into a lot of trouble they couldn't adequately explain as they came into their powers, and adult magicians out in the world were always on the alert for the signs of a youngster in need of rescue. A little glamorie, a little persuasive geas, and the relieved parents were happily sending their "problem" off to be dealt with by someone else. And as for the kids, well, Vickie was pretty sure they were as relieved to finally find themselves in a place where they actually *belonged* as she had been. Vickie had even written a paper once postulating that the legends of "changelings" could be traced to magicians being born into mundie families. The fact that, in legends, changelings were almost universally rejected by their parents was certainly mirrored in the rejection modern mundie parents evidenced in dealing with magical offspring.

Maybe there's something about magic that mundie instincts completely revolt against.

Mom had really liked the paper, and had made it part of her application to St. Rhia's. It was a good theory, anyway.

So far as the parents of the *other* half were concerned—the parents who were themselves magicians—St. Rhia's was the place where their children were free to study and practice magic openly, and where they would get the best magical education to be had in North America. More part of the campaign to keep their nature hidden; at St. Rhia's, their kids learned both magic and camouflage. Eventually, some few, with the right skills, would actually go off and pass as metahumans, joining ECHO, with no one ever the wiser about *where* their abilities came from.

Even Vickie's parents managed that, at least as far as most of the FBI was concerned. Outside of Section 39, except at the very top levels of the Bureau, no one was aware that they were anything other than metahumans—or that the things they stalked were considerably different than "mere" super-criminals.

Vickie hurried in through the ornate double doors of North, joining a stream of others who were making their way from East Quad and the dorms. The contrast between this place and her old high school could not have been greater. Inside and out, it looked like a movie setting. She felt as if she should at the least be wearing one of the academic gowns from a BBC period drama, and not the jeans, white shirt, and blue sweater that were the school uniform for everyone. As she hurried up the handsomely carved steps to her first class, though, she felt herself grinning. Like everyone else, her school day was going to be spent half in academic classes, but half in magic. She wasn't going to have to pretend magic didn't exist, or hide it anymore. *This is going to be great!*

△

Morning classes were ... mixed. Exciting, because she was finally getting to practice and talk about magic and *be* a magician in the open for the first time. Frustrating because no one, literally no one, seemed to talk about how *she* saw magic.

It's the math! she thought, bewildered, as they went on about vibrations and components and stuff that really didn't matter as long as you knew the math. It was as if they simply didn't realize that magic and physics were not only related, they were so incestuously related they might as well have been Borgias. It was as if no one understood that as long as you knew the math, you didn't need the components and ... all of the other rigamarole. Well, the glyphs and diagrams, maybe, because you still had to impose your will on the energy, and that was the easiest way to do it. But the rest? Not so much ...

She wondered if this just wasn't a way to get kids to work and understand spellcasting without forcing them into the math. Obviously it *worked,* since they were doing magic successfully, and all the old grimoires were built around *eye of newt and tongue of dog* and all that sort of icky procedure, so obviously this was how people had been practicing magic since the year dot. But these were modern times, and man had walked on the moon. It was time to modernize. *And wouldn't it be better to start them on the math first?*

But when she tried to talk to the teachers about it, they smiled patronizingly and suggested she was oversimplifying.

The lessons themselves, once she got over the excitement of actually being able to do all of this in public, were ... boring. She'd been doing these sorts of things since she was ten or twelve. This was all *old.* It was the math, of course. When you knew the math, you could always get exactly the same result, at least in this really simple stuff. The Uncertainty Principle really didn't apply when you were lighting candles and Apporting small objects. When you knew the math, you could make shortcuts, and you didn't have to memorize pages and pages of chants and what-have-you. When you knew the math, you not only could do *one* spell, you could figure out how to generalize and do all kinds of spells that were like that one spell.

And there was another fly in the ointment, though it was hardly an unexpected one. She'd figured out within the first half hour that this school was no different from any other. There were cliques. There was an elite coterie of the Very Popular and Very Pretty. There were jocks of some sort (you could tell by the muscles and the attitude), who were part of the Very Popular. The Elite made it their business to try and make life miserable for the Outcastes.

Back in mundie schools, Vickie had mostly kept her mouth shut, her head down, and worn a little glamorie that basically made the Very Popular ignore her. She'd managed to skate along being a lone wolf. You could say that was in her blood, after all ... No one had bothered her. No one had noticed her. Even her teachers had a tendency to forget about her once she was outside of a classroom, and called her "Veronica" or "Valerie" instead of her real name.

Well, glamories weren't going to work here; everyone here her age and some younger could see right through them. She'd already been getting the eyeball from the Elites—and now she was standing just outside the dining hall, knowing that she could stroll in there, find where the Smart Set was eating and see if she got an invitation to sit with them. Which, if she was reading the interest right, she probably would.

Now, this was the first time the Leaders of the Pack at a school had *ever* wanted anything to do with her. And ... it was tempting to let them hook her in. Being popular ... well, obviously it was *fun*. Great parties. Boyfriends. People wishing they were you. And after graduation? Connections. Favors to be called in. People begging to do you favors.

The trouble was, there was always a price tag attached to that sort of gang. Generally it was the one where you soiled your soul by "going along" with things you knew were wrong. And in a place like this, those things were going to be by definition not only wrong, but very sneaky. Vickie could see how *her* skillsets would be very valuable to kids who were doing things they shouldn't be. They didn't know that yet, of course—but if she just went along, she'd be sailing along on easy street until she graduated, and afterwards too.

But she *helped* people, not hurt them. It was what she did. It was what her parents did. Even the Nagy family motto said as much: *Servire et Tueri*. With a sigh—just a little regret, because she knew allowing herself to be roped in by the Pretty People would make her life *so* much easier—she resigned herself to the fact that, tempting as it was ... no. It would be wrong. Oh well. At least she didn't have to *live* here, so their opportunities to cause trouble for her would be limited.

And maybe, just maybe, she could still skate by under their radar as long as she didn't outright reject them. She could always play the Captain Oblivious card.

Right, then. She squared her shoulders and marched into the dining hall.

This wasn't anything like the cafeterias in mundie schools. This was a *dining hall,* with tables with tablecloths and chairs, not plastic picnic benches. Food was served "family style" from platters and bowls on the tables, and the proctors at each end of the long tables watched you to make sure you took some of everything, and didn't just fill up on carbs and sweets.

She headed for the nearest table to the door; it was scarcely a prime spot, it wasn't near the windows and it was far enough from the kitchen that stuff that cooled off fast would probably arrive lukewarm at best. There wasn't one of the Elites anywhere near it. With luck, they'd never notice she was in here, she could get her lunch and get out with no one the wiser.

"Hi," she said, grabbing a chair next to a thin, pale boy who looked a bit younger than she was. "I'm Vickie, I just started today."

She addressed the entire group at the table, who stopped eating and stared at her as if she had spoken in Urdu. Even the proctors looked a little surprised by her choice of seating.

"Uh ... wouldn't you rather sit—" one of them started to stammer.

"This is just fine, thanks," she interrupted, and took a seat, looking around her brightly. "Could you pass the beets please?"

"Are you sure you wouldn't rather be nearer the windows?" the other proctor said, carefully.

"I'm not fussy," she replied, and filled her plate.

That was about all the conversation she managed to get out of any of her tablemates. She tried making conversation herself, but when every overture she attempted was met with nervous silence, she mentally shrugged, exchanged a few dull pleasantries with the two proctors, and just finished her meal. She felt the glares on the back of her neck as she excused herself and went to her locker, though, and she guessed there was about to be a confrontation. The Elites had spotted her attempt to avoid them, and they were not happy about the rejection.

Not surprising really. Rejection wasn't something they had to deal with. It probably stung a lot.

Only the day students had lockers, since only the day students needed them—though these were less "lockers" in the mundie sense and more like small locking closets. Wood, of course, and very posh, polished wood at that. Vickie sensed the bodies closing in around her as she got the books she needed for the next class. So she took her time about it, and made sure she had the door locked securely before she turned.

And feigned surprise at seeing the little group lurking in an arc between her and the rest of the hallway. "Welcome Wagon?" she asked, arching an eyebrow. "I'm honored."

She read their faces and their body language, and reckoned that their next move would be intimidation. *Wow, unforgiving lot, aren't you?* Now, there were a lot of ways to play this. Officially, the use of magic on fellow pupils, except in specific classes, like

magical dueling, was strictly forbidden. Unofficially, well ...
Vickie was pretty sure she knew plenty of dirty tricks she could
get away with.

But that would be wrong. And unethical.

She could handle this physically. She might be small, but she
had a lot of tricks up her sleeve.

They might think they were at a physical advantage, since St.
Rhia's had plenty of classes in all kinds of fighting—she was
enrolled in staff work and was going to be going to that class
next, in fact. She was, however, also pretty sure that she was
probably better than these kids had any notion of in martial arts.

But that would make her the attacker, not the attacked. That
would be wrong too.

However, one thing she had noticed was that there was a
huge hole in the fighting classes, as evidenced by the mere fact
that they were just that. *Fighting* classes. There was not one
single purely defensive class. No martial Tai Chi. No Tae Kwon
Do. And there was her answer. She had been studying Tae Kwon
Do since she was a toddler, as part of the effort to keep her from
becoming Daddy's Little Hostage to Daddy's Enemies. Tae
Kwon Do was perfect for getting out of physical confrontations
smelling of roses.

All righty then, she thought, and smiled up into the face of a
girl who, in any other school would have been Head Cheerleader.
"Well, obviously not," she said, sweetly. "I have a great idea. You
go back to whatever *supah* special elite thing it is you do,
comparing teeth whitening spells and figuring out glamories to
make your hair shine, and I go on to class. I get what I want, you
get what you want. Everybody wins."

Evidently, she struck a nerve, or maybe they weren't used to
anyone actually daring to be insolent with them, because the
girl's face reddened, and she actually was stupid—or unpracticed
—enough to telegraph her intended slap. Vickie was not only
able to easily step off the line of attack, the girl stumbled and
nearly fell into the lockers when Vickie's face wasn't there to get

the slap. And while she was stumbling forward, Vickie was able to slide past the girl and through the hole in the line she made.

Before any of them could react, Vickie was already doing a fast, purposeful walk in the direction of her next class.

If she had any luck at all, they'd decide she wasn't worth the effort of going after.

One could only hope.

△

The pale, thin boy was in her magic lab that afternoon, and the teacher partnered the two of them. And for the first half hour she couldn't get a word out of him, not even regarding the assignment. Finally, when the teacher had gone to the other side of the classroom to help someone else, she grabbed his wrist.

"Look," she hissed, as he went utterly still and stared at her in numb fear, "I can do an Apport in my sleep—and in five minutes. I can show you how to do the same. Talk to me. What the heck is wrong with you?"

"Y-you shouldn't be talking to me," he stammered. "They'll find ou—"

"Haven't you gotten it through your head that I don't give a rat's ass about what they think?" she replied scornfully. "I will go right through the next three years not giving a rat's ass about what they think. How are they getting away with bullying you?"

His jaw dropped. "How did you—"

"Oh *please*. You act like a scared rabbit. This place has rules about bullying, so how are they getting away with it?" She glared at him and he dropped his eyes.

"Because ... nobody cares," he whispered.

"Well I care." She firmed her chin.

But he shook his head. "You think you do, but you won't. Nobody does once they—"

But before she could find out what was going on, the teacher came back to their side of the room and they had to go back to the Apporting exercise. When class was over, he gathered up his books and bolted before she even got a chance to say another word.

$$\triangle$$

"Well?" Moira Nagy said, her fork poised over her meatloaf. "First day?"

Vickie sighed, and stirred her mashed potatoes. "It's better than Chafee. But I'd thought the magic classes would be more of a challenge. I'm practically sleeping through them. It's all stuff I knew three years ago."

It was hideously disappointing, actually, but she couldn't tell her parents that. After all the work they had gone through to get her in?

"They're still evaluating you, kitten," her father said, as her mother's brows creased with faint annoyance. "They can't exactly take our word for what you can do."

Moira flicked a scarlet curl over her shoulders and lost the look of annoyance. "Of course, I should have realized that and warned you. *Every* child is the next Merlin in her mother's eyes. Give it a little time, and they'll bump you up into more advanced classes."

"Yes, but—" Vickie stopped her own protest before she made it. Even her own parents didn't quite understand how she saw magic—only that she saw it very differently from the way they did, and that Vickie's way was startlingly efficient. "Anyway, it's frustrating."

Actually she had come home only to cry a little. She *wanted* to be crammed full of new magical knowledge. She needed it the way she needed air. She just didn't study magic, she *was* magic, and she felt as if she was being starved for it.

But ... brave face. Never mind that there were bullies, just like mundie school, and that she was being put back on training wheels. Brave face. At least at St. Rhia's she was safe to be who she was. Not like some people. That pale kid, for instance.

"This too will pass," said her father, and grinned at her as he shook his blond hair—just like hers—out of his eyes. "Meanwhile, it's meatloaf night, and I bet you get your homework done in two hours or less."

"Or less," she said, and felt at least a little smug about that. "I did half of it in study hall, and like I said, I don't even need to think about the magical part." Then she brightened, as she remembered the one part of the whole day that hadn't been a disappointment. "Oh! And Staff Fighting is *righteous!*"

"Verily," he agreed, and went on to suggest things to her while she listened intently. So intently she forgot to mention the Pretty People thugs and the pale kid that was being bullied, and her concern that she would end up being bullied too. By the time she remembered again, it didn't seem quite as important. For herself, well, it was Tae Kwon Do again. Really, all she had to do was keep evading and eventually they'd just give up.

As for the kid, well, he needed to be willing to *be* helped before she could help him. Still. *I'll keep trying to corner him,* she promised herself before she gave in to the bliss of a DS9 episode followed by a brand-new Charles de Lint novel. It was the first time during a school year that she had *ever* had time for both a TV show and a chapter of a book in the same evening.

And for the first time during a school year, she was going to be able to go to bed at a decent hour—which might have been an odd thing for a kid her age to think about, but then, most kids her age hadn't shorted themselves on sleep so often they had to resort to Triple Red-Eyes to stay awake during the day. No more worshipping at the altar of the Goddess Caffeina.

So ... there was some good.

△

The Pretty People left her alone. Sort of. They didn't try to surround her and intimidate her a second time—which at least proved that the bullies of St. Rhia's were a lot smarter than the bullies of Chafee—but there was a lot of whispering and obvious gossip going on. This, Vickie had expected. And she hadn't been lying when she'd told the pale kid that she didn't give a rat's ass. Maybe—heck, probably—spending so much time in the company of her parents and their peers had given her a certain amount of insulation from what her *own* peers thought and said, and a long view of things. What did it matter, really, when in three years she would be gone, and the only rumors that could possibly cause her any trouble were that she cheated or that she was easy. The first, she could disprove in a heartbeat, and Mom and Dad would back her up. The second, well, any guy or even group of guys that tried anything on her was going to end up singing in the upper registers for quite some time. And that was if they were lucky. She strongly doubted that any of the kids here had ever had to fight for real. If she was actually attacked with intent to harm, bottom line, they would find out she never hesitated, and never held back. She couldn't afford to. She wouldn't *kill* anyone, but there would be people in the hospital and none of them would be her.

Still, when just before lunch some of the whispers finally got loud enough to reach her, she nearly dropped the books she was getting out of her locker in surprise.

"Lipstick lesbian ..."

"Fag hag."

That was the best they could do? Really?

They're dumber than I thought. Why they thought rumors about being gay, or gay-friendly were going to cause her a moment of unrest—well, they hadn't been paying attention. First of all, St. Rhia's had very firm policies in place about homophobia, to wit that acting on it was an invitation for expulsion. And secondly—well—she really and truly did not give a rat's ass.

Then again, this might be 2002, but there were still plenty of people out there with homophobia, and it looked like there was a big fat clot of them right here in St. Rhia's. Just because they were all young magicians, it didn't follow that all or even most of them had exposure to all of the myriad sorts of folks Vickie'd had. If anything, their upbringing might be even more insular than the average mundie and—

Wait a second. Fag hag ... She could almost hear the mental pieces clicking together and solving the puzzle of the pale kid. And that was when she got angry. Because it was bad enough to bully someone, but to do it over something they couldn't help, any more than they could help the color of their eyes, just made it all the worse.

Heck if I am putting up with this shite. The first thing to do, though, would be to verify. Which, fortunately, she was in the perfect position to do. She hurried to the dining hall, and headed straight for the table she'd sat at yesterday, plunking herself down beside the pale boy, who looked even more alarmed than he had yesterday. She said nothing, however, until the proctors happened to be looking away.

Looking, in fact, at the Pretty People who were engaged in some stupidly obvious whispering, giggling, and smirking. Vickie took the moment to lean over and whisper in the pale kid's ear.

"Follow me. Just leave your lunch and follow me. And don't argue if you know what's good for you."

She was pretty certain that he had been cowed enough by the bullies that he would just do what she ordered without question, and she was right. She got up and left the table, acting as if she was upset by the whispers, and he followed a moment later. As soon as they were out of sight and the door to the dining hall had closed, she grabbed his hand and headed for the central courtyard.

"What—" the poor kid gasped, his pale face even paler, as he probably anticipated her taking some sort of revenge on him.

"Hush," she said, put him in the Earth circle with her, and burned through the equations. He gasped as they Apported into the basement of her house.

"But you—but—" His eyes were as big as the proverbial saucers. "How did you—"

"Because I've been doing Apports since I was twelve, I told you," she said, seizing his hand and dragging him upstairs to the kitchen, where she shoved him down into a chair and threw a couple of Cornish Meat Pasties into the microwave. "Here," she said, handing him one. "Now I can talk to you without anyone interfering."

"But I thought—we aren't supposed to leave—" he stammered.

"I'm a Day Student, I'm allowed to go home," she pointed out, and smirked. "And I'm allowed to bring study partners with me. Of course, they're rather stupidly assuming that it's Mom doing the Apport, and not me, and that I'm stuck at school until she gets me. That's not my problem. Who's bullying you? The Pretty People?"

"How—why—" he began, and then his face just crumpled and words poured out of him. Mostly, they were nonsense about how he was going to hell, he was a pervert, and he deserved every bit of it. Vickie let him spew, then cut him off.

"Did you get that crap from your parents?" she said, scornfully.

He nodded.

"And I bet they would tell you that you were going to hell if they thought you were doing magic, too, wouldn't they?" she pointed out. The poor kid actually started, as if she had slapped him.

"But I—but they—"

"They're wrong about both, obviously," she interrupted again. "And if I have to keep you sitting here until we both get demerits from missing class until you believe it, I will." She paused. "Or else I'll tickle you into submission. Either one works."

The second was so absurd he actually laughed weakly.

"Okay. We're good." She grinned at him. "Now, let's get to the important part. We're going to keep anyone from messing with you ever again. After classes, you come back with me; they told me specifically I can bring people home for study partners. I have a plan...."

△

Every afternoon, Vickie and her new "study partner" Apported straight home and went to work. After seeing they really *were* working and not fooling around (and probably realizing more quickly than Vickie had that the kid was gay) her parents left them alone, just setting an extra place at the dinner table for him and sending him back before curfew.

Finally, *finally*, Vickie had found someone who saw magic the way she did! When she explained the whole math thing to the pale kid—Paul—he'd grasped it immediately. In fact, he turned out to be better at it than she was, although he couldn't manage to use modern tech any better than most magicians, so she still had something of an edge on him.

Slowly, and with the help of Konrad Lorenz, Farley Mowat, and other ethologists, she convinced him that he wasn't some sort of perverted monster. And once convinced, he was willing to let her help him.

What the Pretty People were doing was completely counter to the rules, as she had pointed out. The entire problem was that they needed to shine a big fat light on the cockroaches and send them scurrying. And the only way to do that would be to trick them into coming out into the open in the first place.

Paul had wanted to just avoid stirring up a nest of hornets, but she'd convinced him about that, too. She knew how bullies worked. When they couldn't get to him because he was spending most non-school time with Vickie, they'd find some other way to torment him, and the number one target would probably be his room.

Here was the challenge that she had been craving, and she and Paul slaved over both the rules of conduct and the math-

emagic. The rules, because she was dissecting them like a lawyer.
The math, because they were building something so brand new
no one had ever tried it yet, out of the breakdown of the spells
they already knew.

When it was ready, Vickie snuck in one night after both of
them should have been asleep, and they set up the trap. After
that it was just a matter of waiting.

△

"Victoria Nagy."

Vickie looked up from her book, startled. This was study
hall, she was working on her history lesson, and she was so
deeply into it she hadn't noticed the proctor until he spoke.

"Yes?" she managed.

"Come with me. Leave the books." The older kid was stony-
faced, but she knew immediately why he had come for her.
What else could it be? She felt a rush of mingled apprehension
and elation. This, after all, was mostly her magic. If anyone was
going to get in trouble, even expelled, it would be her. She had
made sure it was her signature that was all over it, because Paul
didn't *have* a safe place to go to if he got expelled.

She got up and followed the proctor out of the library, out of
the building, and across the courtyard, as she had anticipated, to
the dorms. Up the stairs to the fourth floor, and out into a hallway, and into an uproar.

This was, of course, one of the boys' floors, but there were
students of both sexes crowding the hall and rubbernecking, and
the proctor had to push through them to get to the area of Paul's
room. A line of proctors was holding the curious back; they went
through that line, and finally Vickie could see the ... damage.

Whoa! It was hard not to be excited. She'd been pretty exact
as to her parameters, but she hadn't anticipated the sheer weight
of nastiness that the Pretty People had brought to the party and
which they had gotten back in their teeth.

It was hard to recognize Lucille, the tall, blond, head cheerleader type, because she wasn't thin or pretty anymore. She was round to the point that her clothing was straining and splitting in places, and she had a face like a frog. The only thing that remained to recognize her by was her blond hair.

Bert, one of the jocks, was black and blue, and on the floor, moaning and holding what looked like a broken arm. A couple of the other boys were in similar straits.

Angela was bald. Bridget had the worst case of acne Vickie had ever seen.

Standing over them was Professor Elba, with a face like a thundercloud. As soon as Vickie entered the cleared area, the Professor rounded on her.

"What did you do to them, you miserable little—" It looked as if the Professor was going to actually *attack* her, and in that moment, Vickie realized who it was who had been protecting the bullies all this time.

Fortunately, at just that moment, the Dean stepped into the space. *"Meredith!"* the Dean snapped. "Control yourself this instant!"

Since the Dean had her wand out—the Dean was clearly one of those magicians who felt she worked better using a wand—Professor Elba backpedaled a step or two.

"This—*girl's*—magical signature is—"

"I've been fully briefed, Meredith, thank you," the Dean replied, in tones of cold neutrality, and turned to Vickie. "Miss Nagy, I have the greatest respect for your parents, as does nearly everyone in the magical world. I find it ... remarkable ... that you would have perpetrated this sort of harm on your fellow students. Quite out of keeping, one would almost say. Explain yourself."

"I didn't perpetrate the harm on them, Dean," Vickie said, as she had rehearsed a thousand times. "They perpetrated it on themselves."

The Dean, a tall, stern woman with hair like cast-iron and a face like a stone statue, raised one eyebrow, slowly. "Indeed? Would you care to explain further?"

And Vickie did. She explained how she and Paul had broken down one of the old Wiccan Sacred Circle spells into its component parts and isolated the sequence that read the intent of anyone or anything that tried to cross the Circle. She detailed how they had broken down the Warding spells that established real-world perimeters. She described how they had worked out how the Mirror Spell that cast back *magical* harm on the caster worked. And how they had put these things all together in order to create something new: a Ward that read the intent of anyone trying to get into Paul's room, and did to them exactly what they were intending to do to Paul or his property.

"Impossible!" spat Elba.

Vickie shrugged, and before anyone could stop her, strolled across the threshold of Paul's room. She stopped, spread her hands wide, wordlessly showing how she came to no harm at all, and came back.

"Impossible!" Elba said again. "You just created a hazardous Ward that would only recognize you and that little pervert!"

Vickie bristled. "That's not true! We did exactly what I said we did!"

The Professor began to shout, or rather, scream, but the Dean cut her off—not by look, or order, but by stalking across the threshold of the room herself. There was a collective gasp, and when she came back out without so much as a hair being out of place, there was another.

"Take the ... so-called victims to the Infirmary," the Dean ordered. "And someone go to the Staff Reading Room, wake up Professor Higgins, and bring him here, please."

Vickie perked up a little at that. *So-called victims?* So the Dean believed her?

But she had to wait in silence while this Professor Higgins was fetched. This gentleman was someone Vickie had never seen before, tall, lean, wearing an odd flat velvet hat and academic robe over a shabby suit.

"Miss Nagy," the Dean ordered. "Tell the Professor *exactly* what you did. Down to the smallest detail."

So Vickie did—but the moment she started, the Professor suddenly looked as if he'd been jolted awake by electricity, and began questioning her—about the *math!* Jarred into excitement herself, Vickie could hardly get the words out fast enough. The Dean listened, looking vaguely baffled, for about ten minutes, and finally interrupted them.

"Professor," she said, politely. "Will this Ward do what the girl says it will?"

For the first time the Professor actually looked at Vickie's work, peering at the doorway over the top of his glasses. "Oh my, yes," he said, sounding as if he had just discovered an entirely new theorem. "Oh my, certainly yes. It reads the intent of those who cross it, and if they are intending something wicked, it bounces them back with as close an approximation of their intended actions as it can manage, wrought on their persons. So elegant for such a youngster! Why, look here—" he began describing some of Vickie's process, and the Dean cut him off again.

"And would you be willing to take Miss Nagy and her confederate as your pupils?" she asked.

"I was about to *demand* that very thing, Dean!" the Professor replied, sounding a little indignant. "As you are aware, I have not had a mathemagician to tutor in far too long, and I certainly am *not* going to permit you to expel the first ones to come along in the last twenty years!"

"Hrrm." To Vickie's relief, the Dean sounded more amused than anything else. "We'll make the arrangements, Professor. Miss Nagy, with me. The rest of you—" she swept the group with a stern gaze. "Disperse, if you please."

△

Paul was already in the Dean's office when they arrived, and the Dean put them both through a fierce interrogation. Frankly, Vickie had seen FBI interrogators who weren't that skilled. Paul obviously began the interview with no intention of revealing that he'd been being bullied, much less over what. He ended it spilling everything. Vickie's role, evidently, was just to corroborate what he said, and reiterate that the magic had been all her idea, though the two of them had worked it out and implemented it together.

Finally, the Dean sat back in her chair and steepled her fingers. "You manage, Miss Nagy, to have neatly skated past every single rule applicable without actually breaking it," she said dryly. "I will candidly admit that I do appreciate your handiwork, and I will be having it applied to every room on this campus, which should put paid to some of the mischief we've had over the years here."

Vickie blushed and ducked her head. "Thank you, Dean," she said looking at her hands, and heaving a sigh of relief.

"There is no room at St. Rhiannon's for prejudice," the Dean continued. "Mister Hunter, your tormentors will be ... watched. They will either genuinely mend their ways, or learn to feign it. In either case, they will no longer trouble you. And to ensure their good behavior, Professor Elba will not be allowed any further contact with them." The Dean's tone suggested that something more was likely to occur regarding Professor Elba, but what that would be, Vickie could only guess.

"As for you two, I'll be rearranging your class schedules so that you will have Special Studies with Professor Higgins daily. I'm sure I can find something you've been sleepwalking through that can be eliminated. There will be no coasting with Professor Higgins, I will warn you in advance. You might just consider this your punishment for unauthorized experiments in magic." The Dean was not joking, Vickie suspected. *I'd rather sweat than coast, so there.*

"Remain here, while I arrange that," the Dean concluded.

"We'll allow the rest of the school to assume you are in here being lectured." She got up and departed through a door in the rear of her office, leaving the two of them alone.

Vickie looked at Paul. He looked back at her. And for the first time since she had met him, he was grinning.

"Fag hag," he said, fondly.

"Homo," she retorted, with a wink.

They fist-bumped. It was going to be a beautiful year.

INTO THE NIGHT

MERCEDES LACKEY

Chicago was actually one of Vickie Nagy's favorite cities. It was August, though, so of course, it was ridiculously hot and ridiculously humid. *That's what happens when your city is on a big fat lake and bisected by a river.* Under other circumstances, she'd have been working her way through the museums, the Adler Planetarium, and the Shedd Aquarium.

Unfortunately, she, Raven, and her parents were here to work. Even her quick run through the Lincoln Park Zoo had not been for pleasure.

Well, there was no question of why FBI Department 39 had gotten this assignment. The local head of ECHO—the Extrahuman Coalition for Humanitarian Operations, the official metahuman organization—had asked for the FBI's help after two of her metahumans had investigated the string of disappearances around Lincoln Park and come up missing themselves. ECHO had itself had been called in after three CPD detectives had gone investigating ... and went missing. Which was after six people around Lincoln Park had vanished. All of them gone without a trace, after doing things like taking out the garbage, going to the corner store, or going out to the car. Three of the six had left wallet, keys, and Blackberry behind in their houses.

While six ordinary people gone missing could have been a serial killer, or even some sort of gang violence, three missing detectives plus two missing metahumans pointed one way and one way only.

Magic.

Oh, it might have been a metahuman criminal, but metahumans usually worked big, and loud. They liked to make a splash. They didn't just quietly murder people and spirit away the bodies. That had been Director Eames's take, anyway, which was why he had assigned 39 to the job. *Mom always said he had good instincts.*

"Finished with your walkabout?" asked her father, as she came up to where the white panel van had been parked. It was a good spot, just off the alley under some tall, overgrown lilac bushes, next to the garage of a currently vacant house. The area around Lincoln Park, once you got past the high-rise apartment buildings facing it, was pretty much residential; two- to four-story buildings, some all apartments, some stores below and apartments above, and the occasional single- or double-family building. Good for parkour, once you found a way up to the roofs. Next to staff fighting, parkour was probably Vickie's favorite thing to do for exercise. And it sure didn't hurt that most of the creatures she and her parents hunted couldn't swarm up walls or leap rooftops the way she could.

"Yep," she said, and climbed into the van. It was cooler in there than in the alley, thanks to Mom, who'd created a little magic-powered heat-exchanger for it. Obviously they couldn't keep the van running to power the AC when it was *supposed* to be unoccupied, and she'd probably pass out from heat exhaustion if there wasn't some form of cooling on it.

It was crowded in here. Moira Nagy had her unruly bright red hair more or less confined in a ponytail and wore a jogging outfit. Alexander Nagy was in jeans, an old vest, and a T-shirt. Raven Stormdance was in a generic gray coverall with a faded nametag that said "Joe." She had to smile every time she thought about her godfather's "name." Because it actually wasn't "Hosteen," it was "Gaagii." "Hosteen" meant "Mister." But when he had first been interviewed for the FBI he had very stiffly told them his name was "Hosteen Gaagii Stormdance," and they'd put down "Hosteen G. Stormdance," probably because they couldn't pronounce Gaagii and didn't intend to try. He'd never bothered to correct them. She had the feeling that he got a big kick out of being called "Mister" any time some bureaucrat with a stick up his ass meant to demean him by calling him by his first name. Even "Stormdance" was just an approximation of his last name, which in Dineh was "Adoolch'itzhizh."

"Well, I guess it's time to get this party started," she said. Mom passed her the three ECHO-tech headsets they were going to use—safe in their hardshell plastic boxes with silk lining. She took them out, one at a time, and held them in both hands, concentrating on the complex equations that insulated the sets from their wearers. It had been fun figuring that out.

She was here precisely because of what she *was;* the only magician she knew of—possibly the only one in the whole world —who could work with technology. That was why Director Eames had let a teenager work with three seasoned FBI agents in the field ever since she was old and strong enough to protect herself. Well, that and the fact that Mom and Raven would fry even common electronics if they touched them, and even Dad, though he wasn't a magician himself, could glitch them after a couple of hours.

And the more complicated the gadget, the worse the damage. If any of the other three members of Department 39, otherwise known as the "Spook Squad," had tried to do *anything* with the high-tech gadgets in this van, there would have been a very messy, and very expensive, serial meltdown. The amount of difficulty a magician could have with tech varied—some, like her parents and godfather, could operate ordinary things as long as they didn't directly touch sensitive electronics, while others couldn't even drive a car without seizing the engine. But that same tech would lie down, roll over, and fetch for Vickie. She couldn't simply work with tech. She could interface magic with it. That part, she was only just beginning to explore, but it had all her teachers at school very excited, though not half as excited as she was.

"This is a better version of the spell to protect this stuff from you guys," she said, handing over the headsets to her mother, father, and the Navajo magician. "It'll hold for about ten hours now. Your batteries will run out before the spell does."

"Well done!" Alex Nagy grinned. He was an exceptionally handsome man, blond, clean-shaven, compact with a lot of wiry muscles. Both her parents were shorter than Raven. *Which is why I'm a shrimp.* But in looks, Vickie took after her father.

"All right, then," Alex continued. "Sooner we get started, the better."

She nodded. All three of the adults were going to split up and cover as much of the neighborhood as they could, using their varied talents and knowledge to try and pick up some arcane traces. Once it was dark, Alex—who was actually a hereditary werewolf, not a magician as such—would come back to the van, shapeshift, and literally *sniff* any magic out, in wolf form. And he would probably be covering four times as much territory as the others. To avoid alerting the neighborhood dogs, he'd carry a charm with him that Vickie had already put another of her spells on. She had given it the rather long name of *We be of one blood, ye and I*, from the *Jungle Book*—the mantra that animals saluted each other with to signal a truce. The dogs would feel it, and wouldn't go ape-shit when a 200-pound *wolf* ran by their yards.

"The guy running the liquor store on the corner knows what we're doing here, and you have permission to use his bathroom," Alex said. "Use the door in the alley, short, short, long on the buzzer, repeat three times."

Vickie nodded again. Besides being a technomage, she was primarily a geomancer, whose talents specifically worked with the earth. She'd be doing a general sweep of the area for as far as she could reach from inside the van—a bit like a radar sweep, but she would specifically be looking for a magic imprint *on the ground*. It wouldn't be as effective with all this asphalt and concrete as she'd like, but she also wouldn't be on the move the way the others were. She could actually sit here in the van and *concentrate*. The others would have to be watching out for non-magical trouble, because even though this was a pretty good neighborhood, it was Chicago, and you could get mugged at night anywhere in a city.

"Time to move out, team," said her godfather, in his deep, quiet voice. One by one they left the van, until Vickie was alone in the dark and the cool. She locked the door, made sure she

knew where everything was, and settled back in the radio opera-
tor's seat far in the back.

She flexed her fingers, reached under the seat for her kit, and
set up her obsidian scrying plate. Time to go to work.

△

Her father came back at dusk, just long enough to shift form, get
his charm-collar on, and slip out again; he couldn't use the
ECHO mic in this form, but he did have a special earpiece
designed to fit in his wolf ear which was also shielded against
magic. At that point, she only had to monitor the check-ins from
her mother and her godfather, and try and pick up ... anything ...
within the limited range her own earth magic could manage,
choked off as it was by asphalt and concrete. It wasn't impres-
sive, no more than a circle of a few blocks in diameter. And it
could only work for something that was actually on the ground.
Disappointing. If they'd been closer to Lincoln Park, she could
have extended her reach all the way to Lake Michigan.

*I need to find a way to hack into traffic and ATM cams. Or
something.*

By midnight, Vickie was beginning to feel the fact that her
sleep cycle was off. The only help for that was a lot of caffeinated
drinks ... which meant that at about 2:00 AM she needed to pay a
visit to the liquor store. To make a deposit, not a withdrawal.

She "disengaged" the heat-exchange spell—a spell, of course,
being a *process,* as she had been told all her life, and not a *thing.* It
needed energy to run, so why waste the energy when she wasn't
in the van? Then, just to be safe, she ran another little spell that
killed her scent. There was no reason to go leaving a trail to and
from the van. It took less energy than the scrying spell, and it
was something she'd only just figured out. *Practice is good.*

The humid heat hit her in the face like a slap with a wet
towel as she opened the rear door and eased her way out, locking
the door behind herself. It felt as if the city was crouching all

around her, steaming. It would be three hours until pre-dawn, and the sun seemed like a distant memory. Vickie knew from experience that this was the longest part of the night, the time when minutes dragged unless you were actively doing something. It was hard to feel like an important member of the team when all you were doing was sitting in the back of a nice cool van. Even if the team couldn't do what they were doing without you.

The signal on the back doorbell was short-short-long-short-short-long-short-short-long. The owner himself, a burly, muscular man in a red T-shirt with a "Paul Bunyan" beard and surprisingly kind eyes let her in, and when he let her out again, he watched her from the door all the way to the alley before he went back into his store, which was awfully nice of him. Not that she couldn't take care of herself. She was a black belt in aikido and was one exam away from being a black belt in staff, and she had a knife on her and with it she could regularly best the saber master using his sword. But she was under five feet tall, waif-like, and he had probably had every protective instinct in his body go off when he'd seen her.

Leaving the alley, she began to slip as quietly as she could through the darkened streets, avoiding the pools of light from the streetlamps. Just in case something was watching. She had every sense cranked up, and she moved in spurts, in an uneven number of steps, to avoid establishing a pattern that anything or anyone who was listening might pick up. *Nature moves chaotically. Only humans move in cadence.* It was good practice, and it forced her to wake all the way up.

It was a good thing that she was being super cautious too. Because she *heard* something trying to get into the van just as she got within eyesight of it, and stopped abruptly where she was, next to a brick wall.

It was not the noise that a car thief would make. It was more like ... the sound of claws trying to pry open a door.

Her palms prickled with sweat, and she pressed herself back into an alcove where someone could leave a trash can out of the way. *I need mage-sight*, she decided. No matter how hard she peered into the slot where the van was, all she could see was a faint gleam of grille and a glint off the windshield, a glint that changed as the van moved. There was *definitely* something there.

Things in mage-sight were visible by the amount of magic they gave off. Because the van had had spells working on and in it, even though they weren't active *now*, it showed up as a ghostly negative image of itself. It rocked slightly, as whatever-it-was pried at the back door. The lilac bushes also gave off a faint glow, since everything living produced a trickle of magic. The aluminum-sided garage beside the van was pretty much a solid black shape—but the alley itself glowed very, very faintly. It was old brickwork, and brick was clay, and porous, and all those pores were full of garbage dust and the microbes feeding on it.

Then the van stopped rocking. And although she listened as hard as she could, she heard nothing at all. If anything, that made her palms sweat more.

Then ... it came from around the side of the van, and she froze.

It was ... more or less humanoid, but it was moving on all fours. Smoothly, nimbly, with a sense of purpose. It was either naked or almost naked, not skeletal, but it gave that impression; there were long claws on its hands and feet. It kept raising its head and sniffing, and now she was *really* glad she'd killed her scent.

Then she got a look at its face. It looked like something the artist H.R. Giger might have designed. Eyeless, fanged, feral. She'd gone from sweating to chilled in the single moment when she'd seen that face. She didn't know what it was ... but she had no doubt that it was murderous.

It made another prowl around the van, then swung its head back and forth, as if it was trying to pick up something. Scent ... *but what if it hunts by heat, too?*

She pressed herself back into the alcove, and realized with relief that the brick was just about the same temperature as her skin. So she froze again, stilling her breath, hoping it couldn't hear her heartbeat. Because her heart pounded with panic. And the thing was too close for her to whisper an alert into the microphone of her headset.

I can't run. And I can't fight. There was no question of her taking that thing on. Sure, she had her athame, her ritual knife that was also a black Fairbairn-Sykes combat knife. But to use it, she'd have to get in close. And *that* thing was nothing she wanted to get close to. She wasn't wearing her 9 mil; *she* wasn't an FBI agent, after all, and the CPD would take a dim view of a teenager packing heat. *If there was something I could grab to use as a staff* ... but there wasn't, at least not anywhere around that she could see. All she could do was freeze, try not to move a muscle, and pray the thing would wander off far enough that she could make a run for it.

This had to be the thing that had taken down three Chicago cops and two ECHO metahumans. *Unless there's more than one of them.*

Just ... don't ... move.

Not moving was probably the hardest thing she had ever done in her life. Every bit of martial arts discipline she'd learned was concentrated on *not moving*, not even to shake with fear. On a hunch, she dismissed her mage-sight for a moment—and it disappeared, although the thing should have been clearly visible, right in the middle of the alley, with dim lights from the garages giving at least some illumination. She brought her mage-sight back up again, and there it was.

Well, that explains how it managed to get cops and metas.

It had moved a few feet down the alley, away from her, but towards the direction where the others had gone. Cutting her off from them. But ... at least it was moving away.

Just ... don't ... move.

Every nerve was screaming in panic as it slunk down the alley. Twenty feet. Fifty. A hundred. Then, suddenly, it alerted to something she could neither hear nor see. Its head came up. And it skittered into the shadows between two garages.

She broke and ran.

She wanted to scream into her mic, but she whispered as she ran, making for the brick apartment building on the left-hand side of the alley. *Got to get up, up on the roofs. If it follows me up there, it won't be able to hide.* "Mayday, mayday, mayday!" she whispered urgently. "Unknown bogie. Visible only in mage-sight. Double-plus ungood. Was trying to get into the van." She went over the wall into the backyard of the apartment building, which was three stories tall, with open balconies at each story. Perfect for getting to the roof. With a grunt, she swarmed up the brickwork; mage-sight worked just fine on this building, way better than real-sight would have been.

"Where are you?" asked her mother in that cold, calm voice that told Vickie she had just gone into maternal overdrive.

"Rooftops," she reported, as she made the leap for the edge of the roof and pulled herself up. "South side, West Dickens. Making for the park." If she was going to have any chance of using earth magic, she had to get where there actually *was* earth.

"Roger." That was Mom. *"Get to the den."* That was her godfather.

She didn't waste any breath with a reply. They knew she would, if she could. Now she had to concentrate on running. With her nerves on fire and the blood freezing in her veins, she ran, and jumped, and ran, and jumped, and at some point she sensed, rather than saw, that the thing was behind her.

It was an alien hunger behind her, and a sadistic enjoyment of the chase. Somehow it knew that she could sense and see it; it relished that. Relished the fact that *this* bit of prey *knew* it was coming for her, rather than tamely wandering within striking distance. The next house was the last on the block; she'd have to go down to the ground to cross the street. But so would it.

She made a leap for the tree she knew was there. Her hands caught the top; it was a young pine, and the momentum of her jump made it bend down and carry her almost to the ground. She let go and dropped, and ran, leaping over the wall into the back yard of the first house on the next block. Through the yard, over the wall, again, and again, until she sensed that it lost sight of her for a moment. And in that moment, she shoved herself into a nook under the steps of the apartment house and froze again, in shadows so dark they were like ink. *Freeze. Don't move. Try not to breathe.*

The nook contained eight electric meters, all of which hummed and ticked, effectively masking her heartbeat. She kept her eyes fixed on the top of the fence.

There was no warning, and no sound. One moment the fence was empty. The next, the thing perched on top. Then it dashed across the yard, and over the fence on the far side. She waited for the count of thirty, then ran between the buildings, over the bit of fence at the end, and came out on West Dickens. Then, she ran, flat out. Ahead of her she could see the tall, ten-story apartment buildings that gave their inhabitants such a great, and expensive, view of Lincoln Park. Her breath burned in her lungs, and still she ran, across North Stockton, and onto the grass of the Park itself. She drew new energy from the Earth, but didn't stop. She sensed the thing had found her trail again, and although it was back among the buildings, it would not be long before it would be in the Park too. Fear had every nerve on fire now. But glowing in mage-sight ahead of her stood the stately brick entrance to the Lincoln Park Zoo, and now she could use her earth magic to good effect. She headed for the lowest part of the wall—ridiculously too high even for an expert parkourist, but not for her. She didn't slacken her pace one bit as she raced towards the barrier—she ran through the equations in a blink and thrust ahead with her hands and an earthen ramp appeared under her racing feet, taking her to within jumping distance of the top of the wall, and crumbling away once her feet left it. She paused only a moment on the top of the wall before jumping down in a tumbling roll, leaping to her feet again and pelting down the concrete walkways. The entire place was alive with the cries of animals objecting to this unexpected intrusion. This was good, it would cover the sound of her running as she headed straight for a particular chain-link-fence-enclosed space. The fence, with its inwardly-curving top, was meant to keep its captives in, not a parkourist out. She went up and over it with no arcane assistance, and landed on all fours in the middle of the Red Wolf den.

"We be of one blood, ye and I," she whispered, triggering the spell, and the growling from the sheltered den-spot stopped. Before the wolves could slink out to meet her, she was down in and among them, deep in the shadows, crouching beside the Pack Leader with one hand on his shoulder. Maybe, *maybe,* the thing on her track would be thrown off. But—

No. There it was, loping towards the fence as if it knew exactly where she was. The big male vibrated beneath her hand with tension, but did not growl. Two of the others whined with terror. She held her magic ready, heart pounding so hard it hurt her chest.

It jumped to the top of the fence, and poised there for a moment. Then it leapt.

In the instant when it touched the ground, she turned the earth beneath it as soft as talcum powder. It unexpectedly found itself buried to its chest; caught off guard, it snorted and was about to spring free when she hardened the earth again to the state of cured cement.

Now it made the first real noise she had heard out of it, a snarl like the tearing of sheet metal. She'd hoped to trap all four legs; only the hind legs were fully caught, the left front was half-buried and the right front was free, and it was clear from its frenzied struggles it had the strength to break out. "I'm in the den; it's caught, but working free!" she shouted into the mic, and dashed out of the den, looking around frantically for anything she could use as a weapon that could give her some distance on the thing. As if by some miracle she spotted an old-fashioned, heavy-duty, iron or steel dirt rake that someone had left leaning up against the den rocks, out of sight of the tourists. She ran for it, feeling all the better for having it in her hands. She spun at the sound of growls and snapping, to see the wolf pack had surrounded the thing, working as a team, one dashing in to snap at the thing's flanks when it was busy with the distractions of another. She dashed in to stand next to the big male, bashing at the thing's face and head and free claw with the wicked tines of the rake. It didn't seem to take much damage, but from the noises it was making, it didn't *like* getting hit, either.

But she could see the hind legs slowly breaking free of the grip of the ground. She paused long enough to try and solidify the earth again, but it wasn't cement, it was just plain dirt, and there was only so much she could do. It *was* going to get free, and when it did—

In a frenzy, she beat at the thing, cursing it in Hungarian, trying not to sob with terror, and backpedaled frantically when it got its other forepaw loose and tried to snatch the rake out of her hand.

She tripped and landed on her ass, staring in horror as the thing began to claw its way free.

Just as a howl split the night, and a huge, black shape, three times the size of the wolves beside her, leapt over the fence, landing squarely on the back of the creature and driving it face-down into the dirt. A pair of massive jaws closed on the creature's neck with a sound of shattering vertebrae, and Alexander Nagy, raging in werewolf form, shook the monster back and forth until it was as limp as a rag and as dead as last year's leaves.

△

Nobody really wanted to have to explain to ECHO and CPD why a girl who looked to be somewhere between the ages of thirteen and sixteen happened to be at a crime scene wearing an FBI consultant badge, so while Dad changed back to human—and into clothing—her godfather made a call of another sort. Local agent Jo Sanchez, who'd worked with them before, came and got Vickie before anybody else arrived. *Plus ten, local knowledge*, thought Vickie, as he stopped, without her even having to ask, at an open diner. He got repaid for his intuition, and his patience, when she came out around twenty minutes later with a big bag and a smaller one, and passed the smaller one to him without a word. "Patty melt, no fries, extra pickles, eat it now before it turns into a chilled grease sandwich."

"You remembered!" Jo said, sounding surprised and pleased. Vickie just grabbed a sandwich of her own out of the top of the bag and filled him in on what had happened between bites. Jo wasn't a magician, but he was a believer; he plied her with questions once he'd finished and got back on the road to the hotel. Finally, he shook his head as he pulled into the hotel parking garage. "That doesn't match up exactly with anything I ever heard of. Though, maybe something Aztec?"

"I'm out of clues and operating on three cylinders," she confessed, grabbing the bag of food from the floorboards, and opening the door. "Your best bet is to join the circus and see what the 'rents and my godfather come up with. Thanks for the lift, Jo!"

Safely in the three-bedroom suite again, she laid out the wrapped cold-cut sandwiches on a tray, got both pots of coffee going, and watched the sun rise, just letting her mind go blank. *I think this was the first time I've ever played tag with something I didn't recognize*, came the unbidden thought. *I hope it's the last....*

About 7:00 AM she heard the keycard in the door and her godfather opened it, followed by Moira and Alex. As soon as the door closed, they started talking, sounding as if they were resuming a conversation they'd been having in the van—in no way would a trained agent ever chatter about a case in an unsecured hotel corridor.

"You were *sure* it wasn't a Skinwalker?" Alex said.

Her godfather shook his head. "Positive. I've never heard of a

Skinwalker able to turn invisible, I have never heard of a blind Skinwalker, and there was no trace of Witchery Way magic about it."

"Confirmed," Moira agreed, and noticed the "buffet." "Oh sweetie, thank you! I wasn't looking forward to having to wait for room service."

"Thank Jo, he stopped at an all-night diner for me—" she began, then got the rest of what she was going to say squeezed out of her by her father's bear-hug.

"First, good op. You didn't panic, you played it by the book. You *also* didn't go running to find out what was snooping around the van when you heard the thing; you held position and observed." Alex looked into her eyes. "Second, quick, what would you have done if you'd been *in* the van?"

"Doors were locked, glass is bulletproof. Assumed I could hold out till you got there, called for help, and grabbed godfather's shotgun and the bandolier and strapped myself into the seat in case it turned the van over. If it pried a door open, I'd have been pumping shells into it until I ran out of ammo." Stormdance's all-purpose weapon was a shotgun that had been sung over by more than one of the Dineh Medicine People, with shells loaded with blessed salt, silver shot, iron shot, deer slugs, *silver* deer slugs, and something that was a secret known only to himself. Since it would have been too conspicuous to carry openly in a Chicago street, he'd carried a handgun with equally creative loads and left the shotgun in the van.

"Good answer." Alex let go of her and passed her to her mother, who kissed the top of her head and hugged her shoulders while Alex made a selection from the sandwiches.

"Well, if it's not a Skinwalker, what—"

Moira interrupted him. "What it is, is dead. Finding out what it *was* can wait. The first thing we need to determine is if there is more than one, and the second thing we need to do is track it back to its point of origin, if we can."

"What's the *official* story?" Vickie asked.

Her godfather smirked around his roast beef. "Metahuman villain, what else? That's the answer for everything that no one wants explained." He turned to Alex. "Moira is going to tackle finding out if this was a solo beast. As soon as you're ready, I could use your nose with the tracking."

Vickie left them sorting out details and closed the door to her bedroom. She might still be needed, but for right now ...

... for right now she was glad she wasn't on the payroll. That bed looked fabulous.

SAVE A PRAYER

MERCEDES LACKEY

W hen Josh opened his eyes, he was terrified; terrified that he didn't know where he was, and terrified that he'd gone blind. The only time he'd ever been in a place this dark was in a subway during a power failure. When you're living on the streets, nighttime is never really *dark*. Whether you're sleeping under a bridge, in an abandoned building, or in a shelter, there's always light you can't block out; from streetlamps, from neon signs, from the lights in the shelter they keep on all night to keep kids from getting out of bed and "wandering."

So he wasn't in any of those places; if he was ... he'd gone blind.

He felt around himself in a panic, trying to pull up his last memory before waking up here. He was lying on cold cement ... and it was just as quiet as it was dark.

Just as it was never completely dark when you lived on the street, it was never silent either. So ... either he'd gone deaf *and* blind, or ...

Now he remembered. Or rather, didn't, because he didn't remember being brought here, wherever "here" was. The last thing he remembered was some people in a blue van passing out bags of fast food. He was the last to get one. He remembered his hand taking the bag, and feeling the warmth of the food inside ... and then, nothing.

He thought he heard a sound behind him, sat up and turned, and that was when he saw a thin, dim line of light at floor level. Was it under a door?

But the relief he felt made him light-headed. At least he wasn't blind and deaf!

His relief only lasted as long as it took for the door to open, and see what was standing there. The silhouettes, at least, because the dim light was behind them, and they were black. Not "African-American" black. Not even tribal African black. They were a black that had no other color in it, and even seemed to swallow up light.

And they were ... monstrous. Like something out of a horror

movie. Bald heads, long, pointed noses, ears, and chins, eyes burning in those black faces, red as hot coals. Arms and legs too long, torsos too short, hunched backs. Joints that were ... wrong. Limbs that could have been rebroken and set to heal badly. Something about them hit him in the gut with an atavistic wave of paralyzing fear, fear that said his ancestors had faced these things in the dim, collective past, and it had not gone well.

Before he could move, they surged into the room and seized him, one and two to a limb, heaved them over their heads and carried him out like some sort of trophy. He got a glimpse of what could have been a subway platform, long deserted, before they carried him into a tunnel. Then, he could only see, dimly, the roof of the tunnel going by.

Frozen with fear, he did not even try to fight them.

Then they came into the light, and before he could think, he was thrown against a pair of metal beams and shackled there, hand and foot, spread-eagled between the two.

He could not see what was behind him, but in front of him was a ring of camping lanterns, half of a Circle painted on the ground inscribed with things he could not read, and four people in those all-over-suits of white Tyvek that industrial painters or people who worked in clean rooms wore. The people had the white hoods up and tied around their faces, and respirators.

And long knives in their hands.

They were talking.

"... you should have seen his face. Stevenson has *never* lost a case like this. He couldn't believe it when he heard the jury verdict. He's already filed a motion to look into jury tampering." The man laughed.

Another laughed with him. "We know how *that's* going to go. Well, we need to get this one done in a hurry. My jury is going to adjourn to deliberate tomorrow. I want the spell to have time to settle into their brains before they do."

The other three nodded, and the first man stepped up to Josh. Only now did he actually *look* at Josh. Finally Josh broke

through his own paralysis to—well, he wanted to scream, but all
he managed was a whimper. "Please ... let me go."

"You'll have to do better than that," the man said, raising his
knife. "He likes screaming."

△

Vickie Nagy sat patiently outside the office of the new Director
of the FBI's Metahuman Division. Specifically, he was assigning
Department 39 a case, and did not like what two of the three
members of 39 were telling him. She wondered if he realized
that she could hear everything that was being said in there.
*Would it be too smart-ass of me to just walk in there and ... yeah, yeah it
would.*

He was objecting to the fact that her parents were including
a fifteen-year-old *her* on the assignment they were supposed to
be *leaving* on ... scratch that, they were now a half hour late.
Missed our flight. Which means we get the jet. Cool. She had absolutely no doubt whatsoever that she *was* going on this assignment, despite the fact that she was a high school sophomore and
not an actual agent, just the offspring of two of the three only
magic-using agents the FBI had. The new Director wasn't
getting any choice. Just like the last Director hadn't had any
choice. And from the sound of things, Mom was about to go into
full demonstration mode.

The new Director's voice rose. *"Agent Nagy, what are you—"*

Her mother's voice was perfectly even. But Vickie could
read the fury just under the surface. The Director should have
known better than to mess with an Irish redhead.
"Demonstrating."

Vickie braced herself, and from behind the door there came
the utterly predictable sounds of a computer hard drive doing a
hard, *hard* crash, and a number of electrical arcs, and—it was a
good thing that the Director's computer had a nice expensive
flat-panel monitor instead of a CRT. At least this time there

wasn't an implosion, the way there had been the last time Mom had "demonstrated."

Good gods, I hope that hard drive didn't spit shrapnel. Wonder if the fire alarm is going to go off this time?

There was the sound of windows being hastily opened, and the smell of burning plastic seeped under the door. But this time, no fire alarm.

Guess not.

The Director's secretary, who clearly had expected this as well, was already on the phone to IT.

"She warned you, sir. Repeatedly." That was Dad. "This is why, if you are going to insist that we use the tech gear, Victoria has to go along. She's the only one of us that can handle tech without it blowing up in her face. She's the only one that can insulate the tech gear so *we* don't blow up what we need to use, and she'll need to renew that protection fairly frequently."

"We *told* you," Mom said, biting off each word. "We kept *telling* you. We're not metahumans. Our abilities don't work like a metahuman's. *That's all in our bloody files.*"

Mom hadn't added, *you cretinous, bureaucratic prat,* the way she had the last time she'd had this argument, but she didn't have to.

There was a long pause. "Send her in."

Vickie took that as the cue for her entrance. She gauged the new Director at a glance. He looked like the original Great Stone Face. There was no sign of a sense of humor in him. No, this was not a guy to be smart-assed with. She took a respectful "parade rest" stance just beside her father, Alexander Nagy, and said nothing.

He looked her up and down while the geeks arrived and began installing his new computer and putting the old one on the cart to be taken away. *At least that hard drive is quite thoroughly destroyed. Ain't nobody gettin' nothin' off that baby.*

The computer her mother had just fried with a touch was impressively, visibly damaged, including massive case dents.

Looked like the hard drive *had* thrown shrapnel; the case had contained it, barely.

"So. Your parents think they need you on this assignment." The way he was eyeing her suggested he was waiting for a response.

"They've needed me on assignments since I was twelve, sir." She kept her face completely expressionless. She considered adding "That's in my file," but ... no. "I'm a mathemagician, a techno-shaman, and a geomancer. I am good at self-defense. I have black belts in staff, aikido, and tae kwon do. I regularly score the same as my father on the indoor and outdoor ranges with a 9 mil. And I'm a traceur in parkour. I can defend myself at need, but more importantly for the purposes of the team, I know not only when to run, and I run very fast, but I can just about run up the side of a building if I have to." She lifted her chin a little. "My mother didn't raise any hostages."

The Director just gave her a long, unreadable look. "Explain mathemagician, techno-shaman, and geomancer."

"Instead of needing to memorize spell-castings or use components, I understand spellcasting in mathematical terms. My mother uses diagrams, chants, and physical objects to impose her will on the physical world. I can do that, too, and sometimes do, but mostly I visualize equations, then work through them to the answer to impose *my* will on the physical world. I can also read someone else's work *as* an equation and duplicate it, without knowing how they themselves achieved the result. That's a mathemagician. I'm one of three that I know of." She took a deep breath. "As for being a techno-shaman, I also am able to interface with technology on an intuitive level, and unlike virtually *every* other magician that I know of, I don't blow the stuff up just by touching it. I can use it like a normal person, *and* I can interface with it with my magical abilities."

"Magicians *do* that," said Moira Nagy, frowning. "Blow tech things up, that is. As I explained."

"Some are more reactive than others," Vickie put in. "My

mother and Agent Stormdance can drive, use electrical appliances and household gear, and don't burn down the house every time they touch a light switch—but I know people who *do* burn down the house just by touching a light switch. But the more circuit boards that are in something, the more likely it is that my mother and Agent Stormdance will fry them. I am able to insulate things like their communications headsets from them in such a way that they still work, but the spell has to fight against them and their innate hostility to tech, and wears off after a while, and I have to renew it."

"We're not metahumans," Moira repeated. "We're something else. We're magicians. And that's why we are in our own Department in the FBI, because there are people—and things—out there that are criminal and also magical, and the Metahuman Division can't handle them."

Ye-ah. The Metahuman Division has gotten their lunch eaten by those things again, or you wouldn't have been told to bring in Department 39.

But the Director was still focusing on something Vickie had said. "You say there are people who can burn down a house by just touching something in contact with the electrical circuits?" His eyes narrowed speculatively. "Can we recruit—"

"How would you get them to assignments?" Moira demanded. "Walk? Ride horses? Borrow an Amish buggy? They *make airplanes crash*. They *stop cars*. They literally live as if they were in the 1850s because every time they touch something modern it destroys itself."

"I can only do so much," Vickie admitted. "I've tried insulating one of them long enough to take a ride into town. It didn't end well, in an extremely expensive fashion." When the Director looked blank, she added, "To be specific, the engine threw not one, not two, but *three* tie-rods, *and* the transmission ate half its gears, *and* it's a good thing that the SUV was rolling to a stop at the time because the last thing that happened was that the power brakes and steering both went in spectacular fashion."

"Oh." The Director frowned. *Another one that doesn't like hearing the word "no," I see.*

"And the last, geomancer, I can 'read' the ground and tell you what's on it and under it to about a hundred feet, and I can make the earth do what I want." She explained. "Like open it up under someone, or bury them. But that's very costly in terms of *me*. Magic operates by the rules of physics and math. It's moving energy, and sometimes matter around. Matter is harder to move than energy. So when I do something that has a physical effect, it wears me out. Sometimes a little, sometimes a lot, just like my mother and Agent Stormdance."

"Why not your father?" The Director frowned.

"Because I'm not a magician. I'm a werewolf," said Alexander Nagy, evenly. "It runs in my family. Rather than *using* magic, I am a species of magical creature. Would you like a demonstration?"

"No, one demonstration is enough for one day." The Director ran his hand over his face. At that moment, Vickie felt sorry for him. After all it wasn't *his* fault that Director Eames had dropped over dead of a stroke last night.

I did warn Eames. So did Mom. So did his doctor, I bet. But he just wouldn't get that blood pressure under control. And it's not as if there weren't metahuman healers who could have helped him do that.

And since Department 39 was an extremely well-kept secret, even in the FBI, this guy had probably thought Agents Nagy, Nagy, and Stormdance were just garden-variety metahumans, like everyone else in the Metahuman Division.

"And we've missed our commercial flight," Moira pointed out. "It's the last one tonight."

The Director grimaced. "Get out to the airport, then, I'll have them warm up the jet. How long will it take you to get there?"

"Fifteen minutes," Moira said crisply.

The Director nodded, as if he was finally happy with something. "Go. That pile of bodies is *not* going to get any bigger on my watch."

△

Alex Nagy was the putative leader of the team, but the reality was that any of the three of them switched out as lead. This time, however, since Alex was the one who'd gotten the full briefing before his wife and daughter had arrived, he was the one who convened them all around the little table in the FBI jet.

"So, this is what was important enough to pull you out of school for a week, Vickie," he said, dropping a folder full of crime scene photos on the table. "The Director wasn't kidding about the pile of bodies."

Vickie was no stranger to photos of dead bodies, even ones as gruesomely tortured as these were. But the number was surprising. "Jesus Cluny Frog ... a dozen?"

"More. Fourteen. They go back about five years, according to forensics, but they stop a year ago." Alex passed the forensics report to Agent Stormdance, the Dineh medicine chief. "And chances are that's only because whoever perpetrated this found another dump site."

Her godfather—whose given name translated as "Raven"—picked up one of the photos and examined it critically. "Ritual torture, made to last as long as possible," he said, flatly.

"That's why we're going," replied Alex. "And that, Vickie, is why we pulled you out of school. These are all teenagers, street kids probably. We've started to ID some of them. There's no one in the office that can pass as a street kid." Her father raised an eyebrow at her significantly.

Vickie nodded; she'd had the feeling her mother and father had been less than truthful about why they wanted their daughter along on this jaunt. She petted her familiar, an enormous British Blue cat named Gray. "Now that I've got Gray, you have a way to keep track of me without a wire, or at least, without an earpiece, which kids are *definitely* going to spot."

"Bingo. We want you wired to record, but Gray will be your backup while we work the other angles." Alex smiled, proudly.

Vickie didn't smile—this was too nasty a situation for her to feel anything but concern and some nausea—but she nodded.

"I'm going to want to stop at a Goodwill and a grocery store," was all she said.

◬

Raven was canvassing the shelters; he passed for someone down-on-his-luck far better than the extremely Caucasian Moira and Alexander Nagy did. Alex and Moira were doing the same, but in the official capacity, all suits and badges. Vickie had dressed down in torn jeans, knitted hat, several layers of tattered sweatshirt and sweaters, and ratty trainers, with a backpack containing pretty much what you'd expect a street kid to have. Everything she wore was painfully clean, but over-sized, faded, and aged. Her recording mic was concealed in the layers of bulky clothing, and she didn't wear an earpiece. Streetwise kids could be good at spotting someone who was wired.

This was the bad part of Boston; it was assumed the street kids had all come from here. They'd been found in the Fall River State Forest, which was a good hour away from here, and across several police jurisdictions. Right now conventional agents were combing the area where the bodies had been found. The Spook Squad didn't need to be there for that. In fact, it would be better if the bodies and any potential evidence were removed before they got there, so they could avoid contaminating the crime scene with the magic forensics they planned to use.

The Fall River State Forest was part of the so-called "Bridge-water Triangle," an area that was supposed to be a hotbed of occult and bizarre sightings and activities. Everything from UFOs to Bigfoot to alleged Satanic activity had been reported in there. The Nagys had never worked a case here before, but at least during Vickie's lifetime, the only fatalities that had occurred there that were not—on the surface, at least—accidents, were cattle and deer mutilations. Not the sort of thing the FBI got involved with, not even FBI Metahuman.

Well, that changed. Vickie walked slowly along the street, shoulders hunched against the cold, heading for an abandoned apartment building street people were squatting in. Supposedly most of them were kids, so that was a good place to start. In her backpack she had a plastic shopping bag with two loaves of bread and a jar of peanut butter to make friends with.

It was pretty easy to tell which building it was. The front was boarded up, and so were the downstairs windows. Like that was going to stop anyone.

Vickie sat down on the front steps as if she was tired, and waited until there was no one on either side of the street for a block in either direction. Then she slipped into the narrow passageway between her target and the next building and made her way into the back. That was where her source had said she could get into the building.

The windows and doors were boarded up here, too, and covered with graffiti and gang signs, but it was easy to spot where one of the sheets of plywood over the door had been loosened. She pried it away, slipped inside, and let it shut behind her, standing in the dark until her eyes adjusted.

The building smelled, like all of these buildings smelled, of urine and feces, mildew and mold, damp, rotting wood, crumbling brick, and lingering stale food aromas. If despair had a smell, this was it. No smell of rotting food though; no food ever stayed around in a place like this long enough to rot. Vickie found herself in a back entrance, with a hallway in front of her. Cautiously, with one hand on the knife she could reach through a slit in her pocket, she set out to make some friends.

△

The girl's name was Sue. No last name. No one had a last name here. Probably "Sue" wasn't even her real name. Vickie squatted on her heels next to the girl while Sue ate the peanut butter sandwich Vickie had made for her in careful, tiny bites.

She's been out here a while. She's learned to make a meal last.

One of the victims had already been identified, the most recent of the bodies. The team had gotten all the relevant details as soon as they arrived, and Vickie had been hunting for someone with information. With access to the background that the FBI could get hold of, pretending that Vickie had been the victim's friend "back home" had been easy. "About Abby, you said you knew something," Vickie said, in a quiet, slightly hoarse voice. "When did you see her?"

Sue finished the sandwich and tucked her empty hands into her sleeves, hunched over on the ratty sleeping bag she was using. "At the shelter. That's the last time I saw her. We both got beds and they said we'd have them for at least a week, so we were both pretty happy. But she got up in the middle of the night, and ... I dunno, I woke up when she did, and it was like there was something wrong. I said her name, and she didn't even look at me. So I figured I'd follow her, just in case, you know, some-body had slipped her something or she was going out to score, 'cause it's a bad idea to go out to score alone. She just put on her shoes and snuck out the back door. Left everything. Out in the alley she got into a van, like a medium blue panel van, and I remember she was talking to someone in a van like that just before we tried the shelter." Sue took a deep, ragged breath. "I never saw her again."

This was the third eyewitness to an abduction, and the third person that had seen a kid picked up by a blue panel van, seem-ingly without a struggle. The first two had been more recent than Abby, but did not have corresponding corpses, so it looked as if Dad's hunch was right, and the killers had a newer dump site than the one that had been found. This was all beginning to add up to a very slick operation. But this was the first time someone had seen enough to make it clear that *something* odd had been going on with the victim.

There was, however, a very large problem; right now there was no way to tell just how the kids had been lured into the van in the first place. There were a lot of ways, magically speaking, that you could use to coerce someone into doing something.

But this was enough information for now; it was going to be dark soon, and it was time to get off the street. Not that she was afraid, except maybe of a gang of six or more, but it was going to be very difficult to explain to the local police how the daughter of two FBI agents came to be in this part of town standing over a mugger who'd eaten his own knife.

Time to pick up some carryout and get back to the hotel room.

She was inhaling takeout Chinese, sharing shrimp with Gray, when Raven got back to the motel suite. "I hope you got me—" the Dineh Medicine Chief began, when Vickie waved her chopsticks at the brown paper bags on the bureau next to the television. "Pork Fried Rice, Mandarin Chicken, and lychee fruit," she said. "When have I ever failed you, godfather?" Then she added, "Don't answer that."

Raven chuckled, and searched through the white paper cartons for his favorites. "Moira and Alex are not far behind. Was your search fruitful?"

"Yes," she said, "And none of you are going to like what I have to tell you."

As if they had heard the cue, there was the sound of a key in the door, and Moira and Alex entered. Vickie got her lack of height from both parents, but she got most of her looks from her father, Alexander. He was a handsome man, compact and slim, with shaggy blond hair, and it was obvious to anyone who saw them together that they were father and daughter. All she had gotten from her mother were the redhead's green eyes and slender build.

"You got food!" Alex exclaimed with relief.

"Figured you wouldn't have time," Vickie replied.

"From your faces, I conclude that the journey to Fall River Forest was unfruitful," Raven observed, as the couple threw their coats on a chair and helped themselves to takeout.

"No trace of anything magical at the site, and only a faint trace of some form of ritual magic, so faint I couldn't tell what it was, except that it was bad," Moira replied with a grimace. "As if that wasn't obvious from the photos. Forensics thinks not only was this was a dump site, but the bodies were cleaned before they were dumped there. I'd agree. Cleaned of magic fingerprints as well."

"Well, I've got something, but let's wait until you're done eating," Vickie told them. "Because it's complicated."

Eventually the Chinese takeout was nothing more than a set of neatly-nested white cartons in the bottom of one of the brown paper bags Vickie had picked up. The team was disposed around the sofas of the center room of the suite, with a map of Boston and the surrounding area spread out on the cocktail table between them.

"Okay," Vickie said, when everyone was ready. "Whoever is doing this is slick. Every single one of those kids was taken from a different spot where street kids hang out. Angela went missing from Harvard Square." She tapped the map. "Tomas from Pine Street. Kevin from Franklin Street." She went through the litany of far-too-many names, tapping the spots where each of them had lived, or at least, the neighborhood where they'd found places to sleep, until they had disappeared. "For the most part, they just vanished; their friends never saw what happened to them. But I did manage to dig up a couple eyewitnesses. And that's the part you aren't going to like."

She described what her witnesses had told her. All three of the adults exchanged a look of dismay. Well, she was pretty damn terrified about it herself, but ...

"Someone has to play bait, and none of us look young enough," Alex said, stating the obvious.

She took a deep, if a trifle shaky, breath, and nodded. This ... was the other reason why she was here. From the time she could understand such things, she had known that the mere fact of *having* abilities like hers meant she had to use them, as metahumans did, to protect people who didn't. That had been a family tradition, in the Nagy line, at least, going back to pre-Christian times. The family motto even translated to "Duty Above All."

"Obviously that someone would be me." She reminded herself that this was not the first time she'd been the bait for a trap, although it was the first time she'd done so in an open urban environment. And it was the first time they'd all gone into this blind.

But she also knew exactly how she would feel if she didn't volunteer, and another kid died.

"We could get an undercover agent," Moira said. "You don't have to do this."

"And first, you'd have to talk the Director into this, and you'd be putting someone out there who hasn't got the first idea magic even exists," she responded, stating out loud what they already knew. "It'd be like dropping a raw recruit straight into a war zone. He won't know what he's seeing, or how to interpret it, and you may not even be able to locate or contact him once he's been snatched. By now the Director has finally read through some of your case files and is beginning to realize how dicey your cases are, and *he'll* know all this, and while you try and talk him into it, kids will be dying." She stopped for a moment, realizing her voice was starting to rise. *Steady, girl.* "So I'll go. After all, this is exactly what you've trained me for, and raised me to do."

Not for the first time, she saw that expression of mixed pain and pride on her parents' faces.

And even though her palms were sweating, and she had a cold lump in her stomach ... it was worth it.

"Hey, kid."

Vickie started, hoping the reaction didn't look too artificial. The voice came out of an alley next to her, and it belonged to a woman in a warm-looking puffy coat standing next to a *(bingo!)* medium blue panel van. She peered suspiciously at the woman, not getting any closer.

The street was mostly deserted; it was too cold for people to want to spend any more time out in the weather than they had to, and it looked like it was going to drop sleet or snow any moment. This was a sad, rather than a bad part of town; so many boarded up storefronts. Which wasn't so bad for the street kids, who could sometimes find their way inside and have a sheltered place to sleep until someone found out, ran them off, and boarded it up tight again. There was only one other thing visible, in fact, besides her. An enormous gray cat.

"Whatcha want?" Vickie asked, hoarsely. She didn't get any closer. No smart street kid would, even if it was a woman, and not a man, next to that van. It would be too easy for someone inside the van to jump out and push you in.

I'm watching, Vickie heard in her head. Good. Gray was her failsafe, her backup, in case things didn't go according to plan. Raven, even dressed like a bum, might have been noticed. Her parents certainly would have been. Another car on the street might have given the kidnappers pause. But who notices a cat?

"Just giving out meals," the woman said, with a smile, and stepped over to her, moving slowly, and holding out a white paper sack with the name and logo of a burger chain on it. Vickie didn't approach her. She waited until the woman was just within reach, took the bag and stepped back, quickly.

And at the same time, she felt the spell hit her.

She and her mother had anticipated this. She was now an observer, wide awake, within a body that was being controlled by the spellcaster. She watched and listened as the woman chattered to her, asking questions ... what was her name, where was she from, how old was she, why was she out here alone, where was she staying. Her body, however, gave the answers Vickie wanted it to, not the truth; the fiction of another runaway, another street kid, escaping from alcoholic parents, hiding out in the former grocery store three doors down. The woman was clearly pleased with the answers.

Vickie assumed that once the woman was done determining that she was yet another kid who wouldn't be missed, she'd be sent on her way, to go to sleep in the grocery and wake up to walk out into the arms of the magicians.

But suddenly, she found herself moving towards the van, as the side door slid open.

Oh shit. They've gotten cocky enough to work by daylight—she thought. And then she was in the van, and without warning, everything went dark.

△

When she woke up again, everything was still dark; black as pitch, in fact. She was lying on damp cement, and her hands and face were cold and clammy. There was a musty smell, and a sound of dripping water. She sat up quickly, and passed her hand in front of her face, and still saw nothing. For one moment, she panicked, thinking she was blind. Then her brain snapped back into high gear and she pushed the button to light up the face of her watch.

Only 8:00 PM. So she hadn't been gone off the street longer than three hours. But the spell that had been controlling her was gone, so either it had worn out, or her captors had taken it off.

Her backpack was gone; she searched her pockets and came up empty. *Of course they searched me and took away anything they thought I might be able to use.* Smart of them, and the reason why she wasn't wearing a tracker or a wire. Of course, they had no idea that Vickie's real weapon was herself.

... I hope.

Because this was slick. Very, very slick. And wherever she was, she was all alone.

The first thing she did was put up her own magical defenses, ripping through the equations that were so familiar that she could quite literally do them in her sleep, so whoever the spellcaster was wouldn't be able to pull any more shenanigans. Then she invoked mage-sight, to see if there was anything she could learn about where she was.

Nothing. Anything living gave off at least a faint glow to mage-sight, and she had expected at least the floor to be crawling with bacteria. But ... nothing. Between when the last prisoner had been here and now, the place had been literally scoured and sanitized.

Someone was being very, very careful. That was ... interesting. It suggested very strongly that this "someone" knew forensics extremely well, and had made sure there was absolutely *nothing* that could link him back to the previous victims.

Well, at least I'm not going to get infected with anything, she thought, and licked her finger and began drawing an intricate diagram on the cement floor in her own spit. When she completed it, she took a deep breath, and slowly, carefully, ran through the Apporting equations, double-checking at each step, until she reached the end. And with a *pop* of displaced air ... her familiar Gray appeared on top of the diagram. She felt faint for a moment as the energy to bring him here dropped out of her, but quickly recovered. *He* was practically blindingly bright to her mage-sight, as was the little backpack he was wearing. There was a limit to what she could Apport right now, and Gray plus that pack was just about it.

I kept telling Moira you were all right, he said, as she unbuckled the backpack and rummaged through it. *But as soon as you were in that van, we lost you to magic-location, and we knew that we had to wait for you to fetch me, she went into hyper-reactive mode.*

Her hand closed on a chemlight; she bent it to break the seal and shook it vigorously. Sure, she could have made some sort of magic light ... but that took energy and that energy was going to have to come from *her*. And any energy she had was energy she might ... she was *probably* ... going to need every bit of.

She got up and walked to the walls. Two sides, the right and the back—she assumed it was the "back" because it was opposite the wall with a door in it—were made of ancient ceramic tile. Impossible to tell what color it was in the green glow of the chemlight. The other two walls were made of cinder blocks, cemented together, with a heavy steel door set into the middle of the "front." In the middle of the right-hand wall, black tiles spelled out the words "Court Street." Gray sat in the middle of the floor, watching her intently.

Vickie went to the steel door, and put her ear to the crack around it. She heard murmuring. It didn't sound like conversation.

Now she rummaged through the little backpack until she found the silk-lined clamshell case that held the ECHO-tech radio and headset. Just as she found them, she felt a distant vibration in the floor under her feet. That cemented her guess. There was only one place she could be. *The subway. This is a deserted station, I'll bet on it.*

She donned the radio, curved the boom of the mic to her mouth and made sure the earpiece was firmly in place before whispering, "Break, break, break."

Nothing. *Dammit.* She knelt, now, and put one hand on the cement floor. It wasn't as good as earth, but there was earth under it. Her reach might be about fifty feet. If there was anything within that distance, she ought to be able to figure out something of what it was.

It was enough. She sensed four sets of human feet ... and twenty or thirty of something dark and evil. The humans stood in a circle around something ... it might be an altar. It might be a summoning circle. But it was extremely powerful, and extremely nasty.

Now what's our move? Gray asked in her head. She considered, sitting back down on the floor and shielding the light of the chemlight from the door with her body. No point in alerting anything out there that she wasn't either unconscious or terrified, and in the dark. *Not that I'm all that far off being terrified.* This was incredibly iffy. If she was on a deserted, abandoned subway platform, it was probably walled off, and her parents were going to have to figure out how to get to her. That would take time. How much time? She had no idea. How long did she have before the people out there came to make her their next sacrifice? She had no idea about that, either. "I have to get you out of this cell and you have to find the team and bring them here," she said, finally, as she extracted her Fairbairn-Sykes knife from the backpack and put it on her belt again. The knife served as both a practical combat weapon and her athame, which should make it effective against whoever and whatever was out there. "So I need to do two things. I need to figure out how to unlock that door, and I need to figure out the spellcasting that's going on out there. I'm the one with the best shot at putting a monkey wrench in the works until the cavalry gets here."

Stay positive. Don't think "if" the cavalry gets here.

She held the chemlight close to the door, and saw with dismay that this wasn't going to be easy. There was no opening to the locking mechanism on this side, and the door fit too closely into the frame for her to try slipping the lock with her knife. She examined the other side, but the hinges weren't accessible either.

"Nazrat," she said, with feeling.

In order to get Gray on the other side of that door, she needed a landing platform—or else it had to be line-of-sight, which wasn't possible, obviously. So she needed the "receiving" Apportation diagram to be on the other side of that door....

She got back down on her hands and knees, and laid her head on the cement next to the door. There *was* a crack under it. Certainly just big enough to slide a piece of paper under. If she'd had a piece of paper.

To keep the panic down, she did as she had been taught. Slowly, and carefully, she itemized everything Gray was carrying, and everything, absolutely everything, that was on her own body. Until she came to the next-to-last layer of her clothing. *T-shirt* ...

It was old, cotton, and worn as thin as paper.

Stripping everything off to get to it, she had it off, and cut a square out of it with her knife. It wasn't the first time she'd used her blood to make a diagram, and it probably wouldn't be the last; the best place to cut was the outside of the arm, and the ferrule of her shoelace worked well enough as a dip pen. When the diagram was complete, she checked it three times, waved it in the air until it was dry, then carefully fed it under the door. She put her hand on the cement near the crack, and ascertained that the piece of fabric was still flat enough to use. Then she looked at Gray.

"You ready to go out there and find them and bring them back?"

The rats that took you got in here. I may not be a dog, but I can follow their scent out.

"Okay then. Hurry back. Tell them what I know. Meanwhile I'll try and figure out how to get myself out of here." She looked at the cell, and shivered. "If they come for me before you get the team here, I want to be on ground of *my* choosing."

Gray looked at her with his head sideways. *And put your clothes on,* he said.

She laughed, weakly, as she was meant to do. And then she ran through the equations, and with a *pop* of displaced air, Gray was gone.

I'm out, she heard in her mind. *We'll be back soon. Save some for us.*

She sat back on her heels, the chemlight clutched in her hands. Gray was gone. And there were so many things that could go wrong. There could be a door between here and the street that was locked and only the people who'd snatched her had the key to. It could take Gray hours to find his way to the surface, hours that she didn't have, because that ritual out there was building up to the point where those people would need their sacrifice, and that would be her. She had no idea how long that would take, only that the clock was ticking. She'd played bait before, but never in a situation so precarious. Never had she been without backup. Never had she heard that "ticking clock" so clearly. She was cold, her throat tight, and she knew this feeling.

It was fear. No, it was terror.

But if she hadn't volunteered ... they'd have grabbed someone else today. Some poor kid that didn't even know magic existed. Some kid that didn't have a prayer, who would have been doomed from the moment these goons got their paws on him. Some kid who had parents, friends, maybe siblings, who would never have known what happened to him until maybe someone found the current dumping spot for bodies.

She tried to push away the thought that if the team didn't get to her in time ... she might be able to fight the mob that was out there off for a while, but not forever. Tried to push it away, but it was ... persistent.

Her eyes stung.

She remembered the day her mother had sat down next to her, very solemn, her expression such that Vickie had known she was going to ask something serious. "Suppose," Moira had said, "You were tied to a railroad track. And we could save you, but the train would be wrecked, and hundreds of people would die—"

And Vickie hadn't even taken a second to think about it. "Then you save the train," she'd said, firmly. And Moira had teared up and hugged her, and she had known then, it wasn't just the right answer it was the *right* answer.

It was only later that she'd understood the question hadn't been rhetorical, the first time she'd asked to come on one of the team's cases, because they needed a technomancer and she was the only one there was. She hadn't known then how rare her abilities were, she'd only known that her parents, and Raven, and the people who were depending on them to *stop the bad guy* needed what only she could do. And things had gotten hairy, and that was when she had actually *realized* why her mother had asked that question.

Because if it came to a choice between saving her, and saving two or more other people, her parents would choose to save the others. They had to. And she agreed with that. In theory anyway.

But when you were sitting on your heels in a cold concrete cell with someone out there about to slit your throat and no idea if help was going to arrive in time....

Then she took a long, shuddering breath, and kicked herself in the ass. They were out there because they were confident she had a good shot at saving herself. They treated her like an *adult,* and gave her the credit and respect of one.

So I'd better damn well act like one.

She knelt down next to the cinder block wall, right where it joined the back tile wall. The farther away she got from those sounds of voices, the less likely it would be that anyone would notice what she was doing.

She couldn't get past the door; she didn't know the lock mechanism, so she couldn't move the pins to let herself out, and the bastards hadn't put an electronic lock on there she could have persuaded into letting her go. She could ram the earth up through the floor, or at least could eventually, and bring down the wall, but that would be extremely noisy, and noise was the last thing she wanted right now. The concrete platform was too thick to get to collapse, and anyway, that would be noisy too.

Can I get through the cinder blocks, somehow? She put her hand on the cinder block nearest the tile wall and the floor.

It ... wasn't much like real earth. But at least it was more like real earth than asphalt was. She bent her will against it, trying to persuade the mixed substances of which it was made to fall apart into its component bits, the way she could with just about any form of earth. But too much of it was "unnatural," the fly ash and clinkers mostly. She couldn't get it to answer to her, and she didn't have time to run the equations to figure out how to *make* it answer to her. She began to taste fear in the back of her mouth again.

Try the mortar. It's got sand in it. Then I can push a block out of the way.

She took a deep breath. *If I do that the whole wall might come down. Which won't be subtle or quiet.*

Still, it was worth investigating. She transferred her attention to the mortar holding the blocks together, and instead of weakening it, she *strengthened* the substance by binding all the sand grains together. Because if—no, *when*—she got rid of the two-block stack, she didn't want the whole wall to come down. She especially didn't want it to come down on her.

I know what cinder blocks are made of. All I need to find is one natural element in these. Something that's not manufactured. Instead of working against the whole block, if she could find something that was fundamentally still itself, like the sand in the mortar ... she bent her will against the block again, this time not *assuming*, but looking and analyzing.

And held back a surge of elation when she found it. Kaolin, a clay. *Now* she had something she could work with, and she did the very opposite of what she had done with the mortar. Instead of binding all the kaolin particles together, she encouraged them to repel each other.

She was breathless and sweating when it finally happened, but happen it did. The cinder block began to fall apart.

The one above it fell, but dropped slowly as the block beneath it crumbled gradually rather than powdering. She caught it before it could make a noise, and carefully dragged it into the cell with her. Then, grateful that she was so small, she crawled quickly out of the hole.

There was light out here, very dim light, from a single battery-powered camping lantern left on the far side of the platform, at the subway tunnel entrance. The platform was about thirty feet long; the cell only took up about a third of it. Below the platform was where the tracks had once been. They weren't there anymore, there was only dirt and the remains of the track bedding. Dimly, down the unused tunnel, Vickie made out a sullen, red light.

She slipped over the edge of the platform and laid her hand flat on the dirt. And *now* her earth magic could give her the information she desperately needed. "Break, break, break," she whispered into her radio, hoping this time someone would answer.

"Go," came the terse reply. She tried not to pass out from relief. At least they were somewhere the radio could reach now!

"Ritual in progress a hundred yards from my location, down subway tunnel," she said. "Four humans, unknown artifact, twenty-seven *svartálfar,* in three groups of nine, walls of subway planted with crude explosives by amateurs."

"Copy that. Making our way towards you."

She waited. But that was not all she could do. Here, with real earth beneath her feet and palm, tainted though it was by decades of city pollution and contamination, there was work she, and only she, could do.

It seemed an eternity, but probably was no more than fifteen minutes, when Raven simply *appeared* on the edge of the platform. She was used to that; the Dineh was the nearest thing she had ever seen to a ninja. Shortly after that, her mother and father slipped in beside them, all of them crouching on the trackbed. Her father had already taken his wolf form. Moira passed Vickie his sidearm.

She felt her spirits soar, and with them, her confidence. *Now* she could take on anything. She was with the team.

"Just in case," Moira whispered. Vickie nodded.

"I think they're about halfway through whatever ritual they're doing," she said.

Moira looked at her askance. "That seems ... long."

"I get the impression they haven't got a freaking clue what they're doing, except that they know if they deviate from it at all it's either not going to work or will have a bad outcome." She thought a moment. "I wonder if the *svartálfar* are the potential bad outcome."

"Less talking," Raven said. "Are you ready?"

She nodded, knelt down a little more, and put both hands flat on the trackbed. Every sense was on fire, vision, hearing, even smell sharpened as adrenaline flooded her system. And not just adrenaline; she pulled on the earth's own energy and filled herself with it until she was just about to burst.

Raven racked a shell into the chamber of his shotgun. Alex tensed all over, crouching to spring. Moira of all of them was the one who stood up, hands held tensely at her side, her hair starting to stand out from the energy she was building.

"Three," Raven said, grimly. "Two. Now."

Vickie *pushed* with everything she had in her. At the end of the tunnel, a wedge of earth and rock thrust up out of the earth, knocking the four people back there down and separating them from the *svartálfar*. It didn't stop until it hit the top of the tunnel. No matter what weapons they had back there, no matter what magic they could command or what that artifact could do, they were out of the combat for now.

But of course, the moment she did that, the *svartálfar* knew they were there.

The twisted creatures turned as quick as thought, but before they could move, Raven unloaded both barrels of his shotgun into them; four disintegrated when the shot struck them, and Moira raised her hands over her head, unleashing wind and lightning. The front ranks charged anyway—and right into a pit of soft sand Vickie had created where the end of the tunnel was. As soon as they had blundered into it, she hardened it, and they were trapped. The ones behind them blundered into them, unable to stop.

Raven racked in two more shells, salt and silver and cast-iron shot, and fired. Four more *svartálfar* fell to bits as Moira's lightning lashed at them, driving them closer together. Two managed to get through their trapped and panicking fellows; Alex leapt for the throat of one, and Vickie drew her Fairbairn-Sykes out of her boot and went for the other. These twisted, malformed creatures of Nordic legend—black as obsidian, and looking like nothing so much as something out of a special-effects nightmare —did not handle the touch of iron or steel well at the best of times, and when that steel was an *athame,* a knife so imbued with magic it practically glowed, the merest brush with it would probably be fatal. At the last minute, in mid-charge, the *svartálfr* realized what it was facing. Its eyes widened, and it skidded to a halt and tried to run back into the tunnel.

Too late. Vickie leapt after it, hitting it in the back with a flying side-kick. It went to the ground, then scrambled to its feet and faced her. She ducked under a pair of wild claw slashes as it fumbled for its own weapon. But trying to draw the stubby sword left it open.

She slashed, cutting its throat.

It fell back, black blood fountaining from its neck, even as the rest of its body disintegrated. She ignored it, looking around for another.

But the fight was over. Those *svartálfar* that were not dissolving away into the aether were fleeing through holes they'd opened up to escape back to their shadowy homeland. Within another minute, the tunnel was empty, the last of the *svartálfar* gone, even the bodies vanished. The only sounds were the muffled ones coming from the other side of Vickie's earthen barrier.

Alex writhed all over; Vickie looked away, as Moira pulled a pair of jeans and a T-shirt from her backpack and handed them to him. When she looked back her father was standing there, human again, clothed and with his FBI badge on a lanyard around his neck, but barefoot. He looked to Raven. "Call it in?"

The Dineh nodded. Alex looked past him to Vickie. "Good job. You can let them out now." His teeth bared in something that was not a smile. "I can't wait to see what we find."

$$\triangle$$

The abandoned station swarmed with FBI forensic techs, although Moira had looked over the artifact on the improvised altar, frowned, and destroyed it before they arrived. Although the four—who turned out to be, of all things, *lawyers*—had been fanatically careful about leaving no evidence back on the station platform, there was plenty at, on, and around their sacrificial altar. And, of course, there was the undeniable fact that they had abducted Vickie herself. And already one of the four had turned on the others and was babbling his mouth off, hoping to cut a deal.

Vickie shook her head with incredulity. "Cases. They were murdering kids to win *cases*."

Raven snorted with disgust. "Lucrative cases," Alex pointed out. "Extremely lucrative. Those weren't off-the-rack suits they were wearing, you know."

"But—" Vickie felt sick. And disgusted. "Ugh. Just ... ugh."

"Look on the bright side," her father pointed out, as they picked their way through the debris on the entrance stairs to the exit.

"What's that?" she asked, as he stood aside to let her emerge, blinking, into the late afternoon light. It was still overcast, but after the dark of the tunnel, it seemed painfully bright.

"They could have been using the same power to go into politics instead," he pointed out.

She shuddered.

THE LONGEST NIGHT

MERCEDES LACKEY

The absolute quiet was broken only by the crackling of flames. Vickie Nagy gave up trying to be interested in her book, sighed, and put it down on the bed beside her. Tucking her legs up under the plush velvet spread, she wrapped her arms around them and rested her chin on her knees, brooding, as she gazed into the fire in the fireplace at the foot of the huge bed.

Under other circumstances she'd have been luxuriating in the comfort. This was probably the best bedroom she'd seen outside of pictures in magazines, *ever,* especially for someone like her, who wallowed in fantasy novels and historical romances. The fireplace was only there for the ambience, not for heat—though these buildings were probably the oldest on the North American continent, the magicians who ran and staffed this very special school kept things nicely modern when it came to amenities. Central heat and air, plumbing and wiring that met every modern standard, even satellite television, although only about twenty percent of the faculty and staff dared touch the TV in the lounge or the sat-dish controller. There wasn't a piece of furniture in here that either wasn't an antique older than the USA, or hadn't been built to look like it was. The dark wooden bed was a huge Tudor canopy number, complete with red velvet bed-curtains matching the bedspread that you could pull shut all around, isolating you from noise, and creating a cozy, dark cave. But there was also a good reading light and her own cassette deck (usually playing classical music) in the headboard of the bed —which also had a cupboard she could stash books in. The mattress was more comfortable than anything she had ever slept on before. There was a faint scent of sandalwood from incense burning over the fireplace.

Her clothing had been put away in a matching freestanding wardrobe. There was a real Turkish carpet on the floor, old and soft and beautiful.

The fireplace she stared into gave off *just* enough heat, and no smoke at all. It had a tiled hearth, and a carved mantel of some sort of dark red wood.

As for the rest of the furniture, there was a real red velvet "fainting couch," and two red velvet chairs that were so cushy you hated getting out of them, positioned on either side of the fireplace. Another wardrobe actually hid a mini fridge, a TV, and a videotape player.

And the bathroom was to die for, with a cream-colored, claw-footed tub deep and long enough that a tall man could float in it without hitting his head or feet. The supply of scents for the water was enough to make even the most jaded hedonist raise an eyebrow.

If this room had been *hers*, she'd probably have considered herself well and truly spoiled rotten.

But it wasn't hers. It was in the guest section of the West Building of St. Rhiannon's School for Exceptional Students, and she was here because her parents, who were FBI agents with the FBI's Metahuman Agents section, had been sent out on a Job, and it wasn't one she could go along for. Which was super depressing, because it was Yule Break at the School, and she *could* have gone without anything getting in the way of her studies.

As long as it was just her parents, and the Job in question was something she could contribute her Talents to, she had gone along on a lot of their cases in the past. But this was going to be something tough; FBI Metahuman Division 39 had sent out three teams on it, and not even her godfather, Agent Raven Stormdance, thought having a teenager along was a good idea. And *he*, not her parents, was usually the one to override protocol and sneak her in because of her Talents.

Super depressing. Not only was she missing a Job, everyone concerned was pretty sure it was going to be a long and involved investigation. Probably wouldn't be over until she was well into the next term. Which meant she was going to be here over Christmas. First Christmas, ever, without her parents. First Christmas alone.

That was why she was here, instead of at home in Quantico.

Nobody thought it was a good idea for her to live at home in their little bungalow alone for several weeks, not even her. Too many things could go wrong—and she was not only the daughter of a pair of FBI agents, and so a potential target for bad guys, she was also the daughter of a pair of pretty formidable FBI magicians, and *definitely* a target for bad guys. No one fancied her becoming Daddy's Little Hostage.

But since she *wasn't* going to officially be a boarding student, the Dean had decided to put her up in the Guest Quarters. She didn't mind not being in the dorms in East Building, not really. For one thing, as an only child, she'd never had to share a room, and she kind of didn't like the idea. She'd seen the dorm rooms, and while they were probably about as nice as her room at home, and even though you were allowed to do almost anything you liked with them, including using transparent, fluorescent, or luminous paint to make star fields on the ceiling if you liked, they were nothing like the guest rooms. For another thing, the boarders all had their own rooms, and at the moment, every room in the girls' dorm was full. That meant she'd have to be doubled up with someone—and she didn't think whoever she got put with would be any too pleased about being saddled with a stranger for a couple weeks to a month, having *her* private space invaded, and suddenly having to share everything.

So she got to luxuriate in the really posh Guest Quarters, which, if it hadn't been Christmas, would have been grand. She'd have full access to the school library and other magical amenities during the break, and she wouldn't have to cook for herself. She *shouldn't* be living here long enough for the novelty to wear off. It should be like a kind of solo vacation, like the going to summer camp she'd never gotten to do. And really, she'd actually be pretty excited about all of this, if only ...

If only what her parents were assigned to wasn't, obviously, a dangerous job. If only it wasn't happening over Christmas. Every time she started to get excited about being here, another wash of worry for her folks drowned it all. Every time she felt anticipation, a reminder that there was just not going to be any Christmas this year made it go flat.

The worry was the worst, really.

They're smart. They're the best there is. Division 39 hasn't lost anyone, ever, not since the end of the Second World War.

She sighed again. Maybe it was just as well she was staying here, in the mostly deserted school, rather than anywhere else, like with either set of grandparents. How could she *possibly* enjoy Christmas when she knew the entire time she'd be all balled up with anxiety? And so would the grandparents. And they'd all be trying not to show it, and trying to keep each other's spirits up, and pretending to enjoy the holiday stuff, when in fact they would *all* be in tense knots and the whole holiday would be completely spoiled for everyone. Besides ... Mom's parents were in Scotland, and Dad's were in the back of beyond in Michigan's Upper Peninsula, and just *getting* her there, with planes booked solid for the holiday, would have required an Act of Congress, almost. And sure, she could have Apported, but then try and explain the sudden appearance of an American girl without evidence of plane tickets if someone in authority got nosy. Trying to take magical shortcuts in the mundane world almost always got messy. Especially when you were under orders not to draw attention to yourselves.

And I bet Mom had that all figured out within five minutes of when they got assigned, she thought, stroking the soft velvet over her knees with an absentminded finger. *I bet that's why she arranged this in the first place.* At least this way she wasn't going to have to put up a façade for anyone. If she wanted to mope here in her room and never go out for anything but meals, she could do that.

Well, I can until classes start, anyway.

And if she wanted to spend all her free time trying to lose herself in her studies, well, she could do that, too. *Think of the bright side. I have Professor Higgins all to myself.*

She stared into the flames, brooding. Why couldn't her parents have been with ECHO, been metahumans, and not magic-wielding, but all-too-mortal, agents of an FBI Division that wasn't even supposed to exist?

If they'd been metas, well, the fact that metas all seemed to share a certain amount of enhanced strength, better reflexes, and faster healing would have made her feel less anxious about her parents and her godfather.

But they're going to be wearing ECHO technoweave, she reminded herself. *They'll be* practically *bulletproof.* And her mom was a healer, after all, since healing spells were in her rep ...

The secrecy was the thing that just *ate* at her. They had not been allowed to tell her anything, not even what part of the country they were going to be in, because they hadn't known themselves. Moira and Alex Nagy didn't often get investigations where they practically had to play Secret Agent, but when they did, every moment that they were gone she lived with a knot in her stomach. And she'd learned what *we can't talk about this* meant very, *very* young, because her own Talents had shown up about the time she started to speak, so her parents had begun teaching her "consequences" at a ridiculously young age. Well, "ridiculous" for a mundie, not so much for the magical child of magicians.

That had its advantages, for sure, as well as its drawbacks. She felt sorry for the magical child of mundies—ordinary people, who didn't know magic existed. Life for someone like that ... at least until they were discovered, and one of the alumni would turn up with an offer "to help your child" ... could range from difficult to living hell.

Hearing some of those stories had really driven home how lucky she was. *Though you would think, in a world where the guy that just robbed the bank is as likely to get nabbed by a psion or a super-speeder or some bloke who can bend steel bars around his little finger as he is by a cop, they might go a little easier on a kid that "does things that can't be explained."*

So far as the parents of about half of the students here were concerned, this was some sort of correctional school supported by eccentric benefactors, and as long as they saw their offspring as little as possible and there were no obvious signs of abuse, the lack of parental access bothered them not at all. Budding mages born into normal families tended to get into a lot of trouble they couldn't adequately explain as they came into their powers, and adult magicians out in the world were always on the alert for the signs of a youngster in need of rescue. A little glamorie, a little persuasive geas, and the relieved parents were happily sending their "problem" off to be dealt with by someone else. And as for the kids, well, from everything some of her friends here had let slip, Vickie knew they were as relieved to finally find themselves in a place where they actually *belonged* as she had been.

So far as the parents of the *other* half were concerned—the parents who were themselves magicians—St. Rhia's was the place where their children were free to study and practice magic openly, and where they would get the best magical education to be had in North America. More part of the campaign to keep their nature hidden, at St. Rhia's, their kids learned both magic and camouflage. Eventually, some few, with the right skills, would actually go off and pass as metahumans, joining ECHO, with no one ever the wiser about *where* their abilities came from. Most, however, would find some other way to be practicing magicians in the world.

Even Vickie's parents managed that, at least as far as most of the FBI was concerned. Outside of Section 39, except at the very top levels of the Bureau, no one was aware that they were anything other than metahumans—or that the things they stalked were sometimes considerably different than "mere" super-criminals.

Most of the time, their job wasn't that much different from a meta-agent, or even a mundie-agent. Investigate the crime, iden-tify the criminal, intercept and arrest. Most of the time, the criminal was *much* more invested in avoiding discovery than he was in fighting back.

But this time ... it could be different. They've taken a three-team Job ... over Christmas. The Longest Night. Bad things can happen on the

Longest Night. Anyone schooled in magic knew that there were "bad" times of the year, when really nasty things could turn up. Samhain—Halloween, to mundies—was the one most people thought of. But the Longest Night, Midwinter, or, as the mundies and non-pagans knew it, Christmas Eve, was far more dangerous. So were the days on the run-up to the Longest Night. Darkness had sway over Light, and on the night itself, had its hold over this half of the world longer than at any other time of the year, and bad things lived in the shadows. If they were off going after something at this time of year ... if they were lucky it was just a really dangerous mundie or meta, that the Bureau thought could only be caught by the "outside the box" method of Division 39.

But if they weren't lucky ... it was something else. It was the "something else" that had her in knots.

But they're the best. And there's going to be nine of them. And Raven promised me he'd keep me updated. There was that. Her godfather was not only the team leader for this job, he knew how she fretted. She'd at least know, if not what was happening, at least that they were all right.

With that held firmly in her mind, she decided she would at least try and read her book. And eventually, to sleep.

△

The central courtyard was covered in about a foot of snow, with neat paths cut through it in the shape of a big equal-armed cross. That was another difference between here and home. When Vickie stepped out into the court, she was forcibly reminded that the school was somewhere in upper New England, not Virginia. Where it was, exactly ... not even her parents knew. You came and went either by Apporting into the central court-yard, or by private plane to an airstrip about a mile from here on private property, and Apported—or occasionally were picked up in an ancient Land Rover—from there. There weren't more than a handful of people who knew the exact location. It was safer that way.

The teachers and students might live in separate buildings, but everyone *ate* in the same place. The Dining Hall was in the East Building, but although she was starving, Vickie paused for a moment to take in the sight of the School resting in the silence, with soft snow falling gently into the court.

It was gorgeous. Like something in a book.

The buildings looked a lot like many of the buildings at Oxford University in the UK, actually; Gothic, but in the pretty way, not the morbid way. Stone made graceful. More of the "dreaming spires" that poets talked about. It was hard not to feel a little awe. The buildings were a gorgeous, pale, pale gray, nearly the color of the raw stone they had been built from, rather than the darker gray of buildings aged and darkened by years and pollution.

North and South were the classrooms, East was the dorms for the live-in students, and West was home to the teachers' apartments, theater, gym, library, guest rooms ... all the other things that weren't classrooms or dorms. The place was set in the middle of an extensive garden. Outside the garden were thick woods that looked really, really old, and impenetrable, although Vickie knew for a fact that the students were actually encouraged to explore them.

Right now everything was softened by snow. The pigeons and doves that lived here on the grounds were all wisely settled in their roosts, and at the moment, so were the ravens and crows that were as much pets here as the tamer birds. Silence hung over everything.

The area in the very center of the central courtyard was *completely* clean, but it wasn't shoveled clean—magic kept the snow off, and for good reason. This was the "landing platform," the Magical Circle that you Apported to when you came here.

The Magical Circle was a construction built of several Circles, carved into the granite paving in the middle of the courtyard; it was one of the most complex permanent Circles she'd ever seen. Literally a Master Piece, carefully inlaid in the granite of the paving, it had been put together by the Founders as one of the first constructions of this School. There were five smaller primary Circles within the huge Circle that enclosed the entire construction, one at each of the cardinal points, and a slightly bigger one in the middle. When someone Apported here, they landed in the smaller Circle that corresponded to their Element. Vickie was North, which was Earth. South was Fire, East was Air, and West was Water. Your magic wasn't necessarily restricted to that of one Element, of course, but you, yourself, always had a Prime Element associated with you.

You didn't *need* to Apport to an Elemental Circle, but it kept things less crowded when there was a lot of coming and going, and it kept the central circle free for mass Apportations. Just in case, for instance, there was an entire class having a Field Trip. There weren't too many day students like Vickie, so it wasn't likely there would be much competition for the Elemental Circles when school was in session, but if there was, well, you activated your Apportation Spell, and then you waited, and when it was your turn, you Apported in.

As Vickie stood just in front of the doorway, the door behind her opened, and Dean McGregor stepped out, a tall, gaunt woman with graying brown hair, wrapped in a worn velvet cloak with a muffler that would have been the envy of a Doctor Who fan wrapped around her shoulders, neck, and head. "New to snow?" the Dean asked, dryly. Vickie laughed.

"Well, we don't get much in Virginia," she replied. "But I've been all over the world, so, not so much."

The Dean chuckled. "I had momentarily forgotten about your parents," she admitted. "Well, shake a leg, Miss Nagy, or we shall be getting cold apple pancakes, instead of piping hot. There is only one cook on duty during vacation, and she is justifiably disinclined to linger about for the sake of someone tardy."

Vickie was exceptionally short, and the Dean was exceptionally tall, so she had to trot to keep up. "What do we do if there's a blizzard?" she asked. "Or if we get sick?"

"If there is a blizzard, there is a small, well-stocked kitchen available to us in West Building. It's right next to the laundry room. Given your self-sufficiency, I assume you can cook?" At Vickie's nod the Dean continued. "You may feel free to use it at any time, of course, although during vacation we assume you will clean up after yourself, as we allow most of the employees their holidays as well as the students. If you are ill, you must let me know, and I'll make sure that meals are brought to you and someone keeps an eye on you."

"Is anybody staying here besides me?" she asked, trying to *not* get a lump in her throat at the thought of being all alone here, with no one her age, for three weeks.

"Not staying the entire vacation, no." When Vickie looked up, she saw the Dean's mouth was slightly turned down. "It seems that no matter how little our pupils' parents may care for them, even the most despised are expected to come home for Christmas. But there are a half-dozen who will be leaving just before the day itself, and returning almost immediately. You won't be left *entirely* alone for most of the break. And of course, there will be myself, Professor Sidhe, Professor Dav of Eastern Studies, Professor Yiu, Professor Stanislova, Professor Hakonen, and Professor Higgins here as well." The Dean smiled as Vickie felt her own expression brighten at the mention of her favorite instructor. "Professor Higgins is looking forward to working with you uninterrupted, so I doubt you will be bored."

By this time they had entered the ornate brass-sheathed doors of the East Building. The Dining Hall was the first door just inside the foyer, a beautiful piece of wood and leaded glass.

Vickie politely held the door open for the Dean, who nodded her thanks, and the two of them entered.

Since the entire School was based on the architecture of Merlin College in Oxford, it was scarcely surprising that the room was monumental by American standards. And it was *stun-*

ning. Wood-paneled, with stained- and leaded-glass windows along one side, the walls featured oil portraits of accomplished alumni any place there wasn't a window, and if the ceiling lacked the vaulting of its model (as well as the three-story height—there were dormitory rooms above it, after all) it still boasted more wood panels with carved borders. There was one long table elevated slightly on a dais at the far end—the literal "High Table" where the faculty ate—and three rows of tables for the students placed perpendicular to it. And they were proper tables too, not the picnic-style common to American schools, with proper chairs. There were lamps placed at intervals along the tables, but although there were usually place settings at each place, right now the tables were bare. Only the High Table had been set. There were also sideboards set against each wall, and one of them was loaded down with buffet-style warming trays. Clearly you were expected to help yourself.

Professors Higgins and Sidhe were already seated at the High Table, along with three other students. Vickie recognized two of them, both a year ahead of her. Naomi McCoy and Ralph Emory. She and the Dean hung their cloaks—cloaks were part of the standard uniform here, which tickled her no end—on a coat-tree at the end of the buffet, and helped themselves. Either the Dean had already known the menu, or she was prescient; there were indeed apple pancakes, as well as oatmeal, scrambled eggs, bacon, fruit, and cold cereal and a few other items. *Pretty much what you'd find at the breakfast buffet at a motel,* Vickie decided. But of course, better. She might have hesitated in picking a seat, not certain what the protocol was during vacation, but Professor Higgins looked up and grinned at her and gesticulated broadly at the chair next to him. Feeling relieved, she made her way around the table until she came to the seat next to him. Vickie was one of the very few magicians, ever, in the entire history of the school, to see magic in terms of mathematical and algebraic equations. Everyone saw magic differently, of course, but because Vickie saw it as math, she was not only able to easily learn and replicate spells, she was able to deconstruct them and derive new ones, or new applications of old ones. The more math and physics she learned, the better she was able to do that. Professor Higgins, who looked very like a hobbit but spoke like an Einstein, was the *only* teacher who saw and understood magic in the same way. She and her friend Paul were his first pupils in twenty years, and he was utterly as delighted to have found her as she was to get him as her mentor.

The two of them chattered like a couple of magpies about mathemagic while the other students who were going to be here for most of the vacation, and the remaining teachers, came in. Unlike meals while school was in session, there didn't seem to be any formality; students and teachers mingled at the High Table, although Vickie was the only one deeply engrossed in conversation with a teacher.

The last to come in was a very young student, much younger than the usual. She looked to be nine or ten at most, when most people came to the school in their early teens. She was very blond, wore her hair in two braids, and looked like a little Dresden doll.

She slipped up to the sideboard like a timid mouse, quickly filled her plate, and sat as far from everyone as she could. "Who's that?" Vickie asked the Professor, who had paused in his discussion to finish his pancakes before they turned cold.

He swallowed the last bite. "Heidi Dortmund," he said. "Sad case, that. Her parents died last year, and her grandmother has charge of her."

Instantly, Vickie felt a surge of sympathy—and a little bit of fellow-feeling—for the little girl. Not that having your parents *dead* was anywhere near the same as having them gone, but ... well the others were chatting to each other and Professor Sidhe, and she was sitting there all alone. Professor Higgins picked up on what she was thinking without her even needing to say anything.

"Planning on acquiring another stray already?" he asked, his eyes twinkling—since spring semester she had been the one to champion her friend Paul against the popular kids in the school who were secretly bullying him. Well, they *had* been popular. They weren't quite so arrogant now that they'd been caught and punished in their covert bullying, and humiliated by Vickie and Paul to boot.

"Oh, I just think she could use a friend," Vickie demurred. "She's kind of young to be here, isn't she?"

Professor Higgins shrugged slightly, and ran a hand through his mop of curly, sandy hair. "There aren't many as young as she is, but I gather circumstances were special for her."

It looked like the little girl was almost done with her breakfast—she'd all but bolted it. Vickie finished hers before the child could escape. The Professor saw very well what she was about to do, and gave her a little wink by way of encouragement, while taking his own sweet time with his own meal. Well, he ate like a hobbit, too; she had never seen anyone who enjoyed food as much as he did, and if he hadn't been a magician, he'd have been too round to fit in his chair. Before the girl could scuttle off, Vickie came over to her chair. To Vickie's relief, the little girl didn't look frightened or alarmed, just wary. Probably not used to the older kids approaching her.

"Hi, I'm Vickie," she said, with an encouraging grin. "You want to help me build a snowman?"

The little girl just lit up. "Yes!" she said, and that was all it took. Since both of them were already dressed for the weather, and had their cloaks and mittens with them, they ran out to the courtyard together to turn words into actions.

By the time the bell for lunch sounded, both of them were snow-caked, and Vickie had a *very* good idea of why Heidi had been looking so cowed.

△

On the one hand, Vickie wished there were two of her, so she could spend time with Professor Higgins as well as with Heidi. On the other hand, at lunch, the Professor had been giving her *very* encouraging looks that she read as "stay with the child." She was used to being extremely active—she not only took Staff Fighting, she was taking Folk Dance and Advanced Free-Running—and it was pretty obvious Heidi wasn't, so by the time supper came along, Heidi was exhausted, and said she was going to go to bed early. After watching Vickie spend all day in the company of the much younger child, the Dean was evidently curious, and intercepted her on the way back across the court-yard to the West Building.

"You are up to something, young lady," the Dean said, although in an amused, rather than accusatory tone. "I should like very much to know what it is."

Vickie hunched her shoulders against the cold. "Heidi's grandmother hates her. Or at least, that's what Heidi says. Heidi says her grandmother never liked her father, and that her grand-mother thinks Heidi is the reason why her parents died." She frowned. "I didn't *say* anything, but she must be the meanest, nastiest woman ever. She treats Heidi like a failing cadet in a military school, and you wouldn't *believe* what she thinks is good reading for a little kid. Brothers Grimm. The original, unedited stuff, with kids eaten by bears, and dismembered, and drowned, and left to die in the woods."

She glanced up at the Dean, and saw that the woman had been taken entirely aback. "Well ... you *have* been busy," the Dean said, finally. "That's more than any of her teachers have been able to get out of her. All we knew was that she was quiet and very unhappy, as what child wouldn't be, who'd been orphaned?" She pondered a moment, then shook her head.

"Is there any way you can figure out how to keep her here instead of going back for Christmas?" Vickie begged, then ran forward to open the door for the Dean. "What if you said she was sick? Like, bad stomach flu? If her grandmother dislikes her that much, wouldn't she just hate having to take care of someone who was throwing up, or worse?"

She paused on the stair that would lead her up to her own room, as the Dean stopped at the foot of the staircase and pondered that. "It's an option ..." the woman finally said, but with some reluctance. "But I don't have to tell you that it is a very bad thing for a magician to lie. Words have power for a mage, and what if we *made* her ill?"

Vickie felt crestfallen. "I hadn't thought of that," she admitted unhappily.

"The trouble is, this is very short notice, especially when we had already set a date with her grandmother when she could be expected home," the Dean continued. "For future breaks, we can easily contrive some sort of excuse—that she needs to catch up on some subject or other, or that there is a school trip. Something we can make happen without any unfortunate consequences for her. But ... this time, I can't think of anything off the top of my head." The Dean smiled encouragingly at Vickie. "It's only for a few days. The grandmother herself set the dates—we had thought that it was only that an elderly woman didn't feel up to taking care of a young girl for very long, or that she thought Heidi would be bored and troublesome, but ... well, your information certainly casts *that* in a new light. But it's not as if she's physically abusing the girl, and Heidi is sensible and knows she'll be coming back here where she'll be happy. I'm sure Heidi will be fine."

Vickie wasn't so sure about that, but what could she say? She went up to her room in a troubled state of mind. Bad enough that she was worried about her parents, but now she was worried about Heidi too.

The first thing she did when she got to her room—besides hang her cloak over a chair facing the ever-burning fire—was to check her message-box. It looked like a little wooden jewelry box, but it wasn't anything of the sort. It was one of a pair, with Apport "landing pads" inscribed inside. She had one, and Raven had one; she and her mentor had made them together. Letters weighed almost nothing, so they weren't hard to Apport; this was more secure than using conventional means to talk, and less taxing than every other form of magic communication.

She opened the lid, and as she had hoped, there was a folded letter inside. With a sigh of relief, she took it out, and settled down next to the fire. It was coded, of course, but it wasn't but a moment and a relatively simple bit of magic to take care of that. She held the pages between her hands, visualized the equations of the spell, said *"Fiat,"* aloud, and the words were descrambled. It was Raven's box that did the scrambling, a bit of techno-magic that she had created, and he ruefully often wished aloud he could duplicate.

She settled down to read it carefully. They were in place, and had set up their headquarters in a rented vacation home. He couldn't tell her where they were, or what they were doing, of course, but he assured her that everything was routine and that so far, other than the fact that there were nine agents on the team, it was proceeding like a normal investigation. Which meant that, aside from the fact that whoever or whatever they were after was using magic or was itself a creature of magic, and they were using forensic magic to track it down, it was just like any other FBI investigation. There was a bad guy, who was doing his best to elude them, but unless they cornered him, Raven didn't see him as a danger to the team.

And then ... she read in between the lines, as Raven would have assumed she would do. They had their own little private code, the two of them, invoking things the two of them shared. It was nothing that anyone other than Mom and Dad would ever have been able to decipher. *Pacific Northwest. Serial killer. Why are so many serial killers in the Pacific Northwest?* Now she understood why they needed a team of nine; there was a lot of territory to cover up there, and if this was a murderer who was striking often, they needed to take him down as quickly as possible. You didn't want to split up in groups of less than three on a case like this.

Strangely, figuring that out made her *less* worried. On serial killer cases, the hunters rarely became the hunted. Serial killers preyed on the weak and isolated, not the strong and united.

She wrote her own quick letter to her parents, which Raven would pass on to them, and just as she had finished closing it in the box, she heard, faintly and muffled, a scream of absolute terror.

There were only two places on the grounds of the School where someone was likely to be screaming, the East Building and the West. And it had *not* sounded as if the scream came from the West Building—which left the East. The student dorms.

It was just pure good fortune that she was still fully dressed, boots and all. Vickie snatched up her cloak and ran for the door without a second thought. She raced down the stairs to the front door, and shoved it open, running straight out into the courtyard.

Just as she left the front door of her building, the scream came again, this time definitely from East Building. As she dashed across the moon-flooded courtyard, the door to West crashed open again behind her; it was the teachers, presumably, responding as she had—but she was too intent on her goal to look back.

She wrenched the door to East Building open; it wasn't locked, since, after all, there really wasn't any place for the students here to sneak off to. The School was surrounded by acres of forest, and most of the kids were city or suburb bred. The building was lit only dimly, all the hall lights dimmed to bedtime-mode, but it was enough to see by. She dashed up the staircase, taking the stairs two at a time, to the first floor, to find a knot of petrified students hovering uncertainly at the top of the stairs.

"Who screamed?" Vickie demanded, looking from one to another.

"I—we don't know!" said the eldest, a seventeen-year-old girl

Vickie remember was named Pomona. "We just heard someone, and came running out into the hall and—"

"And I saw a *thing!*" shrilled Ralph Emory, white as the snow outside. He reached for her arm and clutched it as if it was a lifeline. Maybe because she wasn't the only one panicking. "I think it was a demon!"

At this point, the Dean came up the last of the stairs, and grabbed Ralph by the shoulder. "What do you mean, a demon?" she demanded. "The entire School and Grounds are shielded and warded against demons! It's impossible!"

Professor Hakonen came pounding up the stairs as fast as Vickie had—he was not only the teacher of European Applied Myth, he was also Vickie's Staff Fighting teacher and in excellent shape. "Who's missing?" he demanded, and scanned the little clutch of students. "Where's Heidi?"

"I'll check her room," the Dean said, grimly, and strode off down the corridor. "You question Emory."

Vickie followed on the Dean's heels, but the answer was clear as soon as they were halfway down the hall. The door to Heidi's room stood wide open; from the mess inside, there had clearly been a struggle. The desk had been toppled, as had the chairs, and papers and books were scattered everywhere.

And Heidi was gone.

"Dean!" came the call from back down the hall, and Professor Hakonen ran up to them as the Dean turned in his direction. His blond hair was disheveled and the expression on his handsome face was grim. "Emory is right, he saw a demon—of sorts," the Professor said as he skidded to a halt beside them.

"What do you—" the Dean began. The Professor interrupted her.

"By 'of sorts,' I mean it's something we never warded against, because we didn't think to," the Professor explained, running his hand through his hair in a frantic gesture. "Good gods, we were so—it can only be invoked by someone who knows it, and thinks he—or she—deserves to be punished. That's how it got past our protections. Heidi thinks she *deserves* this, she must, or it never would have come for her."

"For heaven's sake, Nikki, get to the *point!*" the Dean exclaimed. "What *is* it?"

"It's the Krampus," the Professor replied bleakly. "And now it's loose here, it could take *any* of the others if we don't guard them, and if we don't get Heidi away from it before dawn, it will carry her off."

△

Vickie waited in the hall, poised on the balls of her feet, heart pounding. The other students were all in a heavily warded and sealed room, with Professor Sidhe guarding them. But *one* youngster had to be out for this plan to work, and she had volunteered before anyone else could speak up. This wasn't the first time she had played "bait." And her parents would never forgive her if it was her last....

But there wasn't a choice. They had to save Heidi, and to do that, they had to get her out of the clutches of the Krampus, and the only way to get to the Krampus was to get the Krampus to come to them—

It wouldn't come for an adult. It wouldn't come if there were any adults anywhere around. And it wouldn't come for just any youngster, either. It had to be one who had been—naughty—

So she waited in the hallway, all alone, hoping that part of what the Krampus wanted was terror, and the thrill of the chase.

She heard it before she saw it; as the Professor had suggested it would, it materialized in the middle of the utterly deserted hallway, right by the door to Heidi's room, where it had disappeared as soon as Ralph spotted it—because Ralph was old enough to count as an adult. The chains around its waist clinked and dragged on the floor; its hooves made clumping sounds on the wood. She couldn't see it *well* in the dim light, but what she saw was enough. Horns. Tail. And an impossible tongue that lolled out of its ugly mouth and dangled past its knees. But most importantly, she spotted the bulging basket on its back, the straw straining at what it contained. That was all Vickie needed to see. And she had been *naughty*. The Dean had ordered her to go back to her own room and not set foot in East Building until dawn.

"*Hey! Ugly!*" she shouted, making her tone as taunting as she could. "I'm where I'm not supposed to be! What're you gonna do about it?"

The head came up; the thing started panting. And then it launched itself at her, moving much faster than its lumbering gait would have suggested.

She ran. She ran, and behind her, she left tangles of magic, knotty equations she made up on the fly, meant only to slow it down. Because *it* was darn near a primal force, and if she didn't manage to slow it somehow, it *was* going to catch her, and then there would be two to rescue.

"*Think of the Krampus as St. Nikolas's evil twin.*"

That was what the Professor had said, explaining just what it was that they were up against. She knew about Black Peter, of course, the creature who, in some German and English traditions was the fellow that spanked naughty children and gave them coal, but the Krampus was ... a magnitude nastier than that. Really, something only a sadistic German could have thought up. A sadistic German who had been spending the early part of the winter cramped in a dark hut, hemmed in by snow-drifts, with his increasingly quarrelsome family, trying to think of a way to really *make* his children shut up and behave until spring. ...

St. Nikolas rewarded good behavior. But ... that wasn't enough. Not for *some* people. And it wasn't enough for bad children to be pleasurably scared, and deprived (at least a little) of presents. No, for some people, bad children had to be terrified into utter submission, under threats that if they didn't behave, something *horrible* would happen to them.

She sensed, rather than saw, something happening behind her. The Krampus was about to attack! She dodged to the side and went into a martial arts shoulder-roll, narrowly missing being hit by that ... tongue.

Ew! Ew! Ew!

Professor Hakonen had warned her about that, and a good thing, too. That tongue wasn't just obscene, it was a weapon. She got a lot more proactive with her magical tangles as she hit the stairs and jumped down them three at a time as she headed for the basement. The basement, that held the only room big enough for their purposes.

The Krampus was St. Nikolas's hit man. Disobedient children didn't just get lumps of coal, according to the legend. They got a visit from ... the Krampus, who had carte blanche to do whatever he liked depending on how naughty you had been. And he wasn't content just to warn like Black Peter, or give you a little switching, oh no. If you were *lucky,* he whipped you around the room until you bled from a dozen or more cuts. If you weren't?

You ended up in that basket on his back. And he carried you off, and you were never seen again. The Professor wasn't certain what happened to you when he carried off the naughty children at dawn. Some versions of the legend said they were taken to Hell. Some, that they were found later, dismembered, as a warning to other children. Some, that the Krampus ate them.

That was why the Dean had expressly forbidden Vickie to be here, and left. And Professor Hakonen had given her explicit instructions that the Dean was not to know about. And why Vickie was running for her life now, with a demon on her heels. Because when she got to the basement ...

She hit the basement door running, slammed into it, ran down the hallway to the rec area, and slammed through another door, and bolted across the room until she literally hit the back wall of the handball court. Then she turned, back to the wall, just in time to see the Krampus in all its ugly glory come barreling through the door behind her. It was grinning. It was an expression that made her whimper with horror and fear. Then her throat was too paralyzed with terror to do anything; in fact, she was having trouble breathing.

The Krampus reached the middle of the room.

"Now!" the Dean shouted. And that was when the lights went *out,* and the black lights came *on,* and the intricate demon-catcher that she and Professor Higgins had crafted in otherwise-transparent fluorescent paint—the same stuff the kids were allowed to use to paint star fields in their room with—lit up bright enough to make her wince.

It did more than make the Krampus wince. The hideous thing howled, then screamed, then was held rigid in the grip of the spells of five of the best magicians on the continent.

As for the sixth—and Vickie—she and Professor Higgins were unraveling the magic that created the basket on the thing's back. It was very primitive, almost like knitting, and it was Vickie who realized that first, found the loose end, and "yanked" on it. The spell came apart, and with it, the basket. Heidi tumbled to the floor of the basement.

She looked half dead and only semi-conscious. The poor kid had her eyes squeezed tight shut, and was moaning and shivering. Vickie ached to reach her, but right now, that wasn't an option. No passing the boundary of the demon-catcher. Not until the demon wasn't in it anymore.

"Three, two, one. Now!" commanded the Dean, and all those binding spells started tightening, squeezing ...

The Krampus began to shrink, struggling the entire time, but unable now to get enough breath to shriek. There was more than one way to banish an otherworldly creature back to whatever plane it came from, and one—this one—was to make things so impossible in *this* plane that it had nowhere to go but back.

In silence, it got smaller ... smaller ... and then, with a *pop,* it was gone.

Now Vickie and the Dean ran for Heidi; the Dean got there

first, and gathered her up, then began firing orders at the rest of them.

"And *you*, Miss Nagy!" she snapped out last of all. "You are given *explicit permission* to be here at all times. I take back what I told you earlier. You were exactly where I wanted you."

"Thank you, Dean," Vickie breathed. Now she was no longer *naughty*, and thank goodness the Dean had thought of that. Because ... just in case Heidi somehow brought the Krampus back again ... better safe than sorry.

"So it *was* Heidi?" Vickie asked over French toast the next morning. "Professor Hakonen was right?"

Professor Higgins nodded, and passed her the powdered sugar. "As you intuited, her grandmother convinced her she was responsible for her parents' death. And she knew magic was real, of course, so her subconscious was perfectly capable of summoning the worst monster her grandmother had ever told her about, a creature tailor-made to punish a sinful and evil child. That was how the Krampus bypassed our protections. They were never made to hold against something that had been summoned by a child that wanted it here." He ate a bite of bacon. "Needless to say, we've remedied that hole in our defenses."

"How's Heidi now?" Vickie wanted to know. The last she had seen of the child, the poor thing was being taken away to the infirmary. She felt a lump starting in her throat, thinking about how messed up the poor kid must be, to have actually—well— tried to kill herself. Or at least, punish herself horribly. Could she *ever* get over that?

"She'll be all right eventually." The Professor looked at her sharply, and patted her hand. "Don't worry too much; she was as loved by her parents as you are by yours. A few months of emotional abuse by her grandmother isn't going to destroy that sort of foundation, and the Dean is one of the best people with troubled children in our entire community. I think we'll get her set to rights."

"But—what about Christmas?" Vickie asked. "If you send her back to her grandmother, what's to stop the Krampus from coming for her there?"

"The fact that she won't be *going*. We contacted her grandmother this morning and told her Heidi had come down with the flu, and before we could say anything, the wretched woman *demanded* that we keep her here." The corners of his mouth turned down in a rare scowl. "Needless to say ... we are going to ensure she never has to go back to that ... harridan again."

Vickie ate some French toast, already plotting in her mind how she was going to approach her parents about having Heidi with *them* over at least some of the breaks. And meanwhile ... if she could get back to Quantico for a couple hours ... there were some things at the house she thought Heidi would probably like a lot.

Like the snow globe with the slightly-enchanted fairy castle in it, that lit up at night, and had a tiny, tiny fairy princess in one of the towers who'd wave her wand at you. A good thing to look at if you were scared, in the dark.

"Could you take this afternoon off, Professor?" she asked. "I'm not supposed to leave the campus without a teacher, and I've got some unexpected Christmas 'shopping' to do."

△

You might have wondered just what it was that Jack—once known by the code name "Rancor"—had against Dominic Verdigris III. Because by the end of Avalanche *it was pretty clear he was harboring one hell of a grudge.*

This is what.

THE HEIR APPARENT

MERCEDES LACKEY AND LARRY DIXON

O ne day, all this will be yours," Dominic Verdigris III proclaimed solemnly, and gestured broadly with his right arm.

The short, burly man beside him removed an unlit cigar from his mouth, and snorted. "If you're waiting for a Monty Python quote, you're gonna be waiting a long time, Dom."

Verd sighed. "Oh Rancor, you have no sense of humor." He dropped his arm, and surveyed the weedy lot before him. It was approximately five acres in a shabby part of Memphis, Tennessee, fenced in by eight-foot chain-link with razor wire on the top, and a bent-up sign proclaiming "City Property—Keep Out" on its heavy welded-pipe gates. Inside that property was a three-story, square brick building, whose front façade proclaimed that it was "Rogers School." Or rather, "Roger s School," since the first "s" hung crooked.

"So," the man that Verd had addressed as "Rancor" continued. "Obviously this dump isn't what it looks like. And you're the one that's always going on about how much time equals money. We're wasting time, which is money, ergo—"

"All right, all right." Verd frowned. "You have no sense of drama either. Come on."

He led the way around to the side of the building, where there was a much smaller gate, and pressed his thumb into the pipe just above the lock. The pipe clicked, the lock opened, and the gate swung freely. "After you," said Verd.

Rancor examined the pipe before passing through. "Okay. Galvanic sensors. Now that impressed me."

"Prepare to be amazed." Verd adjusted the cuff on his linen suit, where his pajama top had bunched up for a moment, and mimed straightening a tie.

A hidden trigger switch at a boarded-up side door won them into the interior of the building.

It looked inside like what it was outside; a long-abandoned school building, probably constructed in the 1930s with WPA money, too big and drafty to heat and cool economically, and not on property desirable enough that the city could sell it. Light seeped in through the cracks around the plywood over the windows. Many of the windows were broken. The corridor they stood in was floored in split, worn out linoleum. The walls were chipped white paint, with graffiti all over them where kids had broken in and added their personal touches. The stucco ceiling sagged and light fixtures hung precariously from wires.

But ... something was slightly off....

Rancor moved close in to the nearest wall, and got a good look. There was something wrong with the graffiti ...

He turned to look at Verd, accusingly. "No kid did this. This is from an airbrush, not a spray-paint can."

Verd aimed a finger at him. "Well spotted. Not one person in a thousand would have noticed that."

Rancor began examining everything else in the hallway as minutely, and as Verd knew he would, he clearly came to the conclusion that the air of decay was entirely artificial. Only the smell was right, that "school smell" of aged desks and books and old sneakers and too many cafeteria lunches.

He waved a hand at the hallway. "This is all fake."

"Of course it is!" Verd gloated. "Even the black mold is painted on. Now, come along."

He led the way up the stairs to the cafeteria, and watched as Rancor noted all the carefully placed signals that would reinforce to anyone else "nothing to see here, move along." Rancor nudged open a door as they passed, surveyed the bolted-down desks, the blackboards, cracking and falling off the walls.

Perhaps the only thing that gave the game away was that, under all the creaking of thin, warped floorboards and the precarious look of dangling fixtures, everything was as structurally sound as a bunker. If you ignored the sound of walking, and concentrated on the feel, you'd realize that. It had been calculated not to scare away any fence-jumpers or county inspectors, but rather, to bore them, and give a vague sense of unease.

The cafeteria looked to have been stripped of anything useful, including the old walk-in cooler. There was just a hole in the wall where it once had been, and shocks of broken tile edging and chopped-through conduit. Verd led the way inside. Rancor followed him ... carefully.

As soon as they were both in the space, Verd pushed the remote he had in his pocket, and the floor began descending.

Knocked out, splintering boards yielded to metal walls; a new "floor" slid in above them, and the LED lights embedded in it lit up the shaft. Rancor nodded.

"Okay. More impressed," he said.

The metal walls continued for two stories below the level of the school basement. Then the elevator came to a slow and graceful stop. One of the walls slid aside to reveal a corridor that would not have been out of place in any one of Verd's corporate labs. Lights in the ceiling came on at the touch of another button on the remote, sequencing away from them and then splitting down the adjoining corridors.

Verd sighed, and patted the wall. "My first lair," he said, nostalgically. "Home sweet home. You never forget your first, you know. I wanted the United States and then the world, so I set up shop here. Central to everywhere. Drowsy locals. Good infrastructure for moving everything from lab equipment to superbombs by highway, river, or rail. Convenience counts when you're doing high-end crime." Verd traced fingertips on the stainless steel trim. "I've had a lot of bases of operation, but there's just something about returning to your first lair that always feels like coming home. I did some good business here. Good times. Come on, I'll show you around."

"How'd you get your hands on this place?" Rancor asked. "And how the hell do you keep the city from noticing the power drain?"

"Racketeer with a wrecking firm sold it to me, and got me rotating, no-questions illegal labor for the construction work. I installed my own power plant. My design, of course. I don't use every isotope I get just for weapons, you know." Verd chuckled. "Anyway, the racketeer didn't know it was me, of course. It was one of my shell personas. He hardly even had a chance to enjoy the payoff too, before his fatal stroke." Verd shook his head sadly. "I kept telling him, lay off all that butter."

Rancor snorted. He knew more than enough about Verd's ventures into biological research to know that butter had very little to do with that fatal stroke ... unless, of course, butter was the delivery system for some untraceable nanobot that had caused the stroke in the first place. Verd gave the stubby man a raised-eyebrow side-glance in response to that snort. Rancor was the first person Verd had found who could figure out nearly everything Verd was doing, even if he couldn't deduce the means, or have invented them in the first place. But given a tool, he was an absolute genius at coming up with uses for it.

Verd opened the first door on the corridor, and as he did so, motion-activated lights came up inside. His hand caressed the doorframe as they entered. The room had been rigged out as a high-tech garage.

"Remember the Murdercycle?" Verdigris grinned. Of course Rancor would remember it. It had been one of his early favorite assassination tools. "This is where she was conceived, born, improved, and repaired." He had loved the Murdercycle. The only reason he had stopped using her was that ECHO had caught on to what he was doing with her, and not even the color-changing paint and shape-morphing bodywork was going to keep her and her rider from being tracked and caught.

"Now that was a sweet ride." Rancor nodded, smiling slightly. He walked around the room, picking up a tool here, a spare part there, examining everything, while Verd leaned back against the doorway. "We could still use something like that, if we kept it to night rides and switched the venue to high speed, superhighway intercept with a capture vehicle down the road. Hit the target at 120-plus miles per hour."

Huh. Clever. "I'll put that idea on the list," he promised. "We'd need a meta with enhanced reflexes to pull the job though, at those speeds."

Rancor just shrugged. Obviously, such a person wouldn't be him. He wasn't a meta. So he claimed, anyway. Yet Verd thought he detected something in the man's momentary scowl. Jealousy? Envy? Maybe a little anger? As much as Rancor was capable of loving anything, he had loved that bike. And Verd had just suggested he would not be the one to take her to the next dance.

Verdigris smiled, but only on the inside. *Good.* He lived for the feeling that he was successfully playing someone.

Verd decided it was time to move on, and Rancor followed. The lights went out behind them.

Verd displayed the many rooms of his first research facility like the fine gems they were, laying them out for Rancor's admiration. And, grudging though the admiration was, Rancor did deliver it. What was more, he was showing definite signs of desire. He wanted this place, Verd's first "home." He wanted it badly.

Good.

"I've saved the best for last," Verd said smugly. "I wanted to make sure you appreciated this place. I can't leave it to someone who won't use it properly."

Ah, there it was. That little glint in Rancor's eyes that said, "Oh, I am your equal. And with what I do here, you will acknowledge that I am not your underling, I am your partner."

Hmm hmm. Oh, Rancor. That will never do.

He opened the last door; this time, lulled by the rest of the tour, Rancor went in ahead.

Verd slammed and locked the door on him, and activated the intercom.

He waited until the cursing stopped.

"Now, now. I told you this place will be yours, and it will. But you have to earn it first—just like you have to earn the

Methuselah Virus. Yes, I know we were going after that together, but I've gotten a teeny bit ahead of you, and you know how I hate coming in second." Verd laughed. "But you can still have it, and you can still have this place."

He pushed the last button on the remote, activating all the traps. There was one thing to be said about going old-school, in this "old school." C4 never let you down.

"You just have to earn it, Rancor," he repeated, stepping into the elevator. He thumbed a few buttons on the remote. "She has a lot of life left in her, but you need to learn how she really ticks. Tick tick ticks. You need to romance before you can have her, and she is just so sensitive. You have to earn her."

"How do I do that?" Rancor's voice growled from the speaker.

Verd had just enough time to call out before the elevator carried him beyond the sound of anything—voices or explosions.

"Survive the next thirty minutes."

His first lair felt like going home, sure, and even like a first love—but he'd gotten over every girlfriend he'd killed just fine. This was just the prom date of supervillain lairs.

The sound of Verd's laughter echoed up the shaft, and then with the slam of a multi-ton door, was gone.

Here are three podcast stories, one that was omitted from Book One, *two that take place between* Book Two: World Well Lost *and* Book Three: Revolution. *The second was originally an experiment Dennis Lee and I did by doing a story entirely in real time in Twitter tweets. The third is some of John Murdock's background.*

In the wake of the initial Invasion of the Thulians under the control of the Masters, it might seem odd that one of the things ECHO needed to re-

establish was normality. But people who are not touched directly by a disaster—and that was the majority of the population—just want their Netflix back. They just want to go to work and get their designer coffee. They just want to know that those suddenly-scary metahumans can be trusted to keep them safe.

Sometimes they just need a pinup calendar.

STRIKE A POSE

MERCEDES LACKEY

Alex Tesla had an office back. The previous one was still buried under the many tons of rubble that had been the ECHO HQ office tower.

Unlike his previous sanctum, this one had to serve every purpose that the several rooms of his former office suite had provided. Today his tiny desk and computer had been shoved into a corner and the room filled with a folding conference table and chairs scrounged from the wreckage of the complex. Only two of them matched, but at least they were comfortable. Whiteboards were propped up on easels around the table, and a generous supply of whiteboard markers rested in their trays. This return to the primitive made him wince inwardly, thinking of his state-of-the-art videoconferencing video display suite that had made meetings as much entertainment as information.

Around the table were Tesla, Yankee Pride representing the Op Twos and Threes, Ramona representing the Op Ones, Richard Telleman, ECHO's business manager, a trio of lawyers also working in the ECHO complex, two lawyers from the ACLU, the ECHO lobbyist in Congress, and an empty seat. That seat would—soon, Tesla hoped—hold ECHO's own Op Two PR man, Spin Doctor. His powers were not exactly useful for law enforcement, but there was no one to match him at what he did—

"Hey there, guys and girls, the doctor is in the house!"

Alex heaved a sigh of relief as Spin Doctor made his entrance. All heads turned, all eyes were riveted on him. Metahumans were, by and large, very handsome, very charismatic. Spin Doctor, however, took that to a whole new level.

Everything about him was perfect. Only Mercurye could match his chiseled features, his radiant smile, his dazzling baby-blue eyes. His hair, which could only be described as a truly golden brown, was neither too short, nor too long, immaculately groomed, but with just an artful little tousle to keep it from looking too perfect. His suit, of a conservative cut, was of just a pale enough gray to keep from looking like a business suit, and it could not possibly have been tailored more impeccably. To complete the picture, Spin Doctor's voice had been variously described as "Like hot chocolate with a shot of Irish Cream Liqueur" and "Like smoky velvet." He could probably have read the phonebook and been paid to do so. He regularly turned down offers from Hollywood, television, radio, stage, politicians, and pornographers. He had also been offered the position of front-man preacher by one of the biggest televangelist empires in the country. He had turned that down too.

Alex Tesla regularly thanked God, his lucky stars, and any other supernatural entity that might be listening that Spin Doctor had a set of ethics that placed him firmly on the side of the good guys. And so far as Spin was concerned, that meant ECHO.

Spin Doctor slid into his seat, pulled off his dark glasses and tucked them into his breast pocket with a motion that was as smooth and easy as a dancer executing a familiar step, and just as graceful. He interlaced his fingers on the table in front of him and leaned a little forward. "So, problems. I know what *I* have been seeing, but let me hear what you good folks are picking up."

The lobbyist, Gerald Sanders, cleared his throat. "Legislation pending, a whole slate that we are not going to like, but the worst is a mandatory metahuman registration and licensing act—"

"Hold it right there, this is why Spin Doctor asked us here," said the ACLU lawyer with a grin. He was a rumpled bear of a man with a disarming smile. "We are already on this one. As fast as they can propose these pieces of draconian legislation, we are shooting them down."

Alex blinked. "How?" he asked.

The ACLU lawyer leaned back in his chair. "Simpler than you think. There *is* no way to tell a metahuman from a plain old ordinary guy like me, except by the powers. Well"—he amended —"there are some that have got outward signs, like that beautiful blue healer of yours, but most of 'em you couldn't tell from

Joe Plumber. No genetic marker, no weird emissions, no nothing. Sure, most of 'em are pretty, like Mercurye, but so are supermodels. But it goes farther than that. Even when you *get* powers, they aren't always whatchacall—useful in a criminal or crime fighting sense. Like—Doc, who was that example you used?"

"Spoonbender," Spin Doctor supplied helpfully.

"Yeah, him. Okay, he can bend metal with his mind. But only metal he could bend with his bare hands. And he has to be within about a yard of it."

"He makes a very good living bending soft metal in inaccessible places," Spin Doctor added. "But he is not exactly high on anyone's list of people likely to go on a crime spree. As for being afraid of him—" Spin Doctor's shrug was eloquent. "What's he going to do? Threaten to braid the tines of your fork?"

"But if you start mandating registering and licensing metahumans, where do you stop? Do you start going door to door, demanding that everyone prove he or she *can't* do something extraordinary? Do we start registering singers with an eight octave range? Contortionists? People with 'a way with animals'? Where does superb athletic ability stop and a metahuman power start?"

"I see your point," Tesla replied, relaxing just a little. This issue had been worrying him ever since Gerald had brought it to his attention. "Though the part about athletics *is* a touchy one. Various athletic associations debate that one every time someone breaks a world record."

"Leave *them* to that," the ACLU man said firmly. "That's not anything to pass a law about. Then we have the third point, which is that not everyone gets powers from birth. Well, shoot, look at what happened out there during the attacks! We had people manifesting all over the place. But the biggest thing we have on our side is the nature of the enemy in the first place."

Alex started, then controlled himself, realizing that the ACLU lawyer could not possibly know about the alien aspect. At least, not yet. *That* was closely under wraps and "Need To

Know." In fact, he wasn't entirely certain even the President knew yet.

"By which Bob here means that the Thulians were not actually metahumans," Spin Doctor said, tapping the table with his index finger. "They were wearing advanced armored suits, but were not themselves metahumans. So just how do you register that? Add every shade tree mechanic and basement science freak to the list? Any one of them *might* come up with powered armor!"

Alex laughed nervously. "Well, when you put it that way—"

"We have, we do, and we will." Bob spread his hands wide. "It's in our interest to keep you folks able to function so that you don't turn into some paramilitary outfit like Blacksnake. Licensing and registration can lead down some paths we don't want to see *you* on."

Alex winced. He'd been getting stories from the field—stories where Blacksnake had been called in by private property owners and things had gotten ugly. Sometimes very ugly.

"We're on your side, Tesla, as long as *you* lot stay on the side of civil liberties," Bob said, firming his chin and suddenly looking less like a rumpled teddy bear in a suit, and more like a weary lawyer who was going to fight to the death for a cause he believed in.

"Anyone have anything else?" Spin Doctor asked, looking around the table. "No? Then it's my turn. People, we are about to find ourselves with a major image problem. It's going to start hitting us on all fronts. Already there is talk in some cities that they don't want ECHO HQs in the city centers anymore. In fact, they would really rather that we planted ourselves on remote plateaus in Arizona or the Arctic tundra. Never mind that the response time would be atrocious."

Spin Doctor smiled slightly. You couldn't help but respond to that, but this was something that had Alex worried. The NIMBY—Not In My Back Yard—contingent was becoming more and more vocal, and he could hardly blame them. The

Thulians had carved destruction corridors across most major cities as they moved in on ECHO HQs, and no one wanted a repeat performance.

"I have a couple of ideas on that," Spin Doctor continued. "After all, it wasn't only our HQs that were targeted. My people are working on graphics." He rolled his eyes. "You can't do anything without graphics. I think we can keep this one under control, but we might have to move a handful of HQs." He raised one eyebrow. "On the other hand, we are going to make a killing on the real estate market, so there's no loss without some gain. Alex, there are some rumors that you actually engineered this to put push behind broadcast power."

Alex felt his face flushing, and his eyes narrowed. "If I—"

"Good. That's how I want you to look if anyone asks you. Righteous wrath; it's a beautiful thing. But think about what you are going to say. Have it ready, so you can come off as righteous and reasoned at the same time." Spin Doctor nodded with approval. "I'm debating now whether we should mention that the Thulians themselves may have used broadcast power. Sooner or later someone is probably going to try and float that one."

"We should say that *if* they did, they stole the tech, Doc," Ramona piped up.

Spin Doctor considered that, and nodded slowly. "I think that will fly. More righteous wrath, Alex. 'My uncle dreamed this would be freely available,' yada yada."

Alex gritted his teeth. "I can do that." He hated to think about it, but it certainly was possible, and the very idea made him ... furious.

"Now, last of all—a little more image grooming." Spin Doctor grinned. "Ramona, Yank, this is where I need your help, because this is going to involve getting some of your people to cooperate. We're going to be doing a series of photo shoots. Calendars, feature articles. Pushing the sexy angle. It's hard to be afraid of Mr. July—or the centerfold in *Playboy* for that matter, if we can get someone to pose nude."

Yank looked incredulous, Ramona barked a startled laugh.
"You *must* be joking!" she said.

He shook his head. "I was never more serious. I want a
spread of some of your pretty-boys for one of the teen magazines, little bishi-boys. I've got a firm commitment for a calendar
and article for some of the hard-bodied guys—Merc should be
perfect for the leadoff for that—where is he, anyway?"

"Not available," Alex put in quickly, before anyone else could
answer. "He's on personal assignment from me."

"All right ... hmm ... Corbie then. Little black speedo, black
wings, that'll work. Ramona, pick me out thirteen more, they
want a fourteen-month calendar. But the first shoot—" He
grinned even wider. "The first shoot, we are going to remind the
people that ECHO is not *just* fighting and building-smashing.
Our leadoff article is going to be the cover story for *Harpers*,
ladies and gents. *The Sexy Healers of ECHO!*"

⌂

Bella could hardly believe it. She didn't know whether she should
be angry, excited, or sick. After all, she was going to be on the
cover—*the cover*—of *Harpers*. But ... this wasn't what she was
supposed to be doing. And she was *still* angry that she wasn't
back in Lost Wages....

But when Ramona explained it all to her, she had to agree it
made sense, the whole idea, that is. She knew all about spin—she
lived in Vegas, after all. And in fact, since she had started volun-
teering at a little free clinic set up near one of the "war zones"
she had been hearing a lot of negative talk about ECHO. Something had to be done, and she could see this working.

"But why me?" she'd asked Ramona.

"Three reasons." The Op One Coordinator counted them
down on her fingers. "One, Handsome Devil is front and center
on the guys' counterpart to this, and we want someone of ... how
to put this ... 'color' ... to match that cover."

Bella had rolled her eyes. "Okay, and I guess I am the only non-standard-issue complexion in the Medic Corps."

"Two, you're sexy, Bell. You know how to walk, how to stand, how to hold yourself. I don't know where or how you learned that—"

"Anybody in Vegas with a decent set of assets tries out for showgirl sooner or later," Bella pointed out. "Heck, one of the bike cops on our beat was in a show. It's a good second job, and pays better than being a dealer. I actually tried out for a singer too, which I would have preferred, but—" she grimaced. "In either case, I stand out too much to fit in a chorus, and I wasn't a star, so there went that idea. So, what's the third reason?"

"You speak some Russian, you get along with Red Saviour, and we want the CCCP girl Soviette on this to get the Euro-angle."

Bella stared at her. "You want me to what hey?"

"I want you to recruit Soviette," Ramona replied patiently.

Bella rolled her eyes. "*That* will take a miracle. Want me to bring Marx up from Worker's Paradise too? Why me? Panacea and Gilead have more seniority than I do. Doc Shiven is actually the head of ECHO Med."

"Because you have something no one else in ECHO Med has," said Ramona.

"Which is?"

"Two things, actually. Combat cred. And people listen to you." Ramona took a deep breath. "Until now, ECHO Med has been mostly doing Damage Control Officer duty and patching up boo-boos. You were in the middle of the fighting at Area 51, and before that, in front of your fire station, and before *that,* you were an EMT in some of the Combat Zone neighborhoods in Vegas."

"Somebody's been snooping in my records," Bella muttered—but she couldn't disagree.

"And as I said, people listen to you. People, in the aggregate. Panacea and Gilead are good one-on-one. You have command presence. Saviour will respect that." Ramona nodded to emphasize her point.

"All right," Bella sighed. "If you say so. I'll channel Ike Eisenhower and see what I can do."

△

Well somehow she had managed to make Saviour see reason. She still wasn't quite sure how, but somehow, amid all her own amateur spins of "showing the world that Russian women are naturally more beautiful than all the skinny supermodels" and "how do you expect to get men to listen to what socialism is all about if you don't get their attention first?" she had managed to make her case and make it well. The CCCP Medic One, Soviette, was bemused, amused, and entirely cooperative, and thanks to all that Russian military-style training, did *not* slouch the way American girls did. The photographer was very happy.

They all had special ECHO uniforms for the first shoot—*not* nanoweave, since it wouldn't take dye, and fitted to each of them with amazing tailoring. They were all in UN blue instead of black. All but Bella's; the uniform color just made her look like someone had accidentally color-keyed her face to coordinate with the fabric. So instead of UN blue, she got white, which made her really stand out as she knelt in the front line of the group shot, posed as if she was sublimely unaware of the camera, her long blue hair worn loose and tousled around her shoulders.

For the second shoot, they all wore—well, the "classics." What everyone thought of when you said "metahumans." Either their working gear if it was deemed sexy enough, or the spandex beloved by so many writers and comic book artists. Einhorn wore one of her flowing white dresses, looking like an Enya wannabee, Sovie had her CCCP uniform, and Bella, who normally wore the coveralls of a paramedic, found herself holding something that would have fit into a pantyhose egg....

When she put it on, it left absolutely nothing to the imagination and fit like a second skin. It was a white one-piece including gloves that faded into blue on the hands and legs and had a partial cowl that still let her hair show. It also had cutouts. She surveyed herself in the mirror before she sat down so the hair and makeup people could do their thing, and decided that if it was possible, she was keeping the sucker. She looked *hot*. Seven of the other women also had spandex outfits, but ... there was something special about this one.

The last session of the day was the bikini-shoot, and that was when the trouble started.

"No!" Einhorn shouted, stamping her foot. "I am *not* wearing this!" She held up the tiny white bikini as if it was a dead mouse.

"Look—you agreed to this—"

"I am not wearing this!" she repeated, beginning to sound both stubborn and hysterical. "It's not *decent!*"

"Einhorn, there are thirteen more of us wearing the same thing," began Gilead, who in her off hours was as punked out as it was possible to get and had needed to remove most of her piercings for the shoot. "It's not as if you're going to stand out—"

"I am not wearing this!" she cried, and Bella began to feel— something very, very familiar. Psychic pressure. Her eyes widened, and suddenly a great many things about Einhorn began to be clear.

Time to nip this nonsense in the bud before the girl had all of them wrapped around her little finger.

She stalked up to the girl, grabbed her shoulder just hard enough to hurt a tiny bit and shook her. "Alex Tesla is a reasonable man," she said through gritted teeth. "He says this is necessary and I believe him. *We owe him.* Without him, we'd be nothing more than a collection of circus freaks. So you are *going* to wear that suit, you are *going* to smile and look pretty in it, and you are *going* to do so this minute, or so help me, I will strip you naked right now and stuff you into it myself!"

And don't try any of your mind-tricks on me, girl, she projected into Einhorn's mind, watching the girl's eyes widen. *Anything you can do, I can do better.* Einhorn couldn't know that Bella was only a touch-telepath, and couldn't know that Bella herself wasn't sure what she could and could not do yet. Self-confidence and bluff was ninety percent of the game here, and Bella let go of Einhorn before the truth could leak over.

With a squeak, the girl clutched the bikini to her chest and scuttled off to the dressing room.

There was stunned silence for a moment. Then the silence was broken by the sound of one person, slowly applauding from the doorway behind Bella. She turned.

Red Saviour was standing there, looking amused. "I like you better and better, blue girl," the Commissar of the CCCP said approvingly. "Now, I am needing Sovie soon. So be hurrying up with decadent pictures. *Davay, davay, davay!*"

FOR THOSE ABOUT TO ROCK

MERCEDES LACKEY AND DENNIS LEE

S ome people claim they live on coffee. They're pikers compared to me. I'm Victoria Caffeinated Victrix, thanks. I have a minifreezer just for the coffee beans, 'cause I order it in bulk, delivered. Today was a day I was glad I had a lot of back-stock, because I was going to need a lot of coffee. Djinni was out on another solo job and Bell had ordered me to keep tabs on him with Overwatch. Keeping track of the Djinni on solo is a lot like keeping track of a flea on a hot griddle; it taxes even my consid-erable capabilities. Though that's mostly because he hates magic so much.

Jeebus. Hates magic. Yeah, there was that little thing. He and I were not exactly talking right now. We'd had this ... explosion.

Actually, he'd snapped at me and jabbed me in the proverbial gut, right when and where I was most vulnerable. It's as if he has radar for that kind of thing.

This was how it happened. The explosion, I mean. He'd been on another solo job, right after the Goldman Catacombs. Not a surprise, since he recovers faster than anyone I have ever seen. There'd been a news story just before he went out, courtesy of Spin Doctor. We'd both caught it. He thought it was hilarious.

I was in the Overwatch room, he was on the system. "... and for those curious about last night's specTACular lightshow over the Nevada desert," he'd mimicked, "Rest assured, those were your own, your brave, your heroic boys and girls of ECHO on some routine training maneuvers. ECHO, training to keep you, your loved ones, and America safe!" He'd snorted. "Training maneuvers. Gotta love that friendly fire then. Feels good to be out of the infirmary. Was getting tired of Scope's retching anytime a new layer of skin grew back."

I'd been raw, still trying to get over losing Herb, my Earth Elemental friend, on that op. "Remind me again why this thing of yours is supposed to be a *super*power?"

He'd been surprisingly civil. "Hey, Victrix. You better?"

I'd toyed with being honest, decided on a white lie. "If I say 'no,' Spin Doctor will read me the riot act for 'negative impact on morale.' I'm fine, thanks for asking." I just hadn't wanted to open myself up to him.

"Oh screw him." He sounded gruffly sympathetic. "He was pushing me to reveal my real face, for the sake of good press."

I tried to sound light. Probably hadn't succeeded. "It would be, if you look like Brad Pitt. If you look like Emo Phillips, not so much." I couldn't help it. It slipped out. After all, Djinni was the only person besides Bella that ... knew. Knew that what I'd called up hadn't been just this giant rock Elemental, but a very dear friend. "I miss Herb."

There was a moment of hesitation. Then something unexpected. "Yeah ... listen, I'm sorry about what happened to him."

I don't know why I said it ... except that it was true. And maybe he needed to hear that I *knew* this. "Magic has a price. Always does. Always will."

He sounded surprised. "Hey, that's my line."

Finally I asked. "That why you hate it? Everything has a price, you just don't always know about it." I guess maybe I was trying to figure a way to make him understand not just where I was coming from, but about how seriously I took magic. How it was so much a part of me that magic and me couldn't be separated, and I understood the risks I was taking, dancing on the edge of quantum physics as I was.

He'd paused, a long pause on the freq. "That sums it up, I'd say. Professional habit. I like knowing the odds before going in, and magic complicates that. It's hard to give estimates to a client when the potential pitfalls of a job range from 'papercut' to 'complete and utter obliteration of everything in existence.'"

I'd raised an eyebrow over that. What the hell had he—or someone he knew—been tinkering with in his deep, dark past? "I take it you've never worked with a properly trained mage before. Odds of the latter are pretty insignificant most of the time."

The reply I'd gotten was not anything like I wanted. I'd intended it as an opening. I got dissed. "Fine, whatever."

Well one of the advantages of being Overwatch is they can't turn you off. Not without taking out the earpiece, and he didn't dare, not on a job. "Hey. Look, I'm not trying to blow smoke up your ass here. Yeah, things can get nasty, yeah, there's a price, and yeah, there is a quantum uncertainty thing going on, but a properly trained mage has the equivalent of a PhD in Nuclear Physics. Sure, the odds of turning on a linear accelerator and blowing up the universe are there, but they're pretty small. Same thing. A trained mage knows the risks and the costs and knows when to back down on the bad ones. Unless, of course, you're trying to *prevent* the blowing up of the universe, in which case, the risk you take is probably worth it."

The anger in his voice was very real. "And what gives you the right, any of you, to mess with shit like that?"

Where the hell had *that* come from? I was just as angry, how *dared* he? What did he know? And how about all those perfectly ordinary people out there who took horrible risks using nothing more but their hands and their brains? Or all the metas who took risks that *always* endangered the innocent? Wasn't that why ECHO had the Damage Control Officers in the first place? "What gives you metas the right to do what you do? And you— what about you? You weren't exactly fighting the good fight until you got dragooned into ECHO."

His voice dripped with contempt, as if I was some stupid teenager who'd been playing games with the DoD computers in Iron Mountain. "Christ, get some perspective, lady. I'll admit I've never been a boy scout, but I wasn't messing with primal forces. You want to argue the relative morality of what I did with trying to control the fabric of reality? Good luck."

The arrogant, judgmental son of a—oh he'd pushed my buttons but good. "Arthur C. Clarke: 'Sufficiently advanced technology is indistinguishable from magic.' From where I sit there are plenty of people besides mages messing with the fabric of reality. Including plenty of metas."

He had an answer for that, too. "So? I'm hardly defending

any of those douchebags. Magic, science, anything and anyone with the audacity to mess with crap on that scale is an asshole."

I'd snorted my own contempt. "So you'd prefer it if everyone went back to living in caves? You can't pick and choose."

Now his voice just dripped scorn. "You're big with the absolutes, aren't you? Someone who invents the wheel? Good job. Someone who tries to ignite a new Sun in Kansas? Douchebag."

So who had died and appointed *him* Lord High Everything Else? "Look, brainiac, on some level everyone with strong enough willpower messes with the fabric of reality. That's what luck is! You want something bad enough, if there's not enough force opposing you, by damn, you get it! That's why one of the Prime Laws is 'Be careful what you wish for'! Even *you*. Bet you have done just that, and gotten it. Bet you any amount of money you have."

Evidently I had pushed one of his buttons right back. If words were weapons, he'd skewered me with them then. "Right, 'cause you know so much about me! Victoria Victrix, the lady with *all* the answers! Tell me you've got it all down, that you have it all figured out, that you knew what would happen to Herbert!"

I froze. The hurt—it felt like a heart attack for a minute. Finally I managed to say something. "Transmitting your requested info. Overwatch out."

I still heard him, of course, heard the sudden guilt, the contrition, the instant before I shut the comm down. "Shit ... Victrix! I'm sorry, dammit!"

But it was too late.

So now it was two days later, and I was settling in with the closest thing I could get to Tim Horton's coffee (dark roast, pinch of cinnamon on the grounds, double cream, double sugar) and wondering if I could stand to listen to his voice. If he'd skewer me again. Of course I was feeling much, much better now, since Herb was back. In fact, the now-tiny Elemental was perched on one of the desks, watching the monitors curiously.

Bella had been all over me to kiss and make up. I guess she'd been at him ... more directly, because when I put on the headset and opened the feed the first thing I heard was, "Word to the wise—when Bella knocks on your door, get ready to duck, she's got a mean sucker punch. Ow."

I couldn't help it. I felt a smirk coming on. "Jaw hurt?" I asked sweetly.

"Would that make you happy?" His tone was quite neutral.

Honesty, or not? I opted for prevarication. "Yes and no. I'd be lying if I gave an unqualified no. But hey, Schadenfreude. You have a solo job. I'm supposed to inform you because you haven't been checking your email, phone, or PDA. There. You've been informed. You're also on Overwatch at Bell's insistence."

"Thanks." A very long pause. "Victrix?"

I was bringing up my camera feeds. And I was not at all inclined to be anything other than chill and civil. "Yes, Red Djinni?"

"I really am sorry."

I don't often explode. That's Bella's thing. I'm usually ... okay, face it, I am usually huddling in a corner shaking in every limb rather than dealing with anger and confrontation. But this time I exploded. "You're an unmitigated cream-faced spleeny unwashed bugbear. A pustulant boor. A ham-handed, toad-spotted malcontent. A beslubbering, pickle-brained pigeon-egg. A lumpish folly-fallen apple-john. A qualling ill-breeding malcontent. A clouted common-kissing wagtail. A ..." I groped for words. They weren't there. "Damn. I'm running out of Shakespearian insults."

"S'okay. Thanks for putting in the effort." That kind of floored me. What the hell did that mean?

Well, at least I wouldn't have to talk to him for long. "We're supposed to keep radio silence on this one. We only break it if you're in too deep to get out alone." Or alive, but he would know that was what I meant.

"No constant Overwatch?" He sounded surprised.

Well of course I *could*. But ... him and magic. Again. "Nothing you'd accept."

Then he floored me a second time. "What about a magic line?"

The hell? I nearly inhaled my coffee. "I thought you were against me messing with the fabric of the universe."

"I think the universe will hold up to one arcane phone call." When he said that, I almost went to the window to see if there were pigs flying in attack formation over the Varsity.

Okay. Okay. Let's make this the littlest and least intrusive thing I could. "Safest and smallest would be a light charm to link the PDAs and text." Why text? 'Cause the spell to make what appeared on his screen also appear on mine was ... well it was easy, small, and used less magic than lighting a candle.

Which, by the way, is the single most clichéd way to show you are a mage in the entire universe. So don't do it, Okay? Just don't. It only impresses the rubes. It makes the rest of us sigh and roll our eyes.

I couldn't read his voice, but his words were clear enough. "All right, make it happen."

I did. A few moments later I was typing. *Testing.*

Agh! My testicles! This is what passes for Djinni humor.

Okay, it was funny.

Dr. Ruth has a pill for that, I replied. *You want 2027 West Catalpa. Surveillance. Possible Doppelgänger sighting. Definite explosives, hence radio silence. They know there's a bomb maker in there and they know he's using a radio transmitter to detonate, but they don't know what freqs he has his detonators set for. I can't find out magically because I don't know who he is; I don't have anything of his to use as a target. And I can't find out by computer because I don't know his IP address and there's nothing around there I can hack to find it. Which makes the technomancy out on both counts.* I was babbling, over-explaining. Why was I doing this? What about this man made me doublethink myself, made me think I had to explain anything to him? I couldn't help it. It was like scratching at a scab. *Rules. There are rules to this magic stuff. Lots of rules. Unless, of course, you don't mind killing and hurting a lot of people, including random strangers and yourself.*

His reply was ... well ... right on. *Christ, even texting you talk a lot. Alright, objective?*

That was simpler, and required no over-explanation. *Determine if Doppelgänger is in there or not. If not, get Bomb Boy out without him setting off anything. If so, let me know and wait for backup.*

K. I should be at destination in fifteen minutes.

Now ... let me get this straight, here. When I say I have the magic equivalent of a PhD in Astrophysics, I am not kidding. Yes, there are instinctive mages. And some of them, a very few, are very good. Those few are the equivalent of natural athletes, or people who sing opera well with no training. The rest? They're like every yahoo who says "Hold my beer" and thinks he can drive like Mario Andretti or Paul Newman. Not. Gonna. Happen. Oh, they can get where they are going, most of the time, but there's a lot of flailing and flogging and very often, very, very often, there is collateral damage.

And yes, there are the old "Fam-Trad" mages, trained in the traditional manner, by a family or coven member. Things mostly work. They mostly never stray out of the family recipe book. They honestly do not know what they are working with, in the same sense that people drive cars every day and have no idea of the mechanics and physics of an internal combustion engine.

Then there are the people like me, trained in very small, very special schools. I won't tell you where. I *will* tell you that every day from the time I was seven years old, I went to the regular P.S.17 grade school, then came home, and spent another four hours being schooled by my parents. And then from the time I was a sophomore I went full time in a very different school far, far from my home. It was not Hogwarts, let me tell you. It was more like Kiddie CalTech. I attended that special school every day of my life, including weekends, right up to college. And then I went to college. *That* college, one that was *in* a university but ... and I'll tell you what it is. Merlin

College, Oxford University. Good luck finding it. You can look at Magdalen College in the North corner of First Court by the Chapel all you like; if you aren't in Merlin College, you'll never see the door.

So, yeah, it was like that. I did this because my parents determined that I had a double dose of the family knack for the power, and knew it was either train me early and hard, or burn it out before I killed someone. Now, don't get me wrong; I *wanted* this. There were very few times I rebelled, and the rebellion never lasted more than a day or two. You know how prodigies always are, math, science, letters, dance, music—it's not our parents driving us into it, it's us, charging in on our own, sometimes *against* the will of our parents. You punish us by taking away the music, the math books, the magic.

It was in high school that this magic school figured out I was one *rara avis* indeed, a technomage, as well as a geomancer. In short, I could magic machines, the more complicated and computerized the better. I had an affinity for them. Most mages ... don't. Catastrophically don't. Some I know can't even live in a place with electricity without starting electrical fires. The fact that *I* could use them the way most mages use an athame and chants blew people out of the water. Now, actually I had known this for some time, I just figured it was no big deal, everyone else could too, and eventually we'd get to technomancy in the classes. When *I* realized that no, I was the only one and *they* realized what I could do—well—let's just say I ended up with a bit of an ego which bit me in the ass ... but that's another story.

This only intensified my education. I'm a math whiz. And I do technomancy. Which means I can make shit up and know it's going to work. Or to be precise, I know the exact odds of getting it to work. I can improvise *way* outside of the normal things that modern mages do—substituting components and the like. If I don't have what I need for a spell, since I know the math and can deconstruct the original, I can make up a whole *new* spell on the spot that will use what I've got. I can, and do, run calculus in my head, though I always double-check on the computer. This is because, at its root, magic is the ability to move energy in a way that gets things done that you want to get done. The tool for moving it is your will, reinforced by the energies of the stuff you use to make up the spell. Usually mathemagical diagrams in my case; I don't need to use many components these days. That magical energy is all around you; conventional science just hasn't discovered it yet. The energy *you* use to move that energy comes from inside you.

Yes, if you've made the intuitive leap already, I'll confirm it for you. Luck is magic. Energy responding to will, changing reality to suit you.

But there's always a price. *Always* a price. Part of my price to become the technomancer that I am was to have a mere sliver of a childhood. I understood, bone deep, very early in my life, that I was potentially juggling with nuclear bombs. I also understood, bone deep, what the consequences of failure were, because my parents took me on a visit to a very special med/psych ward full of people who had slipped while juggling.

Trust me, you never want to go there.

This is why, when I do the things that have less-than-perfect odds, they're set up so I am the meat-shield between catastrophe and anyone else around.

There is no free lunch. *Most* of the time, the price is sheer, physical exhaustion. Sometimes you end up with a higher price than that. I did once. That is why I am a mass of aching, burning, scarred tissue from my collarbone to my soles. Yet another story.

But I can no more give it up than I can give up breathing. It's me. It defines me. I *need* it like I need air. I never realized how much until ECHO came knocking on my door post-Invasion, and I built Overwatch, and was operating at the height of my powers again.

I say, without false modesty, I am a Robert Oppenheimer of magic. And just as he, I understand the math, and the consequences of not understanding the math completely. He did not embark on the creation of the A-bomb in a spirit of anything other than full understanding of the consequences of failure. I do not embark on spellcasting in a spirit of anything other than a righteous dread of what might go wrong. Ever.

So this is why I see red—pun not intended—when the Djinni acts as if I was some street witch trying to hex her boyfriend's ex with a supermarket spellbook.

Then we get into the fact that not only am I an exquisitely trained mage, I am a mage steeped in magical ethics until it oozes from every pore. Ethical magic is *hard*. You can do nothing without consent. You clean every speck up after yourself. You *think*, a lot, about all the possible ramifications that your alteration to the universe might have.

But I digress.

While I was thinking this over, my screen lit up. *Reading me, Overwatch?*

That's a roger. Something occurred to me. I knew he had headed out without a lot of warning, and that he'd be there a while. *Jeet yet? Yontoo?*

Mwha?

That's Southern for "Did you eat yet? Want to?" I glanced at Herb, who was peering at the screen in a way that suggested he was very eager. He had come back to me, just hours after Red's words had sent me reeling. He was a mere pebble of what he once was, but he had clung to life. He was still with us and he liked Djinni, and ... well, if Djinni was feeling guilt or remorse over what he thought had happened to Herb, it wasn't fair to let him continue to feel bad.

Herb is an interesting barometer for bullshit. I have no idea how he does it, but he always *knows* if somebody is a basically good guy hiding behind the façade of an asshat, or a scumbag hiding behind the mask of someone you can trust. He's never been wrong. Not even when I thought he was.

And he liked Djinni. Go figure.

Yeah, I suppose I could do with something to munch on, why?

You're likely going to be there a while. I've mapped you in the alley and it's not paved. Which meant, of course, that Herb could sneak in through the ground after I gave him a magical shortcut to a spot I knew nearby.

I think sending some Chinese delivery my way might be counterproductive to the nature of this stakeout.

I had something more discreet in mind. Provided you're good with a little visitor of the arcane kind. Herb was jumping up and down and clapping his hands.

Chinese ... elves? I took that as a yes. I went to the kitchen and packed up a small, hardened "lunchbox" of mil-spec steel. It was going to have to survive being hauled behind Herb through the dirt. Coffee in a thermos and a sandwich Bella brought me from the deli. She thinks I don't eat enough. I used a little magic to make it hot and fresh—"go back to the way you were an hour and a half ago" basically. Reverse entropy. Normally I'd use the microwave, but I think Djinni's taste buds are better than mine.

I gave the box to Herb. I had little arcane "landing zones" plotted all over the city these days, in case I needed to send someone—or something—there in a hurry. Without a landing pad, whatever you Apport has odds of 85 percent of ending up a smear on the ground. Or worse, embedded *in* the ground. Herb and the lunch were small, it wouldn't take much out of me. Even better, Herb was magic in nature. Magic critters are easier to Apport. He stepped into the diagram I drew on the counter with the box strapped to his back like a backpack. I'd ask Djinni to bring him home, later, unless he wanted me to Apport him back, or to take the long way back. Sometimes he does. I think he's exploring Atlanta underground. Literally underground.

I ran through the math, sketched more diagrams in the air, said the right sounds, and with a *pop* of displaced air, he was gone.

I went back to the keyboard. *Okay, you hearing something nearby that sounds like digging? Check there.*

You're not sending gnomes at me, are ya?

What do you think I am, a travel agency? Naw, just a Philly cheese-steak and some coffee.

That works. There was another long pause. I wondered what he was thinking as Herb pushed the box up out of the ground. Finally: *What the hell is that?*

Take a good look. I know it looks like a walking lunchbucket; look who's carrying it.

Another long pause, and I swear to you, the text looked angry. *That's messed up, Victrix. Herb was your friend, wasn't he? What is this? Some animated chew toy look-alike?*

Simpler was better. *Hold your horses. It's Herb. It really is. Hell, go take your lunch and talk to him, you'll see.*

Another long pause. *The hell you say. How?*

Well, now that was a tricky question. *Not sure, really. My guess? It wasn't his time.* Simplistic and not my best guess. I don't believe in fate; I've personally changed "fate" too often. Closer to say that Elementals don't work like us. They have different rules. *He used up everything of himself for you guys, but something's kept him here. Like maybe his will. Earth Elementals have the most powerful will of all of the Elements. Herb just could have made up his mind that he was not going, and imposed that on the universe. Of course, there had to be a reason why he would have decided that—*

Like what?

I dunno, our friendship maybe? Or maybe he just wants to see what shit you'll get into next. Could have been either. Could have been both. Could have been a reason I hadn't even guessed at.

Captain Sarcastic had to put in his two cents on it, of course. *So now ... what ... he's your delivery boy?*

I didn't rise to the bait. *He wanted to say hi in person. Other than that ... he hangs out with Gray and does what he wants to do. Right now, that seems to be MMORPGs. He's with the Horde.*

Evidently I said the right thing. *Just shook his hand. Now he's dancing.*

I found myself reluctantly smiling. *He likes you.*

I did not expect the response I got. *Yeah, everybody makes that mistake at the beginning.*

Say what? *Bitter much?* I replied.

Again, a response I did not expect; not from a guy who, from everything I had seen, had an ego that almost left enough space in the room for some air to breathe. *Many hours of expensive psychotherapy have classed it as "acceptance," thank you very much.* Yeah, right. As if the Djinni would ever come within a nautical mile of a shrink if he could avoid it.

I decided it was a good idea to switch subjects. *How's action at the target? All quiet on the western front?*

Immediate reply. *Nothing, I'm getting extremely cold vibes here. How solid is your intel on this one?*

That part, I was sure of. *The DG sighting was a definite maybe. The bomb lab is a hard yes. But our little Nazi sympathizer might not be home.*

Evidently his patience had been stretched thin. *Okay, I'm heading in. Breaking contact for a bit, keep Herb around, he might need to get back to you with a report if I don't come out. Give me ten minutes.*

What could I say? It was his op. The building was all artificial, I couldn't even scry in there clearly. *Roger. Be as safe as you can.*

And thanks, the coffee was good.

It was a very long ten minutes. My only comfort was that Herb was there. If the excrement really did hit the rotating blades, Herb could get through to me quickly. Though small, he still had enough power to do that.

And he did. Before I got a text, I got a message from Herb, as a bloodstone Apported to my desktop. Not good.

I opened Bella's freq. "Bell! Djinni's hurt."

"How bad?" was the instant reply. *"I'm at ECHO Medical, I can add myself to any team that goes out after him."*

"Don't know yet—"

I was about to open Djinni's radio freq in defiance of the orders when I got another text.

Area's secure, Overwatch. Send in the cleaners.

I pulled my little smoke-and-mirrors thing, and called ECHO dispatch using a CCCP freq. "Comrades, this is Upyr, of CCCP. You are to be havink man down, Comrade Krasny Djinni. He is to be sendink me at safe distance, and is to be tellink me to be havink cleaners and medic sent." ECHO proper did not know about Overwatch. ECHO proper was not going to learn about it until Tesla gave it the official blessing.

"Roger that, CCCP Upyr." They didn't ask what a CCCP op was doing out of their neighborhood, and I broke the freq. When ECHO Medical got the buzz Bell would handle it.

All this took seconds. I texted back. *Herb says you need a Band-Aid. Scrambled ECHO Cleaners with Bell in tow.*

Wouldn't mind if they rushed a bit.

My heart jumped into my throat. Okay, I knew he was able to heal himself crazy well, and I was still kinda annoyed with him but—

You okay? I responded immediately.

The reply did not comfort me. *Not really, the guy knew how to use that machete.*

My heart nearly stopped. *Shit, Red! How bad?*

Pretty bad, I can see ... well, parts that I shouldn't be able to see.

I wanted to swear and didn't have time. Instead, I got on Bella's CCCP comm. When she answered the thing, I could hear the siren in the background. "This is beink Upyr, Comrade Blue. Your man down is nyet good. Is being cut half open." This was for the benefit of the others in the response vehicle.

"Roger. Spasiba, Upyr." Off-mic I heard, "You heard the woman! Floor it!" then the comm clicked off.

I got back on the keyboard. *Got the pedal to the metal. You should be able to hear the sirens soon. Stay with me, keep typing. What about the mark?* I didn't want him to pass out. He was experienced. He knew what to keep pressure on, how to make his body help him, and he would as long as he could. He was his own best aid at the moment.

Oh, HIS parts are all over the place now. He didn't leave me much choice.

I was going to type anything to keep him alert. *And DG?*

No sign of him. Hope the cleaners pick up his scent.

A pause, and I was about to try and prod him when more text came. *Herb's not dancing anymore. He just keeps looking at me.*

You made him sad. I'll explain it to him later. Now ... that was way, way oversimplifying. Herb was an Elemental. He might be child-like, but he was no child. He understood very well what Djinni had just done, and—although I do not know this for certain, I am quite sure that either an Elemental Herb knew, or even Herb himself, had killed in the past when someone had tried to coerce him, magically. They did that. That was what Red had been afraid of. You'd fight to the death, too, if someone tried to enslave you. And Herb was an *Elemental*. They are nature spirits. As in "Nature, red in tooth and claw." They are well acquainted with innocent violence. These are not happy peaceful little stone Buddhists.

So Herb was not sad that Red had killed someone. He was sad that Red had been hurt, and sad that Red had been forced to kill someone and that—which the text "he didn't leave me much choice" told me—had made Red feel guilty. What I would explain was why all of this had happened, why it had been need-ful, and that humans felt guilt even when we did needful things.

He might act with the open emotions of a toddler, but his understanding was completely adult.

Another message from Herb. A roughly truck-shaped rock Apported to my keyboard with a click. I breathed a sigh of relief.

But Red ... Red didn't know what I knew, or what I meant. And the last text I got from him as Bell and the crew reached him made my heart ache.

Guess he likes me less now. Told ya. Everyone makes that mistake in the beginning ...

WAITING ON

MERCEDES LACKEY AND CODY MARTIN

This might have been the best motel John had ever stayed in in his entire life.

Vickie had guided him to it, after having him leave the beater rental van, pick up a newer rental van, and visit a mega-mart. It wasn't just a room, it was a whole two-story suite, one of those "extended stay" places. Three bedrooms and a bath up, one bedroom and bath, a living-room-thing, and a real kitchen down. The fridge even came stocked. With beer. And other things, but the beer was what interested John most after that little adventure in the "abandoned" missile silo with the Thulian base in it. He'd been listening to the radio on the way back to KC, and the explosion he'd helped create had made the news, which meant that John had been very eager to not make himself available in the immediate area. Someone might have noticed an athletically built fellow with some interesting bags and a beater van in that no-tell motel. *Can you say "terrorist profile"? I knew you could.* So now he was an athletically built fellow in newish clean athletic gear, athletic bags, and a name-brand rental van, with the story that he was waiting for his sports team—sport unspecified—to arrive, and they were all going to be living here in a fancy suite motel. Now someone just had to think of a sport that would have a lot of Russians on the team. He didn't think Pavel was going to go unnoticed.

John closed the door behind him, noted that Vickie had gotten a suite that was as secure as a motel could be, and let his guard down, a little. He chose the downstairs bedroom, which had a king-size bed, dropping his bags on the floor. "Nice digs. Still with me, blondie?"

"Five by five, tall, dark, and waterproof." The voice in his ear sounded relaxed, almost cheerful. *"It's easier to hack their stuff than the Roach Hotel, oddly enough. I'm on channel 99."*

"A-ffirmative." John retrieved a cold beer from the fridge—local swill, but he wasn't about to complain—and plopped down on his bed with the remote in hand. A smart-remote, so this TV was equipped to surf, which meant he could treat it like a computer of sorts. "An' we're up. Start feedin' me whatcha got."

"Tesla and Marconi got me a translation program, so all that stuff we downloaded is cooking at a rapid rate. There definitely is a big staging area somewhere there in KC. Saviour is sending you a team, hence, the suite."

"How big are we talkin' 'bout here?" He took a long draught from the beer, looking up to the TV.

"Well, this is where the trucks that deliver Thulian smash-and-run teams are coming from for this area. So big enough to load the trucks. More staff than the missile silo. Staff to repair the armor and maybe the Robo-wolves and Robo-eagles. Didn't seem to have anything for Death Machines."

John had read briefings on the mechanical horrors that the Thulians fielded, but he never had had the unpleasant opportunity to fight against them. "Nasty customers, their Robo-whatsits?"

"Pretty damn. Uh, look, I can do something called 'retro-scrying' if I have a piece of stuff that came from where I want to look. I was gonna call up the fight that the Misfits had down in the Catacombs after I lost their feed and before I got it back. I could do that now and you could watch it while I burn it to memory. Want?"

"Certainly." He retrieved a fresh beer while Vickie did whatever mumbo-jumbo she did to make this stuff happen. "Got any relevant AARs an' dossiers I could browse in a sidebar?"

"Yep, got the analysis ECHO did on the downed eagles from the Slycke caper. Use the scroll-down and page-down buttons on your remote, this hotel rig is set up for reading email." The screen split into two windows, one with text popping up and the other with some ... interesting patterns at the moment.

"You're a peach."

"I can't do a lot in the field, Johnny. I kinda gotta make it up with what I can do in here." She was muttering something too quietly for him to hear, but it didn't sound like English, so he didn't pay a lot of attention to it. *"Did I ever tell you that magic on the computer*

level is basically math and physics?" She didn't wait for him to answer. *"All that high-level physics stuff running around these days says that pretty much everything in time and space is connected, you just have to bend things around the connections and you're looking at what you want to."*

"Y'know, this all sounds like it's a helluva lot higher than my pay grade. Hey, I'm still gettin' paid in things other than beer, right?"

She chuckled. *"Right now you're getting one meeeeeeellion Polish zlotys a day."*

"By my math, I might be able to buy a few popsicles with that. If I find someone that's nearsighted."

"And you call yourself a Marxist!"

"Not in the slightest, cupcake." He leaned back, propping his head up with a pillow so he could still drink and watch the television. "Anyways, keep goin'."

"I do have something of interest for you besides your wallet and the intel. KC is a beef-packing town. There's some very nice T-bones in the meat drawer if you can cook. Aha." The patterns on the screen resolved into a static image. *"And here we go. Connection between now and then, my rig and the Catacombs established. And rolling."*

At first, there wasn't much of interest to see—except for the rank upon rank of power armor down in that enormous vault, and the Misfits wandering around among the silent giants like kids in a museum. He was getting an overhead view, which was interesting, and probably better than the original camera feed would have been. "So, why are they called the Misfits again?"

"We," she corrected. *"I'm part of the team."* She sighed. *"No one else will have us but Bulwark. He makes a habit of trying to save people. Particularly the ones no one else believes in."*

"Huh. Kind've a raggedy looking bunch. And y'all have that Djinni guy with you?" John had heard about "the" Red Djinni during his time on the run; the criminal element and people like John seemed to intermingle regularly.

"Red … has his moments."

"Don't we all—" John was cut off when the doors in the vault slammed shut. A structure smack dab in the middle of the room seemed to change, and very quickly the Misfits were fighting Robo-wolves and Robo-eagles. They got split up immediately; the three girls, Bella, Harmony, and Scope, were under attack by the birds, while one wolf chased Djinni and one chased Acrobat. "Jesus, those things are mean. Besides blowin' them to hell an' softenin' them up with fire, what weaknesses do they have?" John was already looking for joints, ammunition magazines, power cells, anything that could be exploited. It was becoming increasingly hard with the flurry of action on the screen.

There's a pretty good AI in there, and we think that the wolves had an uplink somewhere. The wolves are fangs and claws, the eagles are beak, claws, and an energy gun in their mouth that uses a different mechanism from the Thulian power armor arm-cannon. They've got IR and UV vision, night vision of course, the usual ability to camera-zoom in tight on a target. Bella found out that if you shoot that area in the eagle's mouth where the gun is, you have a good chance at making whatever they use as ammo explode the head. The eagles DON'T seem to have radar; when Scope shoots out their eyes later, they collide.

"All the sensors located in the head? Whatever do they use for a processor?"

From the wreckage, the processor is buried deep inside the body, the sensors are all in the head.

"Well, that's a pain. But, y'knock out the head, ought to be easier to pry the bastard apart."

Right about then, Bulwark, who had raised his force field, was driven to his knees with a grunt as the wolf on him pounded the outside of the field. *Yeah, that looks harsh. Bull's power isn't like a sci-fi field; energy applied outside gets some transferred inside.*

"Jesus! Any casualties on this op? I hate surprises."

Thanks to the powers that watch over fools, no. Bull was pretty messed up with a lot of internal injury, Scope nearly ruptured her eyes, and Bell was drained down to just about nothing. And Djinni looked like one of those carcasses hanging on a hook over in the stockyards. But every-

body lived. Oh, watch this, this is how Djinni takes out his wolf." Red was looking a little worse for wear—and naked—but certainly not as bad as Vickie had made him out to be. John saw how he ended up matching her description. The meta paused, measuring up the Robo-wolf, and then pounced on its neck. His hands dug into a seam that had formed where the contraption had taken a beating, and then his hands seemed to distend and harden into grotesque claws, while his body somehow grew a kind of encasement that was part insect carapace and part rhino hide. The wolf did *not* like this turn of events, and started to buck and turn to try to dislodge Djinni. It was vicious and fast, but finally a shower of sparks erupted from the seam, and the wolf slumped to the floor.

"Well, I've gotta say, I've seen some eight-second rodeo riders that would've had a helluva time stayin' on for that ride."

There was silence for a moment on the other end. Then, *"Holy Jeebus Cluny Frog on a pogo stick. I—wow. Uh, Okay, this is where I got the feed back."*

This version was one-sided, John couldn't hear what Vickie was probably saying, but as the weird protection sloughed off, leaving the Djinni raw and bruised but looking reasonably like a human again, if a skinned one, Red said something in Russian.

"Okay, rewind. I'll show you Bull and Acrobat taking out theirs." This was a little more straightforward. Acrobat teased the wolf into chasing him, returned on Bulwark's signal, and the two of them working together got the wolf impaled on the gigantic sword of one of the more primitive suits of toppled armor.

"Those damned things were carrying swords? I never really thought I'd dislike Nazis more than I already did, but I'm learnin' new things every day."

"We are pretty sure that's something like Version 1.5. They hadn't figured out how to make energy cannon yet, or maybe how to get the stuff small enough to fit in an arm. So since these things were supposed to be terror weapons, they just gave them honking big swords to mow people down like a John Deere harvester."

John shook his head and finished his beer. "If they had come out with those things a couple of decades earlier, they could've still done some nasty damage."

"Rewind to Scope taking out the two birds with a couple good shots."

This was even more straightforward. Despite being under fire, despite a lot of hysterical screaming and shouting, and with Bella finally pouring enough of herself into Scope that she went the color of skim milk and passed out, Scope managed to take out the "eyes" of both birds in mid-dive. Unable to see or correct, they crashed into each other.

"So. Dat's dat. More shit went down with a Death Sphere that was probably operating on AI, but you already know how to take those out, and I have the camera feed on that. I'm not looking forward to when they figure out what we're doing and make improvements."

"Tough customers. Remind me never to play 'Raiders of the Lost Ark' with you, though."

"Trust me, this was not my idea, nor would I have sent in one small team." The second window closed, leaving John with the report on the downed eagle from outside Atlanta. *"On one level, I am glad Tesla is gone. He made some piss poor decisions."* Her voice sounded curiously hard, even a little angry. *"I know they say not to bad-mouth the dead, but those were my teammates he put on a suicide mission down there."*

"Ain't this grand adventure we're all on just one big potential suicide mission, though? We all gotta die sometime, kiddo. An' sometimes ... we gotta let some folks die to save others." John looked away from the TV, finishing his beer in a long draught.

"And I don't have to like it, and I aim to prevent it where and when I can."

"Y'know somethin' that just struck me 'bout those damned eagles and wolves? They aren't nearly as effective as the rest of Thulian arsenal, 'cept for one task."

"Bet I can guess, but tell me."

"Terror weapons. Power armor suits, flying death orbs an' whatnot are frightenin' enough. But those robots are just goddamned scary on a primordial, primitive level." He shook his head, taking another swig of his beer. "Imagine a pack or a flight of those things bearin' down on ya."

"That was my thought when I saw them. And think of the intimidation factor in a parade, or standing bodyguard over a leader." He could hear Vickie typing over the link. A second later, in a little window, was a photoshopped image of Hitler with a wolf at either hand and an eagle above him.

Got to hand it to the Kriegers, they know 'bout presentation.

Another window opened and dossiers of CCCP members appeared in tabs across the top. *"Your team. Saviour has you on command on this one."*

"Oh? She couldn't have been too happy 'bout that one. You an' Blue blackmail 'er or somethin'?"

"Unter pointed out how no one else could pass as a Murkan. So I hear."

"Georgi must be goin' soft in his old age. I'll get caught up on all of 'em in a bit. I'd offer ya a beer, 'cept I don't think y'can work teleportation—wait, can you?"

"Yes, within reason. Only in my case there's no 'tele' about it. It's magic and not psionic, it's called 'Apporting' and I need a landing strip. In other words, I need a prepared area where I'm sending things, or they tend to end up as a smear on the floor. I can bring stuff to me safely enough; it's sending them off that's hard." She chuckled. *"But I don't need your beer, thanks. Sorry about the generic brand, it was all I could get the hotel to stock. But I found a package store that makes deliveries, so say when you want one and I'll have 'em bring up a case of Guinness and some wodka for the comrades later."*

"Much obliged." John continued to scan the files and information that Vickie was sending him, but his mind was elsewhere. *She really is a friggin' witch. If she can do all of this, just with a computer and some hand waving and chanting ... what does she know about me, without even breaking a sweat?*

"You do realize that in magic, it's TANSTAFL, right?"

"There Ain't No Such Thing as a Free Lunch?" *Girl knows her Heinlein.*

"Da tovarisch. I go through a lot of calories. I build up a bunch of magical batteries to use in an emergency."

"Kind of the same thing that happens with Blueberry with her meta-healin', right? All the energy has to come from somewhere."

"Exact-a-mundo. Very big bad stuff means I better have reserves. VERY big bad stuff means I may need backup." She sighed. *"So far, that is what makes the computer stuff work so well. Don't need a lot of energy to move electrons around. It's amazing what you can do when you know the math. Like ... okay, look at this—"*

A new window opened; it was a DoD document with about ninety percent of it blacked out. *"You can get that via Freedom of Information. Real useful, right?"* The sarcasm was thick.

"Only math I was ever really good at involved calculating bullet weight and drop, but I think I follow what you're sayin'." He scanned through the large blocks of black, only picking out some inconsequential words and bits that gave nothing away. "Yeah, right. There's a 'but' here, right?"

"You bet. Oh, this is the doc on our dear departed friend the 'Echo Janitor.' Now what I can do, since I know the math, is I can tell the image I have in my computer, 'Become what you used to look like before they blacked out all that stuff.' Watch and learn." Slowly, letters, words, resolved out of the black, as if the ink was dissolving away. *"I can do this with a real document too, but on the computer image it costs less in energy because I am moving a few electrons, not actual ink."*

"So, the image and the original hard copy are connected, then? I'm still confused by this crazy stuff."

"Laws of Similarity and Contagion. The Law of Similarity says 'If A looks like B, I can make it act like B.' Law of Contagion says 'If A was ever in contact with B, I can make either one look like the other and affect the other.' Both of those are what make voudoun dolls work."

"Christ, voodoo is real, too?"

"One of the more effective real-world magics. Djinni, Bull, and I just recruited a voudoun houngan from New Orleans."

"I don't know what that is, but anyways. With the effects of these two laws, you can get into a lot of places and see a lot of things that folks don't want others to see. Corporate espionage made easy, research files, government dossiers ..."

"Very true, o wolves. Howsomever, there are not too many people who do what I do. I only know of me, actually. Most magicians make tech go all wonky." There were more typing sounds. *"Even my folks don't do this for the FBI. Mom is a standard witch; uses standard spells, mostly nature-based, does some healing and glitches probability, what you'd call 'hexing.' Dad is a werewolf, which makes him great for passing as a guard dog."*

Werewolves, too? Hell, an' here I thought I had a decent handle on how the world was, even with Kriegers blowin' it to hell.

"There just aren't a lot of magicians around, way fewer than people with powers. But we've been around a long, long time. Anyway ..." The window with the document closed. *"That's part of what I can do."* There was a long ... a very long ... pause. *"I have mentioned a time or two that I am paranoid, right?"*

"You? Never!" John imagined Vickie wishing for a few busts of The Heroes of the War of Northern Aggression to throw at his head right then. "Paranoia is just heightened awareness of danger, t'me. I assume Blue gave you enough of a rundown on how much runnin' around I've done the past few years."

"Ah ... er ... uh ..." Another long pause. Then, in a very small voice, *"I've got more. On you."*

John's blood turned to ice in his veins, but he did his best to sound casual. "Oh? Well, all the good stuff is fabrications and all the bad rumors are true." He took a sip of his beer, hardly tasting it as he waited for her to continue.

"So, you really turned down the head cheerleader for the Senior Prom?" A note on the page of his senior yearbook opened in a new window. *"You made a good-looking Sergeant."* What looked like his entire Army file took its place.

"I still would."

"And then there was the 'little accident' they arranged for your squad in Panama."

Another redacted file replaced the Army file, and the black dissolved away from the words.

"So that was how they got you into that secret program of theirs. I dunno why they picked you out of the rest for that ... but I can prolly find out if I keep digging. There's a block on a lot of stuff." She sounded a little annoyed, maybe disconcerted. *"I'm better than their blocker, it's pretty brute force stuff, I just need to be careful and sneaky and finesse it. I can get past it if I work at it long enough, but I kinda have had a lot on my plate."*

"I would've thought you'd know already. Seems like the rest of my history is an open book to ya, kiddo."

"Well ... it could be. It took me a long time to dig out this file. That blocker again." The cursor hovered over the window she had just brought up. *"A lot of stuff isn't in computers, or is in computers it's harder for me to crack. I only just got this one before Tesla was murdered."* Another sigh. *"How angry at me are you?"*

"Not very. Can't blame ya for lookin' in on someone that you're doin' Overwatch for. Much."

"Knowledge is a shield. The more I know ... the more I can shield myself. Or you." The cursor continued to hover. *"You want to read this? You want me to stop digging, or keep going?"*

John shook his head. "Don't need to read it. I went through it, one day at a time. Keep diggin'. Never know, might find something I can use."

"That's a good part of why I'd do it, Johnny. If they get hold of you again, I want to know how to crack you out."

"So, have you told me everythin' y'know 'bout ... well, shit, me?"

"I can send a full file copy with the Commies. Or you can read it onscreen."

"Don't send it with the team."

A folder icon popped up in the corner. *"At your leisure. But once you close this connection, if you want to look at it again you'll have to ping me. That's a link, not a copy. None of the things I'm passing you are actually on the hotel net."*

John scanned the beginning of the first file. It was an operational report; the status listed it as a failure. It was dated for five years ago, and the location was Albuquerque—

Retrieval: Subject 371 Project Metamorphosis. John Murdock. Status: Failure. Subject neutralized agents and escaped....

△

New Mexico. John was lost in the desert, somewhere in New Mexico. He had no supplies, no water, and didn't know how far away from civilization he was. His clothes were tattered and burned; it was nighttime, and the temperature had plunged as soon as the sun went down. He was trained to survive in extreme situations, but between the drugs coursing through his system and the state of shock he was in, he could hardly think. *I think I might die out here. That's a laugh. Get away, and turn into buzzard food. The Invisible Man in the Sky has a helluva sense of humor for someone who doesn't exist. If I do die, at least I won't do it at the hands of those murdering bastards.* John felt the bile rise in his throat, dizzied by the sudden flare of emotion. After what seemed like hours, the sensation passed. Everything was blurring together. The chattering of his teeth, the pain in his shoeless and bleeding feet, even the cuts and burns that covered most of his exposed skin.

There was a moon, a full moon. It rose, fat and cold, over the mountains. It stared blankly down on him, as indifferent as the eyes of those "doctors" that had done such terrible things to him, to all of them.

More blurred time. The moon was higher. And he heard the sound of a motor. An engine.

The crazy impulse surged through him to bash his head out on a rock, to immolate himself, to do anything to kill himself. Suicide was a better option than being taken *back*. And they would surely want him back. He was too expensive to just let die. After what he'd done? More than ever. He was too tired to fight, and too tired to try to kill himself. Instead, he just collapsed onto his hands and knees, silhouetted by the sudden flash of a vehicle's headlights.

He expected to hear barked orders, see the glint of the moonlight or the glaring headlights off the barrels of weapons. Instead he heard a stream of profanity. Then "Buddy—are you from Alpha Centauri?" John craned his head upwards with an effort to see the driver. It was a man, late '50s to early '60s. He had a crazy beard, with hair flowing out from a straw hat all the way down to his shoulders. A Hawaiian shirt, cargo shorts, and sandals completed the picture. "Oh man ... you look like hell, what'd they do to ya? They been interrogatin' ya? Torturin' ya?"

"Somethin' like that," was all that John could manage to croak out. He lifted a hand up towards the driver.

The fellow grasped it, then took him by the elbow, and helped him to his feet. "We gotta get ya outa here. The MIBs'll be here any minute. Dontcha worry, I won't let 'em take ya back." The man half-carried John to the passenger side of the vehicle; it was an old Jeep, and despite its age was in fairly good condition with almost no rust. "You know, you're lucky I found you when I did. This desert can swallow people whole, especially this far out. Only reason why I came around this part was the big fire to the east. Big ol' jets of fire, huge columns of it shooting up into the sky like volcanoes erupting! Was that you?"

John shook his head wearily, pointing to a canteen on the dash. "I don't know what it was. I just remember guys in suits and them takin' me somewhere."

The man handed him the canteen without a moment of hesitation. "It's electrolyte solution, you prolly need it. Black suits and black shades, right? What'd they pick ya up for?"

John drank greedily from the canteen, gasping for breath long enough to say, "My good looks."

The man cackled, and shoved the 4-by in gear. He turned off

his headlights. "You musta seen somethin'. UFO?" He pronounced it "you-foe." "Landing? Close encounter? Third kind? Lizard men? Or the Grays? You gotta watch them Grays, man, the lizard men'll only dissect ya, the Grays ... they got ... probes."

"I don't know the why, pal. Just that I don't wanna go back." John did his best to keep his seat as the Jeep rolled over the bumps and rocks. "What's your name?"

"We don't use names, man. Safer. Ya can call me Sandman."

"Right. I owe ya, 'Sandman.' I was as good as dead out here."

"You ain't lyin'. MIBs count on the desert t'kill anything that tries to get close or get away. Ya gotta have good survival trainin' t'be out here."

"In my condition, I don't think there's much that trainin' could have done." He shook his head, then changed the subject. "Where are we headed? Anywhere but here is good enough for right now, but I'm the curious sort." His wits were starting to come back to him now that he had hydrated and was at least momentarily safe.

"Ya done with that canteen? There's 'nother under your seat, an' a baggie fulla meal bars. We're headin' fer Albuquerque, but I'm gonna drop ya at the edge. Well, first we're gonna make a stop where the Black Helicopters can't spot us, I'm gonna get the kit, and you're gonna patch yerself up and take a spare shirt an' pair of pants. An' shoes. Then I'm gonna loan ya one-a my spare bikes an' ya can pedal yer way into town."

"You're a saint, Sandman. I don't know how I can repay ya. In fact, you helpin' me might've been the start of some trouble for ya. The worst kind."

Sandman cackled again. "Put yer hand on the outside of the Jeep door."

John did. The surface felt ... odd.

"Stealth paint. I don't show up on radar, man. 'Struth. Mighty Wing's gotta Corvette he stealthed with the stuff, he makes runs at a hunnert-ten an' the cops never tag him. An' I ain't gonna say nothin' about this on the net, man. Two peeps can share a secret, three, and it ain't a secret no more. Right?" Sandman cast him a sly look. "Yer my secret. I helped one-a the MIB's prisoners! I bin hopin' fer somethin' like this fer twenty years!" His grin showed white in the moonlight.

For the first time in what felt like years, John smiled, and then slept.

△

It felt like John slept for years; entirely too long, and not long enough at the same time. The only thing he saw was fire and blood in his dreams; he woke up to Sandman shaking him awake.

"Okay, brother. I took the route 'round Robin Hood's barn, just, ya know, to be sure. We were south of ABQ in case ya didn't know. I went west and north and around and we're on the south side of forty right now, on Central." He cackled a little. "They call this the 'war zone.' You can prolly tell."

Tattoo parlor, Vietnamese restaurant, pawn shop, beauty parlor, all in the same tiny strip mall, all burglar-grilled except for the tattoo parlor, which was open. Gas Station with bars on the cash box. Burger joint, taco joint, Mexican grocery, all closed at this late an hour, all with cages.

"I can drop you about anywhere along here with the bike, you can bike straight up Central to the Uni, and get public transport there."

"This is pretty close to where I need to be. I still can't tell ya how much I owe ya, Sandman. You're doin' me a solid." John looked at the bike in the backseat. "Don't think I'll have a chance to get your bike back to ya, unfortunately."

"I get 'em cheap at cop auctions. There's always another twenty-buck bike out there." Sandman shrugged.

"Let's pull off into an alley. Better if I get out that way than out here in the open."

Sandman took a right at the next corner and pulled into—

well it wasn't an alley, it appeared that Albuquerque didn't exactly have alleys, but it was behind another strip mall where dumpsters were lined up, smelling of things best forgotten.

"Here's as good as it gets, brother," Sandman said, a little wistfully. "I kinda wish you could tell me more, but hey, probable deniability, right?"

"Safer this way, compadre." John hefted the bicycle out of the back of the vehicle, then held out his hand to Sandman. "Time for me to go."

Sandman shook it heartily. He had a good handshake. "Safe journeys, brother."

"I like that. Safe journeys to you, Sandman." John grinned lopsidedly. He wished that he could do more to show his appreciation, but time was against them both.

Sandman reached into his back pocket and stuffed something into the breast pocket of the vest John was wearing. "Stopped on the way, you were out and didn't wake up. Figure you can use this."

Without waiting for an answer, he waved, gunned the engine, and drove off. John reached into his pocket, and was surprised to find a wad of hundreds in his hand. There was a small bit of metal sandwiched in the cash, about as big as a large button. It was a scorched and tarnished badge in the shape of a star, red with a golden hammer and sickle in the middle. *Now what in the hell would he give me this for?*

It didn't take long for John to pedal to where he'd rented a long-term storage shed. Inside was everything that he'd need to get clear of the trouble that he was in. Forged documents, extra cash, disguises, some basic necessities, and an unregistered pistol. He'd paid for the rental for several years in advance, in cash, up-front, with a few extra bills slipped to the manager to make sure that things weren't disturbed. In this part of town, that wasn't that unusual. After doing what John had done the past few years, he'd learned that being prepared was a reward in and of itself. Readying everything into a single backpack, John closed and locked the shed for a final time. *Time for the hard part; getting away.*

$$\triangle$$

The thing about a university is that an abandoned bicycle will get snatched up before the seat has a chance to get cold—and the public transportation will generally take you to the train station if there is one, and the bus depot. Since universities are full of students who know nothing about an area, the public transportation stops are generally plastered with route maps. John sat in the back of the bus, and tried to look as relaxed as possible. He was still partially dehydrated, burnt, and cut worse than a piece of roadkill, and coming off of a laundry list of drugs that the doctors had pumped into him. He was a bundle of nerves, but did his best to appear disinterested in everything. There were maybe eight people on this thing, and most of them looked almost as beat-up as he did. The only two who didn't were a couple of teenagers more concerned with eating each other's faces than anything around them. Despite everything, John almost allowed himself to feel good again. Just being around people, normal people, after what he'd been through ...

He shook himself out of it. The bus was approaching the train station's stop. No one else was getting off at the stop with him. He shrugged on his backpack and pulled his cap lower over his eyes. Taking a deep breath, he made his way off the bus and into the main building. The building had a vaguely Pueblo vibe, like many public buildings in this part of the country. The inside was institutionally clean, but still had the rundown feeling of a place that no one wanted to spend too much time in. John located the ticket counter and paid for the earliest train that would take him to Kansas. It was scheduled to leave in about two hours. He'd worked out his "grand escape" on the bus ride over. He'd get into Kansas on the train. From there, he'd either hitchhike into Oklahoma, or just stow away on a semi going in the right direction. Same would go for Texas after Oklahoma. From there, John would cross the border into Mexico, and do his best to disappear in South America after that. If anyone was looking for him, they'd figure he'd take the direct route, bus straight down to Las Cruces and from there to Juarez. Juarez really *was* a war zone, and it would be easy for him to get lost there, so ... if there was pursuit, his picture would be all over the border guard post by then. The more twists and turns he could put between himself and any pursuit, the better.

After purchasing his ticket, John found a dark corner seat in the waiting room. All the seats next to it were either broken or covered in vomit; luckily, the original owner of the vomit had probably already been shuffled off. John kept his head low, but made sure that he kept his eyes on everyone. It wasn't very hard; this early in the morning, there were few people occupying the terminal. Just some custodial staff and a couple of fellow transients. John wanted nothing more than to sleep again, but he was still too keyed up. One thing he did need, though, was water. Lots of it. He spent his time waiting by getting water from a machine, and then filling the empty bottle at a nearby water fountain. No telling when he'd get a chance to rehydrate again.

That's where everything went to hell.

"Hey, buddy."

John turned, slowly. There was a transit cop standing behind him. "Look, buddy, I've been watching you for a while. You've probably drunk close to a half a gallon of water." The cop actually looked concerned. "That's not good, you know?"

"Honestly, I'm fine, officer. If it's all right with you, I'm just gonna sit and rest for a while until my train comes in." John made a show of holding his ticket up, slowly; transit cops at terminals spent a lot of time clearing out drunks and the homeless that would take up space trying to sleep under a roof.

But the cop was shaking his head. "Look, you obviously aren't from around here. You're probably sick and don't know it. Heat exhaustion ... swine flu ... diabetes ... all those things will make you drink like that and the last thing I need is to have to clear you out when you have a seizure or pass out or start vomiting like the Exorcist. Look, come with me to the aid station and we can get you checked out. There's plenty of time before the train. If you're okay, no blood, no foul, and if you're not, we find out before you become a problem."

John was stuck. If he argued with the cop and made an issue of it, the cop would *force* the issue. If he ran, he would need to find a new way to get clear of New Mexico. And he certainly was *not* at the point where he'd kill a cop in cold blood just to save his own hide. "Alright, officer, if ya say so."

The cop kept up a running monologue about some college kids who'd gotten heat stroke and put the whole station into an uproar. John really wasn't listening. He was trying to keep track of where possible exits were. His eyes were darting to cameras, exits, obstacles, anything that could be used as a distraction or a weapon.

"Alrighty, here we are. I'm just going to finish a quick check at the front desk, and then we'll get you sorted out. Just sit tight in here for a few minutes." The cop smiled, showing John to a seat in front of his desk. John sat quietly, running over his options mentally, looking for a different one. He could still slip out, quiet-like, if he did it now ...

Four of them came into the room at once, from both doors. They slowly walked in, locking the doors behind them. Four men in identical black suits and sunglasses, all of them in their mid-thirties. Walking clichés. *Sandman would die to see these guys.* John immediately tensed, but stayed seated. The men were all very casual in approaching him, self-assured. *Goddamnit! How the hell did they find me so quickly?* John was the first to speak. "So."

"So, John. You left quite a mess, you know. Some very important people spent a lot of time and money on you and the others, and now most of that has gone up in flames. Literally!" It was the shortest of the four men that spoke, a redhead with a severe jaw. He chuckled to himself. "You're going to come back with us. You suddenly became much more valuable, with the destruction of the Facility. More than valuable enough to overlook everything that happened back there. And, as they say, 'The Program must go on.'"

"I don't want any part of it. Not anymore. I'm *done*, goddamnit." John stood out of his chair, backing up to the wall. Three of the "suits" thrust a hand into their jackets, obviously going for pistols. The redhead was the only one that didn't, instead motioning for the others to hold off. "It don't matter what you offer me, it ain't enough, and it ain't ever gonna be enough."

"John, you're talking like you have some choice in this matter. You most assuredly don't. Despite your recent ... changes, you can't kill all of us before we kill you." He walked over in front of John until his face was mere inches in front of John's. "I've read your dossier. You're good, or you were. Losing it over a skirt? You've lost the plot. Besides, even if you were still good ... I don't think you have it in you to kill us." That same self-assured smirk.

John leaned forward the barest few centimeters, his face betraying no emotion. "I just escaped from the Facility. To do that, I had to kill several hundred people. While tied to a table, waiting to be executed. And right now I don't have a goddamn thing to lose but my life, which you're gonna have one way or another. Do you really think I don't have what it takes to end you?" The redhead's expression broke, and John saw the man's eyes go wide as he fully appreciated the situation. There was still a chance ... still a chance that these goons would back down.

But then he saw the redhead reach for his pistol and all bets were off. John immediately clamped his hand around the bulge in the redhead's jacket. John squeezed—hard—and the weapon fired. The round passed through the suit jacket and hit one of the government goons, wounding him. John had been unconsciously breathing quickly as soon as the suits came into the office. He felt as if his body was a tuning fork that had just been

struck the right way. Putting all of his might into it, John shoved
the redhead away from him. Somehow he flung the man far too
quickly into one of the suits behind him. They both violently
crumpled into a heap as they crashed into and dented a large
metal filing cabinet, sending papers flying. John and the others
were momentarily stunned, and John could practically hear his
whole body humming. It was the closest he'd ever had to being
high on something like coke or meth—like being drunk, but
with everything operating with full clarity and at high speed.
Amped up. *Jesus ... these 'enhancements' are more than the docs ever
promised.*

The other two suits reacted before John had snapped out of
his daze. One ran towards him with a blackjack raised. It looked
like he was moving a little slower than he should have been. John
quickly raised his left arm to block the overhand strike, but his
timing was off; he moved too fast and was out of position when
the blow landed. John was staggered backwards, and his oppo-
nent pressed his advantage, raining blows on John's head and
shoulders. Every counter John tried, he overextended himself,
punching or kicking too hard, blocking too fast and early. John's
left eye had closed up, and he could feel blood flowing freely
from his scalp. He was backed up against the wall, and the suit
that had been shot had joined in trying to subdue him. John
roared and grabbed the blackjack-wielder in a tackle suddenly
and carried him into the opposite wall. Somewhere in the back
of his mind, he noticed that the cinder block wall of the office
cracked and deformed when they impacted. John started
pounding the man's midsection, still shouting. He immediately
stopped both after looking up to see the man's vacant eyes; the
back of his head was—flat. And blood was splattered all over the
wall around it. John gasped, stepping back and away from the
body; it slid messily to the floor.

The injured suit behind him got his attention, shocking him
back to the present out of his self-horror. "Bastard!" He raised a
pistol at John, leveling it with his chest. Moving faster than he

knew he could, John was upon the suit almost instantly. He spun the man around, and then twisted his pistol arm behind his back, jamming the gun into his spine. There were popping and snapping sounds as sinew and bone gave way to John's brute strength. The man started—well it wasn't screaming, exactly, it was more like a high-pitched whine through clenched teeth. *I've already killed one. First one's expensive, the rest are cheap. Screw it.* John forced the man to fire the pistol repeatedly, emptying the magazine. Since the muzzle was pressed deeply into the man's back, the shots were muffled.

The redhead made the mistake of getting up, instead of playing dead. The suit he had landed on didn't need to play; he was most certainly dead, neck broken by the impact. "You ... fucking ... asshole!" Redhead was cradling a broken left arm, his pistol still in his right hand. "We gave you a way back in! You could've been made! Helped us stay on top ... but you threw it away! Any one of us would've killed to have the opportunity you had, to be what you've become!" He then swung the pistol towards John. Still moving with blinding speed, John drew his 1911 from his waistband, lined the front sight up with the redhead's chest, and fired four times in rapid succession. The man crumpled, whimpering, without ever getting a shot off. John slowly walked over to the man, picking up and shouldering his backpack.

"You wanted to be like me? Wish granted, shithead. Now we're both dead men." John fired the pistol a final time at the man's face, finishing him. He reholstered the pistol in his waistband, moving the jacket to cover the exposed grip.

Is this what it's going to be like? Is this what I have to do? Is this what I might become?

No time for that shit now.

John heard and *felt* the suit with the broken neck get up. Slowly, he turned around. The man's neck was still at an odd angle. That is, until he used his hands and snapped it back into place with a sickening pop. "What? You thought they'd only send chumps to bring one of *us* back?" The man didn't wait for a reply; he simply charged, wordlessly and without expression, moving just as fast as John could. John caught him just in time, locking his hands onto the man's shoulders. They were equally matched for strength and speed. John brought his knee up between them, and then flexed his leg as hard as he could. The man was kicked out less than a foot—damn he was strong!—but it was enough to break the grip that they had on each other.

Time slowed down for John again. *He's like me. That's what they want from me. Some sort of obedient, Frankensteinian bastard.* Everything that John had been through in the last two days blurred through his mind in a tumble of jumbled images, all out of sequence. The training, the fighting, the running, the drugs, his escape ... *her* ... All the rage came swimming back to the surface, surging through him, overwhelming him. He didn't notice the fire forming in his hands, crawling up his arms and shoulders. He was still too amped up from his enhancements, from all of the fighting. He saw the man through a red haze, someone not unlike him. That only made him hate the suit even more, their similarities. John screamed once, and reached for the man. He knew he wanted him dead, but didn't know how he was going to make it happen. The wanting was all it took, though. A giant stream of fire erupted from John's hand; it engulfed the man, fanning over him and splaying against the wall behind him. Before John could even think to stop, the entire room was on fire. The man was a charred cinder on the ground, still twitching. The enhancements ... they seemed to make it harder for John to control himself when he was amped up.

The scene around him resembled the Facility far too much for his liking ... *I need to get out of here.* Less than two minutes had passed since the men had walked into the room. It felt like a life-time. John opened the door that he had first entered to get into the office ... and came face to face with the transit cop. John was faster on the draw, however; more practice, and more opportunity to put that practice to use. He had a bead on the cop's center of mass before the cop had even cleared his holster. Behind him the office was on fire, flames licking across the ceiling tiles.

John slowly raised his aim from the cop's chest to his forehead. "Just let me go. This isn't a great day for either of us, right?"

They both had to choose. John desperately did not want to shoot. This wasn't some Program goon, this was just a regular joe, an honest cop. The guy wasn't in on the score. Hell, he had wanted to *help* him. But, right now, he was an obstacle. The cop had to choose, between a dangerous man and the fire behind him. He couldn't deal with both. And if he chose wrong, he might end up dead and able to deal with neither.

The fire alarms went off, and so did the sprinkler system, which didn't seem to be doing anything to the fire in the office. "So? What's your call? You're decent. You tried to help an asshole like me, and that's a lot more than most would've thought 'bout doing. I'm just tryin' to get clear." You could still see that there were bodies in the office, even through the flames. The cop's eyes widened, shocked. Had he known the goons were in there? John had the feeling that he hadn't. "Trust me," he added impulsively, "This was way, way past yer pay grade."

There was another of those moments, where time got slower, or John got faster, and he could practically see thoughts flashing behind the cop's eyes. Then the man reached out with an empty, open hand; John kept from reacting. The cop grabbed his shoulder and pulled him into the corridor, then shoved him towards the exit. "Get! And grab anybody you run into and get them out too!"

John nodded. There wasn't anything that he could say. He'd had two decent people go above and beyond to help him in less than a day. There just weren't words for something like that. So, without another word, John disappeared into the station, and out, pulling a couple random strangers who were reacting to the alarm with bewilderment out with him. Looked like he'd have to find another way out of town.

△

"Yo! Daydreamer!" Vickie's voice in his ear kicked him out of memory. *"I've got incoming CCCP in less than an hour. Uh ... one of 'em's the Bear. I have a food delivery service showing at your door in fifteen."*

John shook his head to clear it. "Christ. I'm not sure that there's enough vodka in this dry little town. Not to mention Chef-Oh-Boy." He thought for a moment. "If you can get some diesel and noodles with ketchup delivered, I think it'll suffice; not sure Ol' Pavel could tell the difference twixt any of 'em."

Vickie chuckled. *"Hell if I know ... but you're the one that's gonna have to stow the case of cans."*

John sobered. "Hey, Vic?"

"Roger?"

"You know everything in that file. An' I suppose any other files you've dug up on me. Are we still cool? This Overwatch only works if we're both in on it, after all."

Vickie's voice softened. *"Cool as a cucumber, bonehead. It's not just what's in your file. It's what you are."*

"... and what am I?" John's voice had the barest hint of pain in it, longing to be understood. Save for Sera, no one knew him the way Vick did.

"A helluva man, and my friend. The guy I trust at my back. More, the guy I trust at Bell's. Now get ready for incoming food and Commies, in that order."

"Roger, dodger. And ... thanks, Vic."

He heard unaccustomed warmth in her voice. *"De nada, big guy."* There was a buzz of a doorbell at the door of the unit. *"Huh. Early. Twenty buck tip. Don't be a cheapskate."*

"Oh, don't worry. This is comin' outta the 'operational

budget.' Just another thing for Nat to yell at me for. I'm pretty sure she has a list, by now."

Vickie laughed in his ear all the way to the door.

Meanwhile, there were more iterations of the Program than just the one that John Murdock was in—or the ones that Sera and John rescued Zach Marlowe from. The rot ran deep.

FURTHER ON UP THE ROAD

VERONICA GIGUERE

The thick concrete walls, painted over with gray to hide the scorch marks and occasional blood smears, could take a beating almost as well as Nova could. Half a meter thick and reinforced with metal, they extended half a kilometer from the central column that housed Epsilon Base. At the end nearest to the door, an ionic cannon hung from a ceiling mount, smoke curling from the short barrel after its most recent volley. The ring of blue-white light had faded, and only the tang of ozone remained.

At the far end of the tunnel, the girl they called Nova stood barefoot in the center of a red and white target someone had painted on the composite floor. The fresh coat hid most of the fatal mistakes suffered by others who had stared down the same hallway. Her close-cropped hair, fine ebony curls only a few shades darker than her skin, sizzled and smoked from the burst that came from the ionic cannon. Patches of her nanoweave bodysuit had melted, pulling too tight and making breathing difficult. In some places, the fabric had lost all integrity, exposing evidence of past burns and the shiny smooth scars they'd left behind.

Nova tasted blood on her dry, cracked lips. At least she could still stand. The blast had lasted for nine seconds, two seconds longer than the last time they had put her in the firing range. She had tasted blood that time, too.

"Reciprocation in ten seconds." The voice from the speakers embedded in the ceiling barked the order, ready to begin the countdown at the three-second mark. "Target at two o'clock, three hundred meters. Blue cross."

The eleven-year-old girl pivoted to her right and squared her shoulders. Her entire body brimmed with potential energy, the persistent hum and crackle along each synapse setting her nerves on fire. Pain numbed the underlying terror, forcing her to focus on the metal plate that dropped from the ceiling.

The voice called out the countdown in short, loud bursts. "Three."

Her teeth began to itch, beginning with her bottom molars and deepening into her jawbone.

"Two."

Her vision blurred, facial and ocular muscles struggling to mask the agony that coursed through her body. The skin beneath her fingernails burned, and blood thudded in her ears. She could feel the white-hot needles jabbing into the soles of her feet, but she remained motionless on the painted target.

"One."

Maybe if I held it in, I could make it all go away.

"FIRE!"

Two years of intensive training and psychological programming reduced the inner voice to a frightened whisper, and the girl they called Nova saw the blue cross with startling clarity. The searing pain, thousands of tiny knives stabbing beneath her skin, all stabbed at once, and she thought that the energy would slip away from her control. In the next instant, it rushed from extremities to core, bubbling and boiling in her chest. She swung both arms forward, palms facing the target, skin enveloped in a gauzy haze that hummed like a power station. Index fingers flexed and her thumbs came together, and a tiny sphere of light and heat blossomed between her sweaty hands. Whorls of plasma swirled within the rapidly expanding edges.

For the briefest of heartbeats, Nova wondered what would happen if she could catch the fire between her fingers and pull it back in, let it consume her. In the next heartbeat, the energy erupted from her hands, surging towards the target in an amalgam of fire and electricity. The metal plate puddled to slag at the far end of the tunnel.

Nova fought to stay on her feet in the center of the red and white target, klaxons blaring in the concrete tunnel. Protocol mandated that subjects remain in place before the handlers gave her permission to approach the exit. Otherwise, they would fire the ionic cannon again, and she would become a puddle, just like the blue cross she had hit moments ago.

"Live-fire exercise concluded," the bodiless voice called over the fading whine of alarms. "You are cleared to leave the perimeter."

Her arms fell to her sides, her thoughts nothing but numbing stasis. Again, training and conditioning forced her feet to move forward, even as her entire body trembled in the wake of the violent discharge. Nova walked past small lumps of metal that littered the floor from previous training sessions, the newest addition still smoking as she passed it. A thick yellow line on the floor separated her from the only exit. She stopped, her bare and blistering toes on the edge of the paint.

The tiny voice whispered in the space behind her eyes. *This is a coffin. A big concrete coffin. Someday, they might not let you leave.*

A heavy metal door beyond the yellow line slid open. Nova snapped to attention when a grizzled man in gray and black fatigues entered, flanked by two guards in full combat gear. One of the guards held a long pole with a fat nylon rope at one end, while the other carried twin insulated tanks in a backpack harness, the connected hose and sprayer held between thick insulated gloves. Nova knew from a singular experience during her first weeks at Epsilon Base that the subzero concoction in the tanks would bring her to a sudden, painful, and icy stop if the guards suspected her to be a threat to the general.

She willed her breathing to slow, even as her skin on her fore-arms and hands began to blister and crack in the aftermath of the release. Complete compliance would get her out of the tunnel. Anything less would earn a reprimand, or worse.

General Mixon stopped just behind the yellow line. Nova maintained the appropriate expression of obedience and submission expected of all Program subjects. She forced her right arm up in the appropriate salute, even as the remnants of nanoweave chafed against the ravaged skin on her shoulders and chest. Pain did not preclude subjects from showing proper respect to senior officers, especially the general.

He nodded, a curt gesture of approval. "Good showing. Do you have any injuries that would require medical attention?"

"Thank you, sir. No, sir, I have no injuries to report." Eyes forward, words crisp, and salute steady, the lie flowed like air from her lips. At this stage, subjects who reported injuries for medical assistance beyond what they could treat themselves in the barracks suffered additional consequences disguised as treat- ment. Nova had treated plenty of burns and contusions with her basic kit stowed beneath her bunk, even without having the regenerative abilities of her fellow trainees. Today would be no different, and she would return tomorrow for fresh wounds to bandage alongside today's injuries.

The general showed no sign of disapproval at her words. One meaty hand as large as her face motioned for the two guards to exit. "Very well. Gentlemen, have the team reset and prepare for the next trainee. Nova has concluded her exercise for the day."

The men on either side of the general saluted and exited the room. General Mixon remained, the ionic cannon looming over his right shoulder. She held herself in the stiff, formal salute, fighting the full body tremor that threatened to shake every inch of her body. Whether it stemmed from fear or exhaustion, she couldn't tell, but Nova could not afford to appear weak now.

"At ease." The general nodded and began a slow circle around her, shrewd eyes taking in every detail of her scorched uniform and blistering skin. When she stood tall, her head came a full eight inches below his shoulder. His solid build marked him as one who had not set his own fitness aside in his command of the facility, its operatives, or its subjects. Muscular forearms and powerful hands had exacted more than one punishment on a recalcitrant trainee as an example to others who might consider disobedience to be an option.

In her first week, she and nineteen other subjects had watched the general take down an operative with nothing but raw strength. Only a black body bag had been necessary to remove the enormous beast of a man afterward. The general had stood in front of twenty children, wiping his bloody hands on a white towel as if nothing had happened, the barest hint of a smile on his lips.

No matter how often Nova thought of ways to end her time in the Program, she never considered putting her body in the general's hands.

Once he completed his circuit and faced her, his stern expression relaxed into something friendly, bordering on paternal. The warmth only increased her discomfort. "You've made remarkable progress, Nova. Your skills are a testament to your resilience and tenacity."

Failure is not acceptable. Failure means death. "Yes, sir. Thank you, sir."

The man gestured to the metal door, motioning for Nova to walk ahead of him. She moved quickly, the chill of the floor stabbing up through the soles of her bare feet. Nova willed herself to maintain the efficient stride drilled in her during the first weeks of training. Eyes forward, arms at her sides, breathing slow and even, even as her thoughts raced through a myriad of questions and scenarios. Had she failed part of the training today? Did the general find her performance substandard compared to her previous sessions? Had she done something to warrant a reprimand that only the general could give?

"Your unique abilities and dedication to your training have impressed everyone, including me. I've watched you meet and succeed at every exercise this week, and it's clear that you have the potential to do even more. There isn't anyone else here at Epsilon Base with your skills, and that makes you special." He moved up to walk next to her, taking slow steps to account for her much shorter legs and spent muscles. Nova tried to remember if she had ever seen him with other subjects, but she could only recall him watching from a distance through thick observation windows or on a balcony overlooking a combat arena. Guards and high-ranking trainers had always surrounded him, barking orders while he nodded in stern silence. Now, they walked together, alone in the corridor, and he knew her by name and ability.

"Thank you, sir." Nova didn't know what else to say, but she couldn't stay silent. Eyes forward, she stayed at his elbow as he walked down the long gray hallway. It ended in a solid gray wall, the options available to go left or right. With the general at her side, she dared not assume one path over another. She slowed, knowing that the rush of adrenaline through her veins had blocked the post-training pain for only a short time. Terror could stave off the rest for a little longer.

"This way." The general indicated the path to the left, and the acrid odor of disinfectant met her nose. Memories of post-training medical treatments flashed in her mind, part necessity and part cruelty for those who couldn't heal themselves or struggle through their injuries with basic medkits in the training barracks. The meager contents of her stomach began to curdle and her pulse doubled. Nova felt certain that anyone in the hall could hear the staccato beat of the blood in her ears. Her feet continued to move in spite of her fear, staying in step with the general past closed doors and silent rooms.

"Your performance today has ended the first stage of your training, and you've earned my personal attention. In my time here, few others have impressed me the way that you have." A note of a smile crept into his voice, dangerous comfort that she refused to accept in this unfamiliar space. "In fact, you are going to become part of my personal security retinue."

Nova understood personal security, but the last word escaped her vocabulary. A flicker of confusion must have passed over her young face, because the general chuckled and patted her abused shoulder with one meaty hand. "You are special, and I've chosen you as someone to become even more special. Not a subject, but an operative. A soldier in an elite group, under my personal command."

At the end of the corridor, a pair of reinforced doors slid open to reveal a massive operating theater, shiny metal surfaces and dozens of people in pale green surgical scrubs. They all turned as one to salute the general, who continued to push her forward through the doors and into the room. The soles of her feet burned against the icy sterile floor, and she could feel the tremors beginning in her belly and spreading out into her chest and legs. Two of the green-suited figures moved to take her, and she saw the man with the tanks in the backpack harness standing ready just inside the door.

Bile rose in her throat and her knees gave way as soon as the men in surgical scrubs took her by her arms. Her training regimen had bled out all of the fight from her, and Nova hung limp as a third figure found a compliant vein and inserted a needle attached to a long tube. Her mind fell further and further from her body as something hot and sweet burned up her arm and spread over her chest. Pain dissolved, leaving only terror, and the general's smile filled her vision before everything went black.

Only then did the pain return.

△

In spite of the general's promise to make her part of his personal security team, Nova did not lay eyes upon the man for more than five years after their last meeting in front of the ionic cannon. Much of those years passed in a pharmacological haze, her body held in a strange kind of stasis while the doctors and researchers put it through the process of augmentation and enhancement. When they didn't have her on an operating table or in one of the recovery pods, the trainers put her through an excruciating regimen in any one of the "danger rooms" that they used for live-fire exercises. The cycle repeated, the only constant being that Nova grew tall and lean as the years passed.

And angry. More than anything, Nova grew angry with each passing day.

Scars ran the length of her arms and legs, taut muscle doing more to highlight them than hide them. Nova caught her reflec-

tion in one of the shiny metal doors a few days after a particularly intense day of training, and it took her a full minute to
realize that she was the young woman staring back. Shaved head,
clenched fists, broad stance, it was enough to make her jump
back in fear.

Is that what they're trying to do? Make me like him?

As training progressed, the treatments became fewer and far
between. Never having enough energy to fight the efforts of the
doctors and researchers in the infirmary—they always took her
after the last round in the danger room, after the last burst of
energy had left her body and she could barely stand on her own
—Nova had developed a reputation of being compliant.
Whether this caused her to experience less pain than others
during the treatments, she didn't know.

She didn't speak to anyone at Epsilon Base, not unless they
spoke to her. Since that first and last meeting with the general,
they had kept her separate from the other subjects. The private
cell and toilet, the carefully cultivated shelves of books, even the
food that they brought rather than have her join others for
meals, all of those amenities served as control under the guise of
favoritism. Rather than ask why, Nova consigned herself to
watching and listening, taking in every detail in case it might be
useful later.

For what, she didn't know. She had forgotten so much since
her arrival at the facility; her mother's face, her favorite food,
even her real name had turned into a blur of syllables hidden
somewhere in her memories. Since realizing the amount of time
she had lost to the augmentation procedures and recovery, Nova
had promised herself that she would remember as much as she
could about Epsilon Base, the general, and the Program.

In the recent weeks, her danger room exercises had consisted
solely of bouts with the ionic cannon, powerful bursts at longer
intervals. The augmentations and enhancements didn't stop all
of the burns and blisters, but they kept her injuries to a mini-
mum. If they cut her, she would certainly bleed, but few of any

kind of blade got close enough to try. Every training session worked her to near-exhaustion, followed by debriefings and a cursory medical examination to address any abnormalities. Experimentation had ended; sooner or later, they would end the danger room exercises and take her out in the field.

Today, she finished her bout with the ionic cannon and reported to the infirmary for the perfunctory examination. As one of the nurses applied a healthy layer of salve to the worst of the burns, the doors opened and a team of operatives rushed in. One hurried to Nova and nodded at her injury. "You can walk?"

The question struck Nova as odd, considering that the burn was on her forearm and the fabric covering her legs had no scorch marks or tears. The ionic cannon was predictable, and she could contain the energy alongside the tiny fragments that her own body naturally harbored. To prove a point, she slid off the exam table and stood before answering. "Yes, I can walk."

"You'll need to run." The familiar rumble of the general's voice came from the back of the group. As the cluster of operatives parted, Nova could see the gray-green fatigues and the gruff expression. One of the massive hands held a thick metal rod, the end capped by a fat rubber disk. She snapped to a salute, the gesture earning her the faintest of smiles.

"With me, Nova." The group arranged itself to allow her a place at the general's right arm. The operative who had addressed her shared a few terse whispers with the nurse, whose eyes widened and head bobbed in rapid, terrified understanding. Nova's gaze swept over the six other operatives standing around her. Their expressions, calculated dispassion and efficiency that almost mimicked boredom, had hints of fear and uncertainty around their eyes and the corners of their mouths.

To her surprise, the general shared that same bit of trepidation and uncertainty. Nova said nothing as the group left, her energy and focus on the man to her left and the rapidly changing environment. They jogged down unfamiliar hallways and up stairs hidden behind panels that masqueraded as solid walls. Two operatives always preceded her and the general, giving them a silent 'all-clear' before they climbed another set of concrete stairs or hurried down a sterile corridor. As they climbed, Nova could feel the floors and walls vibrate, and a series of emergency lights flashed a silent warning along their path.

In the last stairwell, Nova felt one of the general's meaty hands rest heavy on her shoulder, and for a moment, she froze in place. Memories of the one unlucky operative and the single body bag flooded back into her mind, and she wondered if she had failed to meet the general's standards during this new simulation.

Then, she heard a raspy breath and wheezing, and the round rubber disk of the general's cane came down on the step in front of him. She shifted her weight and pushed herself up, supporting the older man's weight as they climbed the remaining steps. Nova kept the edge of the cane in her peripheral vision, doing her best to quell the too-familiar voice behind her eyes that screamed in the eerie silence.

You can run. You owe them nothing. You are more than he is, and you can run. Run!

The little voice screamed at her, but it knew nothing of what the other men could do. Until she stood alone with the general, she wouldn't dare run. The heavy hand on her shoulder steadied her, forced her to focus on the immediate situation. Her ears tuned to the scrape of metal against metal, her body feeling the thrum of tremors that shook the earth around them. Ahead of her, a sliver of light illuminated the landing and the two operatives preceding the general. They slipped out, and Nova held her breath, waiting for the door to open again.

The stairwell shook and chunks of concrete rained down around them. Behind her, Nova heard a grunt and a crash, followed by the groan of metal straining against its supports. She reached for the railing as the general's hand pressed down on her ravaged shoulder. They could not go back down the crumbling stairs, but she had no idea what lay beyond the door. Something so massive that it made the very earth quake, but what else?

"Go," the general wheezed, forcing her forward and up the remaining stairs. She put out her hands, feeling the rough metal surface of the door. Nova leaned into it, something at the base keeping it from opening freely. She pressed and the door gave way, tracing an arc in the blood of a fallen operative. A pair of boots attached to bloody fatigues confirmed the kill. Nova held up a hand before stepping into the hallway. Her nose twitched, and her body stiffened as an all-too-familiar odor met her nose.

You knew it would be a coffin. This is what death smells like.

Scorched concrete. The tang of ozone. A mixture of burning hair and flesh, coupled with the stench of melted plastic. Nova flexed her fingers against the warm metal of the door, even as an inappropriate sensation of glee began to tickle the back of her mind.

Not your death. Their death. His death.

The whine of an unfamiliar weapon met her ears, and Nova glanced through the sliver of space between the door and the frame, halfway between the metal hinges. The soldiers that carried the energy cannons stood even taller than the general, and their armor gleamed in the flicker of the emergency lights. She counted three, but another deep thrum within the walls reminded her that there could be more beyond this corridor.

The general pushed her shoulder. "How many are there?" He failed to keep the tremor from his voice or his outstretched hand. It fluttered against her neck like a frightened bird. The motion threatened to set off a fit of laughter, but she put one fist to her mouth and held up three fingers on her other hand.

"You have to lead, Nova. You must go first, to preserve everything that we have here." He turned to keep as much of his bulk behind her as possible, more of his weight on the cane rather than her shoulder. She felt the push forward and the rush of adrenaline forced her from hiding, and she stood face to face with this new enemy. Polished metal helmets hid faces, but Nova fixated on the burning center of the shoulder-mounted cannon.

The leader stared down at her, head and shoulders looming above her. Nova tensed, enhancements keyed up, senses heightened. Anticipation tickled the length of her arms and legs, and she smiled with a strange relief. It could end here, for her and the general and the rest of them, and she hadn't done anything but survive for this long. The nervous laughter burst through her lips as a strangled sob, and she felt herself smile in spite of the unavoidable destruction less than ten feet from where she stood. The three metal soldiers stared at her, the whine of their cannons a faint whistle as destruction raged around them.

Failure means death.

The thought made her giggle and her smile widened. Relief washed over her.

"GO!" Behind her, the general's voice roared, and he shoved her ahead of him. She stumbled, and the motion broke the bizarre truce. The cannon whined and the center pulsed, growing brighter by the second. Nova realized that the general held her upper arm in one of his meaty hands, using her smaller body as a shield. She felt the air crackle around her and the light in the center of the cannon spilled out and around her.

The burst of energy resembled the discharge from the ionic cannon in the training room in image only. She struggled to gather it within her core, so it danced along her nerves, searing every inch of her being. Nothing spilled out; instead, Nova willed herself to drink it in, huge gulps until she felt certain it would drown her and burn her in the same instant. Time seemed to slow, the flare of energy so hot that it became ice, and she shivered under the strain of holding just one more drop.

The cannon stopped, the center dark. Her vision had narrowed to pinpricks, with blurry edges that left her able to only see one of the suited soldiers. They studied her, heads tilted, their posture almost identical to that of the general's soldiers in the concrete tunnel as they waited to see what would happen next.

Death means freedom.

Rather than focus the release of energy forward, Nova threw her arms out and her head back, her wiry frame at the epicenter of the massive explosion. It surged outward, light suffusing everything. The general's hand tightened on her shoulder and released, and his howl ended abruptly as another wave of energy pulsed from her core. The trio of soldiers disappeared, armor puddling to slag in seconds. Earth scorched beneath her now bare feet. Nova sought the last bits of energy stored within and forced them up and out. The fiery vision in front of her grew dark, and her body sagged to the scorched earth with profound relief. Nova felt the last bits of consciousness slip away, and she crumpled to the ground with a peaceful smile.

△

Nova woke at the bottom of the crater, a thin film of dust and dew crusting her exposed skin. For a brief moment, she stared up into the night sky and wondered if this sort of view greeted everyone in the afterlife. She drew in a deep breath and pain flared in her chest, followed by a rush of razorblades along her spine and over her limbs. A sob burst through her lips, but she could do little more than roll herself to one side and pull her knees up. The full moon gave her a view of muted color, and her eyes adjusted to the limited light. Lying on the ground, Nova took in the charred earth and the lumps of ash and slag that circled her. The crater curved up for a half meter, tufts of blackened grass at the edges. Everything around her smelled like soot, and every bit of her body hurt.

Pain meant that she had survived. The lump of ash and bone nearby meant that the general had not. The thought made her smile, and the ache in her chest lessened. Nova willed her body to relax, fingers uncurling centimeters. Blood thudded in her ears and bits of light danced in her vision when she tried to move her head. A high-pitched tone whined in the space behind her eyes, but she strained to listen for anything that would tell her that she wasn't alone under the never-ending blue sky.

A low rumble echoed in the distance, vibrations moving through the earth and shaking bits of dirt and rocks down the side of the crater. The sound and movement faded, then started again, and she counted thirty seconds of silence between the faint roar and rumble. A horn blared in the distance, followed by an even longer and lower rumble than the first few sounds. Nova's pain-addled consciousness struggled to put a name to the sounds, even as the slight breeze tempted her to slip back into the bliss of unconsciousness.

Truck. More than one. Convoy.

A new sensation flared within her chest, adrenaline making itself known in the midst of her injuries. Nova took a cautious breath and rolled to her hands and knees. Gravel and dirt found their way into the raw swaths of skin on her palms and forearms, but she could push herself up if she kept her motions slow and controlled. Counting the seconds it took to stand up helped her focus on the singular task, and she exhaled as she straightened and surveyed the land beyond the crater.

Floodlights made the land beyond her patch of destruction as bright as midday. Remnants of a fence topped with razor wire separated her from what appeared to be another military installation. A line of 18-wheelers had formed on the ravaged asphalt a few feet past the fence, their cargo covered with heavy burlap and secured with heavy straps. Two figures in fatigues hurried past each truck, one consulting a handheld tablet while the other barked orders on a beaten walkie-talkie.

Nova shrank down to her hands and knees, assessing the distance from the crater to the nearest truck. She could make out enough space between the tie-downs to fit her burned and abused body, although she didn't know what waited beneath the dirt-brown covers. Her muscles tensed and she readied herself to sprint the short distance to the truck. She had no idea where it was going, but she was less concerned about the destination and more worried about putting as much distance as possible between her and what remained of Epsilon Base and the Program.

Eventually, someone would return to salvage what remained of their precious projects. She didn't want to be here when they did.

So, she ran. Enhancements keyed up, adrenaline throttling back the screaming pain, Nova bolted for the nearest truck as the engines came to life and the lead vehicle started to move. In less than a minute, she had crossed the broken road and scrambled between some secured crates. The pair of soldiers had moved on down the line, and the floodlights went dark as the truck ahead of hers began to move. She moved further between the crates, hoping that the person responsible for loading them had made sure to tie them down for the ride. The floor under her gave a shudder, and she lurched towards the rear of the load as the truck moved to follow its comrades on this unknown journey.

Nova held her breath, waiting for the crates to shift, but they stayed in place. She gave a small sigh of relief and sat, back against warm metal and knees to her chest. Under normal circumstances, she would have stayed awake and vigilant throughout the dark ride, but her body finally succumbed to the need for rest and she drifted off, lulled to sleep by the steady rhythm of the truck as it took her away from the Program and towards some new and unknown destination.

$$\triangle$$

She woke when the convoy slowed and came to a stop sometime in the early morning. Nova heard conversation over the distant crunch of tires on gravel, and she sat up straight in the dim light. Now that the sun could peek through some of the cracks, she could make out the insignia on the crates, but she didn't know what the triangle with the horizontal line through the top meant. It certainly didn't look like any insignias she had ever seen during her training. Nova traced the lines with a finger, but stopped when the conversation grew louder and boots crunched the gravel close to her hiding spot.

The footsteps paused, and the conversation faded to low words that Nova couldn't quite make out. She pressed herself further into the space between the crates and forced herself to breathe slowly through parted lips. Could she run? Would there be any place to run? Would the people guarding the convoy shoot to wound or kill if they saw her running? If they caught her, what would they think of her burned and bruised body, not to mention her Program-issued suit that clung to her form in melted, frayed pieces.

"Hey, you okay?" a voice whispered from the other side through the spaces in the crates. The speaker sounded like they wanted to keep anyone else from hearing her question. "No judgment, I just wanna help if I can."

Nova hesitated, then answered in a hoarse whisper. "Where am I?"

"Atlanta. ECHO campus, near the storage units." The owner of the voice shifted and poked her face into the space on the other side. To Nova's surprise, the girl didn't look too much older than she was. "You hungry?"

The first words made little sense to her, but the question reminded her that her last meal had happened before her training, hours before the attack at the site. Her empty stomach burned at the thought of a meal. "Sort of," she lied. "Are those soldiers out there?"

"Sort of," the girl responded, but her answer carried more truth than Nova's words had. "You don't have to go with them if you come with me, though. I know a safe place for people like us."

"Like ... what?" Nova drew back, instantly suspicious. She didn't know why this girl thought they had anything in common.

"Runaways. Girls wanting to put distance between us and people who wanna do bad things to us." She put a hand to her ear as if she could hear voices, then mumbled something that Nova couldn't make out. Another nod, and she reached a hand into the space between the crates. "It's safe, I promise. I ain't gonna hurt you, unless you try and hurt me. Okay?"

She hesitated, looking at the outstretched hand. She had been willing to give up everything a day earlier, so what did she really have to lose? Nova took a deep breath and reached for the hand, feeling the girl's warm dry palm. An odd sense of relief flooded through her body, and she felt tears burn her eyes. Fighting back the urge to cry, she crawled between the crates and emerged in the early morning light. Humidity engulfed her, but her ravaged skin welcomed the cool sensation. The girl put an arm around her waist to keep her standing, and she helped Nova around to the back of the truck.

"I'll be back for the rest of the supplies later this morning," she called to one of the soldiers. He waved her off, as if he saw teenagers crawl out of supply convoys every day and thought nothing of it. She nodded at a beat-up van off to the side, where someone had already loaded a few of the crates in the back. "We'll take that to HQ, and get you something to eat. If you don't mind me sayin', you could probably use a doctor. Sovie's one of the best. You speak any Russian?"

Nova shook her head, shock threatening to set in. "No, why?"

The girl shrugged and opened the passenger side door. After helping Nova into the seat, she shrugged off her jacket and placed it over Nova's shoulders. She plucked an energy bar from the glove compartment and thrust it into her hand. "It'd help, but most of 'em speak good English. You pick up all of the important swear words in a day or so."

Nova unwrapped the bar and took a small bite, the simple act of chewing more difficult than she had anticipated. The girl slid into the driver's seat and buckled up. "I'm Mamona, by the way. You got a name?"

She swallowed and waited for the beat-up van to rumble to life. As they turned out of the gravel lot, she allowed herself to relax against the seat and take a deep breath. "Nova," she said, hands in her lap. "They called me Nova."

ALL MINE

DENNIS LEE AND MERCEDES LACKEY

The girl was very young and thin. She could have been any age from eleven to fourteen. She might have been biracial, but her dark, straight, short hair gave no clues, and her coloring could have been due to Mediterranean descent, Greek or Italian, or even Spanish. Dr. Marcus Dufresne only knew her as "Subject 0067." The hospital scrubs all the subjects in the Program wore were baggy on her slender frame. From here, he could not see her eyes.

She stared fixedly at a small, foam ball resting between hands flat on the surface of the table where she sat. Every visible line of her radiated tension and effort. Watching her was, frankly, boring. Finally, she let out her breath in a sigh. "I can't," she said, or rather, whispered, apologetically.

"Yes, you can, Sixty-seven," came from a speaker in the room; a stern, harsh voice. "Two hours ago, you threw a pitcher full of water at Eighty-eight's head. Now you claim you can't lift a tiny foam ball. You aren't trying."

In another child, that might have elicited an angry response. Not from this one. The girl looked up at the speaker, and a slow tear trickled down her face. Now Marcus could see that her eyes were a sad, deep, dark brown, like the eyes of a beaten puppy. "I *am* trying," she whispered. "My head hurts, I'm trying so hard."

"No, you're not!" the voice snapped. *"You're useless! Worthless!"*

Instead of rebelling, the girl shrank into herself, and her features froze into a mask of terror. Her mouth opened and closed, but no sound emerged.

Through the one-way mirror, Marcus watched as another slow tear ran down the girl's face. There was something there. Something familiar. It sparked a brief twinge of despair, a distant memory. He pushed the thought away and glanced back at his tablet, intent on recording the brain wave activity that blipped steadily from the device attached to Subject 0067's cranium.

"There you have it," said the Project Lead, Dr. Joseph Garvey. He was an ugly man, and his looks were not improved by facial and cranial scarring. He had clearly had some cosmetic surgery, but the ropy keloid scars that remained testified he had at one point been severely burned. The injury had to have been substantial; enough that his left arm was either completely cybernetic or in a cybernetic sheath. The arm hummed at times, and when Garvey lifted something heavy, it whined. Hydraulics, perhaps. It threw Garvey off balance when he walked, but it was strong enough Marcus had once seen Garvey crush the edge of a metal table during a heated discussion with another of his under-lings. "She's perfectly capable of throwing cinder blocks at people when she's frightened enough, but she can't seem to lift a grain of rice otherwise. And her psychometry is erratic and weaker than we'd like. She can only backtrack about a week before it becomes useless. Think you can do anything with her? You did wonders with Fifty-nine and Seventy-two."

"I'll have her up to speed by your deadline," Marcus murmured, still studying the oscillating waves on his tablet. "This one is different, to be sure. Look here." He turned the tablet towards Garvey and pointed. "There's a strong undercur-rent to her efforts. She might not have the baseline strength others have, but she's still developing. Still, look at the regularity of it. She's displaying a resonance that no one else has before. It's solid. I can work with this."

Garvey studied the tablet. "That resonance may be the prob-lem. Something's holding her back. Can you turn it off?"

"I suppose I could," Marcus said. "Not the first thing I would propose, though."

"And why's that?"

"It might play havoc with her natural development. You run the risk of it strengthening her ability now, only to have it burn out." Marcus paused. "Oh, and it might kill her."

"What's your point?" Garvey said. "If she dies, we can get more."

"It just seems a waste of a perfectly good subject. Call it instinct. I think there may be much more to this one than a common foot soldier. I'm thinking of the long game here."

Garvey sniffed at Marcus's objections. "When has that ever been an issue? We need working operatives *now,* not at some nebulous point in the future. Besides, children obey; teenagers rebel. They're better for our purposes when either young or old enough to be trained to respond to commands by a superior."

"This one might be different," Marcus argued, although he kept his tone flat and uninflected. "There's potential there for more. Her behavior suggests you might mold her well into adult-hood as the perfect operative. If you play this right, she'll follow your orders until her dying breath."

Garvey waved that away. "Operatives *now,* Doctor. Not in the future. Invisible, obedient operatives. No one ever pays a damn bit of attention to children. No one thinks of them as metas."

Marcus shrugged. "As you wish. I can start her on the cock-tail immediately." He swiped at his tablet a few times and began to input notes.

"Test Subject 0067," Marcus said, as the tablet dutifully began to record his voice. "Note vitals and tailor the usual cock-tail to her specifications. Standard monitoring apparatus." He paused, and shrugged again. "Ignore elevated risks of compro-mising her immune system, shock, and death. Subject 0067 is expendable."

$$\triangle$$

Virtue huddled in the corner of her bed farthest from the door. The room was scarcely big enough to hold the bed and a tiny bedside table with a tablet. She had wrapped herself in her blanket and was hugging her pillow, knees to her chest. *They* never allowed her any tissues unless she was actually sick, because they had discovered the little fairies she'd made from them hidden under her mattress. So her sleeve had to do for her sniffles and her pillow to dry her tears.

A gentle tap on her door made her stiffen. "*Querida,* it's me," said a soft, accented voice, and she relaxed, relief flooding through her.

"Ramon!" she exclaimed. "It's okay—"

She didn't need to go any further. The door opened long enough for a lean, tall, Hispanic man in a janitor's coverall to slip inside. He was carrying a teddy bear and a box of tissues.

She reached for the bear first, as he sat down on her bunk, slipped his arm around her shoulders, and held her, pulling out a tissue for her. "Were they very terrible today, *chiquita?*"

"They keep saying I don't try," she said plaintively into his shoulder. "But I *am*! I *am* trying!"

"You do not need to convince me. I know you are," Ramon replied. "I wish I knew how to help you," he added, in frustration. "But I do not. I wish I could take you away. You could be a sister to my little Maria."

"I'd like to have a sister," Virtue said, for what was probably the millionth time.

"Well, you know I am taking night classes to make my English better, and I have just read a story in my English class about sisters," Ramon replied, drying her eyes gently with a tissue. "Once upon a time, there was a beautiful queen. She wanted a child very badly. One day, while a fairy was listening, she stuck her finger while she was embroidering—"

"What's embroidering?" Virtue interrupted.

"It is making pictures on clothing with colored threads and a needle," Ramon said patiently. "It makes clothing prettier."

Virtue examined the hem of her scrub sleeve and sighed. She would never have pretty clothing....

"So she was embroidering, and stuck her finger, and before the blood could soil the sleeve, she held her hand outside the window, so the drop of blood fell on the snow outside instead."

Virtue did not ask what "snow" was. Ramon had explained that to her, and she had looked up pictures on her tablet.

"*Oh*, the queen said. *I wish I could have a little daughter with lips and cheeks as red as blood, and another with skin as white as snow,* she said, and the good fairy, who was listening, and knew she was a good and virtuous queen, nodded, and said *Let it be so....*"

Marcus let the cold water run over his hands and felt that familiar surge of numbing clarity as the chill set in. He wondered if it was enough, and considered the prospect of a good long shower in freezing water. It had been another bad day, but numbing it away was hardly going to solve his problems. He had just spent hours fruitlessly trying to stimulate Test Subject 0067's brain activity with a diverse barrage of challenges, ranging through electrical, chemical, and even emotional triggers. Nothing seemed to elicit more than a passive blip on his monitors. The remnant spikes he observed in her brain activity after her rare episodes of explosive power suggested she was on the cusp of something unprecedented. There was something in that subject that defied prediction, as if she was on the verge of actually *evolving* into something entirely new. Maybe not *homo superior,* but certainly no longer mere *homo sapiens.* The sharp, staccato spikes that streamed across the screen of his tablet suggested something more to him than neuronal synapses dutifully firing off. They seemed to cry out in a muted rage, shackled and tethered mere inches away from a satisfying and violent release.

He sniffed in distaste. Violence was chaos; it was unrestricted emotion vented out through destructive channels. He had always preferred the calculated order he could impose on his reality. He was a scientist. He loved the elegant task of posing questions and systematically designing and executing experiments to prove or disprove them. Done correctly, conclusions drawn from experimentation could be absolute and overpower any counterpoints founded upon flimsy, nebulous beliefs and pre-existing notions. Any truth could be uncovered by the collection of hard facts. Marcus had never let something as prosaic as morals or emotion lend its voice to the process.

Until the day Emily had told him she was sick, the day Marcus had discovered another part of himself.

Marcus grunted as he pushed the thought away. He didn't have time for it. He had promised Garvey a working assassin before the end of the month, and he was no closer to that goal than he was to his own freedom. It was a long-standing joke in academic circles how most scientists were little more than indentured servants—slaves really—but having now served under not one, but *two* well-funded madmen, Marcus had to wonder when his life had crossed that undefined line from lampoon to full-fledged horror show. He had barely escaped the clutches of Dominic Verdigris III with little more than the shirt on his back, but—he *had* escaped. And he still drew breath. That was something at least, an achievement of sorts, something he was incredibly lucky to have, and he knew it. But there was the problem. How had he been so euphoric from his escape, so grateful for his new-found freedom, that he had stumbled so carelessly into the hands of another crazed scientist?

Still, at least here he was able to continue his own work, to some degree. While Marcus could draw many similarities between Dominic Verdigris III and Dr. Jacob Garvey—in their paranoia, their obsession with success, their indifference to human life—at least Garvey was less hands-on in his approach. He more-or-less trusted his subordinates to do the work and get his results. Their lives depended on it, after all. Verdigris had never been so trusting. It really was a miracle that Marcus had managed to escape.

Be grateful for small "favors."

It helped that Garvey didn't seem to want to be here either. It wasn't just his disdain for his researchers or his impatience for positive, repeatable results. Marcus suspected Garvey approached all aspects of his life in a similar fashion. He could feel it coming off the ugly man in waves. There were more important things to attend to than the unpredictable surges of power in filthy, disgusting, *unreliable* children! Garvey wanted adults who were *like* children in that they could be easily controlled, but were otherwise responsive and predictable. Marcus had long suppressed the notion of correcting Garvey's misplaced notions. The last thing anyone, man or child, could be was *controlled*, at least in any real way that mattered. Frightened, perhaps, cowed into a superficial state of submission to escape the threat of pain. But short of lobotomizing them, Marcus couldn't see any way to fully control a sentient being. People were too damn stubborn for their own good. Marcus often wondered what the world would be like if people simply obeyed their betters, trusting that the smarter person knew what was best for them.

Emily had never obeyed him. Emily had been something of an annoyance, really. They had been orphaned at a young age, and it had fallen to him to look after her through years of foster care. Between their schooling and the constant moves from one home to another, it had been his duty to make sure she was protected. It was the last promise he'd made to his parents. She was only nine when they passed. He remembered telling her the news, rather bluntly, and the awkward days that followed; she an inconsolable mess, and he the helpless older brother, clueless as to how to make his sister stop crying. She was sensitive—too sensitive, he thought. When she wasn't sobbing over their dead parents, she was trying to find ways to help the other kids in their foster homes—and worse, making *him* help too. Why should they care about kids they were never going to see again? Soon, they would be moved, and again, and again. They could never find foster parents who could handle both Emily's weakness and his strength. He thought of her as a burden and secretly wished that someone, somewhere, would finally release him from the thankless task of being the only guardian she could ever have.

The day Emily told him she was dying was also the day she finally thanked him, for everything he had ever done for her.

She had always been so different. Where he had excelled in his studies, she never seemed to have the focus required for anything academic. She followed her heart, flitting effortlessly from one endeavor to another, throwing herself into whatever cause, whatever fight against injustice struck her as earth-shattering that week. In that contest, Marcus supposed she was the leader, not him. She was always sure of herself, fully in the moment, and she propelled herself through life with sheer drive.

Until the day she just ... stopped.

Perhaps he should have seen it coming, should have recognized the signs early. The blackouts, the sudden lethargic episodes—they should have been a warning of things to come. How had he not taken notice when a girl who never stopping talking, never stopped moving, suddenly resigned herself to sit quietly in the corner of his laboratory at midday, her head nodding, fighting off inexplicable exhaustion? He didn't even have time to take her to the doctor; his experiments had to come first, of course. So when the diagnosis came in, anaplastic astrocytoma, a rare form of brain cancer, for the first time in his life Marcus had felt a wave of rage and a burning sense of injustice. It had slammed into him, a sucker punch to the gut, a roaring in his head, unlike anything that had come before. The bitter taste of every prior failure paled in comparison: when he had been passed over, repeatedly, for foster care, for scholarships, and even the lost feeling that seemed so overwhelming at the time when his parents had quietly passed away in their hospital beds ... nothing could have prepared him for this.

She was just a young girl. A young, earnest girl who had fought for everyone else, every day of her life, despite having nothing herself. Not even, it seemed, an older brother who gave a damn about her. She had nothing to call her own, except her drive, her will to fight, and now even that was slipping away. After she had told him the news, it shocked him how weak she looked, how frail, almost translucent and ethereal. She was dying, and she could do little more than flash him a weak smile and tell him it was going to be all right, that maybe it was just her time. He remembered peering at her, wondering where his sister had gone. Where was the girl who had once rallied an entire school of self-absorbed high schoolers to action, setting up an impromptu blood drive in the wake of one of the worst hurricane disasters to hit the East Coast? Where was the strong, passionate voice that had once cried out against the rise of violence towards women on campus in her freshman year at college, leading a giant protest down Main Street and up the steps of Convocation Hall? She was nowhere to be seen. In her place was a ghost, a mere wisp of the vibrant soul that had given him the strength to go on, for all those years. She was dying. Where was the justice in *that?*

He remembered it so clearly. He remembered himself gasping as she thanked him for taking care of her, for looking out for her, ever since their parents had been taken from them. She was thanking him, when he should have been thanking her. What had he given her, really, that she had not returned tenfold? He remembered reaching out to do something he never remembered doing before. He drew her into his arms and held on for dear life. And he had never really let her go.

She gave him something else that day. A purpose. From that moment on, he had devoted his research to her. In retrospect, he realized he had made some startling advances in the field, but it wasn't enough. Of course it wasn't. There simply wasn't the time, and no one, no matter how brilliant or driven or lucky, could solve something so overwhelmingly complex in a few short years. She held on longer than anyone thought possible. It seemed there was still something of a fighter in her yet. Even now, years after she had slipped into perpetual sleep, Marcus was still looking for his answers.

So much time had passed, and still he was looking. And what was the cost? All that she had given him, was there anything left?

His humanity. He had ignored it for so many years, only realizing its value when it was far too late. What little was left felt like it was slipping away. He almost laughed. He wanted to live. He *needed* to live. For her, for Emily. But to live, he had to do some terrible things. To live ...

Marcus caught another glimpse of himself in the mirror. This time, he didn't look away. The hard lines that defined his lips, his chin, his cheekbones ... they might have been considered handsome, but his eyes ...

They held nothing.

They were his eyes, but not just his. He had seen them before, in another face. They were hollow. Dead. He blinked, and winced, watching Garvey's eyes blink back at him.

△

"... but the horses slipped on the glass mountain, and never reached the top," Ramon said, holding Virtue tenderly, as she held the bear. She sighed, and more tears escaped her. He paused in the story, for she usually hung rapt on his every word. "What is the matter, *mi corazón?*"

"I feel like that," she replied, as he gave her a tissue to blot her tears. "All the time. Like I'm on a glass mountain, and no matter what I try, I can never reach the top."

He fell silent, unable to think of anything to say to help her. He had no idea what it was they were trying to get her to do— and even if he knew, these special children, they could all do things that were like magic, and he felt as helpless in his ability to advise them as he was to save them. All he could do was hug her shoulders, wait to hear if she said anything else, and then continue the story. Maybe she would find some clue to help her in the tale. It was, after all, a story about how to do the impossible.

"And all the while this was going on, the king's son was wandering with his oxen...."

△

Ramon closed the door quietly and stowed the bear and tissues under the drape on his cleaning cart. He would have loved to leave both there, but he knew the consequences of doing so would be dire for both himself and the little *muchacha*. He did not mind punishment for himself ... but it would be more than punishment for her. She would lose her only friend in this horrible place, *and* they would be even harder on her, if that was possible. They had not resorted to beating her—yet—but he had no doubt they would do so if they thought they would get better results.

The mere thought put him in a rage, a rage he quickly clamped down on. *Results!* Children were precious jewels, the hope of the future, and these men were treating them like ... like cans of beans. *Worse.* Like helpless lambs in a slaughterhouse. He seethed, and was so preoccupied he didn't sense the presence behind him until he straightened up from the cart. And by then, of course, it was too late.

It was one of the *scientists*. They wore no nametags, of course. That way if "something happened" none of the underlings could identify them. And they all wore thick goggles that obscured the upper halves of their faces, which would make picking out pictures almost impossible. But Ramon had names for all of them. "The Boss." "The Sneer." "The Nervous One." To Ramon, they all were uncaring, brutal bastards, but this particular scientist chilled him to his core. He never seemed to betray anything about himself. Even his voice was hollow and monotonous. Ramon had named him "The Cold One."

He thought for a moment about greeting him as if nothing was going on, but that in itself might be a betrayal that something was going on. "The staff" were supposed to say nothing to the scientists. Like slaves of old, they were supposed to keep their eyes down and move aside. So that was what he did. He dropped his eyes and touched the cart to roll it to the side so the scientist could pass.

The Cold One didn't move. He stood in place, his hands clasped behind his back, his goggles fixed firmly in place on Ramon. He tilted his head, a curious gesture which Ramon took as quizzical. It was the first hint of emotion he had ever detected in this man.

"You are not allowed to disturb the test subjects," The Cold One said.

Ramon felt a chill. He had been seen. He had heard unsavory things happened to those who did not keep their heads down, to those who meandered from the razor's edge of their duties.

"I heard her weeping, *señor*," Ramon said. "I only went in to see if she was hurt."

The Cold One's head tilted further askew, and Ramon fought down a scream of terror when the man took a step forward, followed by another, and another, until his goggles were near enough Ramon could peer past the tinted glass to see the hard, unforgiving eyes beneath.

"You are not allowed to disturb the test subjects," The Cold One said again.

"*Por favor* ..." He reminded himself that his father's father's father's father had fought the Spanish. That his father's father had fought the Nazis. That his own father had been a talented boxer. That he came from a line of fighters. It helped ... a little, enough to keep from shaking in tooth-rattling terror of this creature that seemed more like a *thing* than a man. And to manage to choke out a few words, a quote he had heard ... somewhere. "No man stands taller than when he stoops to help a child in need."

The Cold One continued to stare at him. Ramon sniffed, stifling a sigh of relief when the goggles finally dropped, only to shudder in fear as The Cold One's gaze came to rest on Ramon's cart. Ramon watched, paralyzed, as a gloved hand reached out and pulled away the drape, revealing a box of tissues and Virtue's teddy bear.

The goggles rose, and Ramon saw the man's eyes again, boring into him.

"You've done this before," The Cold One murmured. "Tell me, Custodian Tomaso, just how tall do you need to be?"

The words came out of him before he could stop them. "As tall as the *muchacha* needs me to be." He gritted his teeth, but it was too late. The words of defiance were out, as was the secret.

"Ah, a man of compassion," The Cold One said. "You don't approve of what we do here, do you?"

"They are *children*—" Again, the words escaped him before he could stop them.

"It is not your *place* to approve or disapprove!" The Cold One barked. Ramon felt his resolve falter as he bent beneath the strength of that icy gaze. "It is not your *place* to do anything more than clean and maintain the infrastructure of these facilities! You are merely a tool—one that performs its duties, keeps its head down, and does not interfere with the delicate projects destined to shape the future of this nation! Is that understood?"

Later, Ramon wondered what had come over him in that instant. Perhaps it was hearing his *querida* referred to as a "delicate project." Perhaps it was time when a man was past all fear. Perhaps it was the spirits of his ancestors, deciding to step in and strengthen his backbone. Perhaps none of these, or all. But he suddenly straightened and said, "You know *nothing* of children. You do not know that when you starve their hearts, you break them. You do not know that when you do not comfort them, you kill their spirits. And what you do not know is breaking *her*. Soon she will be useless to you. Is that what you want? Can you make a *delicate project* out of a thing that is broken?"

"As a matter of fact, I can. You assume we want them whole, with anything resembling spirit. Frankly, our job would be much easier with their backs broken. I can mold something soft and supple. I can ..."

The Cold One took a step back from Ramon and rested his

hands on his hips, his head down, as if struggling with indecision.

"*Señor ...*"

"Shut up. Just shut up."

The Cold One stood still for a long time. Ramon struggled against his need to retort, that to break Virtue would be to shatter her like a delicate porcelain figure, and there would be nothing left but shards too small to piece together. Finally, the scientist relaxed, and turned to walk away.

"You should really be more careful when you make these visits," the scientist said. "There are eyes everywhere, you know."

"*Señor ...*"

"Call me Marcus."

"That's ... that is not allowed ..."

"You're right, so try to do it only when we're alone, will you?"

The Cold One walked away. Ramon could only stare after him.

△

Crystal clear surveillance footage played on the video monitor. Everything visible, from each stitch on Marcus's coat to the tiny beads of sweat on Ramon Tomaso's forehead. This was the third time Garvey had played the footage for Marcus, and he froze it as Marcus walked off camera, the sharp patter of his footsteps growing faint in the distance.

"So. What am I supposed to make of this?" Garvey asked, rhetorically. "That you are encouraging insubordination in the help? Giving the nod to the contamination of my subjects? Is this why we're getting poor results from Sixty-seven?"

"I'm guessing you wouldn't have been so forgiving with him?" Marcus said.

"He's as good as dead," Garvey seethed. "Everyone here is easily expendable. Why do you think I go through the trouble of vetting everyone in this establishment? He's no one. At least, no one that will be missed."

"No one?" Marcus asked. "No family?"

"He did have a daughter, but she died a couple of years ago. He's taking a class or two but if he disappears the school will assume deportation. There's no one left to question his disappearance." Garvey's eyes narrowed. "Or yours, for that matter."

Marcus sighed, and shrugged in a helpless gesture. "I don't suppose you'd be willing to hear me out," he said.

Garvey was on him fast, faster than Marcus would have expected from a burn victim with a heavy metallic arm that swung him off-balance when he turned too quickly. In a flash, Marcus felt the powerful grip of steel fingers throttle him about the neck and heard the shrill whining of hydraulics as Garvey picked him up and slammed him back against the wall.

"You know," Garvey began, "I'm sure it has not escaped your notice that I am not a *patient* man. I have worked long and difficult hours to get where I am. I've sacrificed more than you can imagine to achieve what I have, of myself, and yes, of my *staff*. So don't think for a moment I have any reservation about simply turning you inside out if I think it will help me in the slightest."

Marcus grunted in pain and tried to speak, but could only manage a hoarse cough.

"Oh dear," Garvey said, relaxing his grip. "I seem to have broken you. Pray continue, Dr. Dufresne. Please, convince me not to kill you, Subject 0067, and this meddlesome janitor right here, right now, and move on to the next subject."

"Y ... y ... you ..."

"Really, man, you need to speak up," Garvey said. He released Marcus, who fell to the ground in a heap, breathing heavily and holding his throat in pain.

"You're ..." Marcus wheezed. "You're missing an opportunity here."

"Oh, this should be *rich*," Garvey sighed. "You have thirty seconds. Convince me."

Marcus exhaled, drew a few deep breaths, and began.

"I've done a full analysis of her resting power. That's what we've been seeing, that mature, low-level resonance that's always in play when we record. We almost got the full read, once. It was coming back to rest after her last display, but we were too late to get a decent pattern. We need to have a recording *during* a full telekinetic flash. And the closest we've come since is when we threatened to throw Subject 0013 into the sensory deprivation tank for a week. The green one. The one the subjects call 'Gremlin.' She seemed to have some concern for the boy. What if we could use that? Run the scanners, get a full reading, *just one*, and I assure you everything you need to unlock her talents will be found there."

Garvey knelt down and pulled Marcus in close by his shirt.

"And how do you propose we do this?"

Marcus glared back at Garvey, and told him.

△

The attendants brought her in, dropping her unceremoniously in her chair. Test Subject 0067 slumped forward, face and body rigid with apprehension, her hair already clumping with nervous sweat. Without a word, Marcus stepped forward and attached the sensor to the base of her neck. There was a soft click, followed by a gentle hum as the device flared to life.

"There now," Marcus said, stepping back. He brought his tablet up and checked her vitals. All systems seemed normal, and the steady, resonant waves began to oscillate across his readouts, like clockwork. "I think we're just about ready to begin."

Test Subject 0067 stirred and gave him a furtive glance.

"No tests today?" she mumbled quietly.

"And why would you think that?" Marcus asked, his fingers tapping his tablet, queuing up the standard equilibrations and baseline monitors.

"Because ..." The girl hesitated, and looked about, flinching as she caught her reflection in the one-way mirror. "Because you're in here, with me. Not in there." She pointed at the mirror. "You're safe in there. In here ..."

"You think I'm in any danger?" Marcus asked. "Really, Sixty-seven, you've hardly done anything dangerous. Yet. I'm in here today to try and change that. I think we can give you a nice little boost and see what you're really made of. Would you like that?"

The girl didn't answer, at first. Finally, she nodded. Clearly she had learned it was best to always agree.

"Very good," Marcus murmured. "If it helps, you might be happy to know that today we're not interested in hurting you at all."

Slowly, the girl raised her head. There were tears in her eyes, and a wild hope.

"R-really?" she said.

"Really," he answered.

"No shocks?"

"No shocks."

"No gas?"

"Not a bit."

She stumbled through a wavering sigh of relief and gingerly wiped away her tears.

"Thank you," she whispered. "Oh, thank you ..."

"No, I thought we would do something a little different today, Sixty-seven." Marcus looked over at the mirror and nodded. "It seems you've made a friend here. I thought you could use some company right now. Would you like to see him?"

The girl looked simultaneously elated and terrified. "I don't have any friends! Don't hurt Gremlin! He doesn't even know who I am!"

"Oh no, no," Marcus said. "No, no, no, not Subject 0013. I don't think he'd provide the ..." Marcus paused, scratching his head theatrically, "... the *depth* we would require for today's agenda."

The girl stared at him.

"I don't have any friends," she repeated. "The other kids don't talk to me, they ..."

She paused as the door swung open, and a man strapped firmly down to a gurney was rolled in. He was frightened, shivering, his hands clenched into tight fists at his side. He turned to look at the girl and tried to give her a reassuring smile. Instead, he looked frenetic and crazed.

The girl screamed. "Ramon!"

"Yes, Ramon," Marcus said, waving the attendants out of the room. He strolled over to the gurney, looking down at the struggling man with a curious tilt of his head. He glanced up, and the girl shrank from him, sobbing uncontrollably.

"P-please ..." she stammered. "D-don't hurt him! Oh please, don't hurt ..."

"Then show me!" Marcus barked. "Show me what you can do!"

"Yes! Please! I'll do anything you want me to! Just ..."

"We're out of patience, Subject Sixty-seven! You have power! You've used it before! We want a full demonstration, *now*, or ..."

Marcus paused, as Ramon stopped struggling and glared up at him.

"Her name is Virtue," Ramon hissed.

"I do beg your pardon?" Marcus said.

"Her name is Virtue," Ramon repeated. "She's not some number. She's a child, and she has a *name*!"

"Of course, she does," Marcus agreed. "Very well. Where was I? Ah. *Virtue*. We want a full demonstration, and right quick. If I have to ask you again, I don't think Ramon here is going to have a very good day."

Virtue's eyes overflowed with tears, which ran unheeded down her cheeks, dripping onto the front of her smock. She shook, her hands clenching and unclenching. The blood drained from her face until she was almost the same color as the smock itself. "I ... I can try ..."

Virtue braced herself, laying her hands flat on the table in front of her. Completely rigid, she stared at the foam ball on the table before her.

Nothing happened.

Marcus picked up the scalpel from the tray beside him and jammed it into Ramon's shoulder.

Ramon's whine of agony was drowned out by Virtue's scream. *"Stop it! Stop it! Leave him alone! I'm trying, can't you see I'm trying?"*

But the balls didn't move. Not even a fraction of an inch. Clearly this was going to require an extraordinary level of stimulation.

He twisted the scalpel, and with clinical precision, dissected out the brachial plexus, laying it bare to the air. Ramon's screams rang in his ears, and Virtue—*Sixty-seven's*—screams echoed them on a higher note. Marcus fought down an urge to join them. This was getting out of hand. For once, he was thankful for the goggles and the half-mask that Garvey made all the scientists and technicians wear. Keeping his hands steady from shaking was one thing, but if anyone could see his face they would know. They would see his doubt. He glanced at the mirror and could feel Garvey's cold eyes staring back at him. Marcus felt an odd tingle about his neck, where Garvey had so callously wrapped his metallic fingers around the day before.

He struggled with indecision, staring down at the screaming man, at the exposed nerve bundle glistening with a sheen of blood, and the blood dripping down the shoulder, onto the stainless steel of the gurney, and from there to the floor. This ... this was wrong. People weren't ... things, objects to be manipulated and broken. They weren't disposable. Were they? They weren't, surely. *Were they?*

It seemed an eternity, but then one, singular, sharp sound broke his concentration. A sharp rap on glass.

He looked up at the mirror. He felt Garvey's impatience. He felt what little tolerance Garvey had for him rapidly coming to an end. In a moment, Garvey would summon security, and he would die along with the janitor.

It was only a janitor. No one of importance. The man's last link to anything had died along with his daughter in a school bus crash. No one would care when he was gone—no one except the single person Marcus *needed* to goad into the full eruption of her potential.

Him, or me. Or him and *me.* It was no choice at all. He couldn't die. He had too much to do. For Emily.

With a single swift incision, he slit the carotid artery. Blood fountained over the edge of the gurney in a long arc. Marcus felt something snap inside of him. He had done it ... dear lord, he had done it ...

He glanced at Sixty-seven, bracing himself, expecting to see the horror of the moment consume everything else on that young, frail face. She would likely be crying. Those who witnessed her last episode swore that her eyes had lit up in a brilliant silver flash, so he braced himself for that as well. Instead, he saw something else.

She wasn't Sixty-seven—*Virtue*—anymore. In her place, he saw another. He saw Emily's face.

And it was angry.

After that, there was nothing but incredible, excruciating pain as he smashed into the wall behind him. Then into the wall to the left. Then to the right. The ceiling, the floor, and the ceiling again. And now, barely conscious, he felt himself flung through the one-way glass, smashing it, to land in a shower of shards at Garvey's feet. His body was screaming, bent in odd angles. He was screaming as well. He heard himself stop, coughing, wheezing, and he stared, astonished, as a bloody froth erupted from his mouth.

Above him, Garvey peered over his tablet and flashed him a grin.

"Reading complete," Garvey said. "Well done, Dr. Dufresne."

Marcus stared back at him.

"You look dreadful," Garvey noted, sighing. "Those wounds are clearly ... oh, what is the word ... ah! Mortal. I doubt you would even last the trip to the infirmary. Still, you never know. We do perform miracles here, don't we?"

There are no miracles, Marcus thought, sinking into the black.

Familiar sounds penetrated the deep and formless blackness. The steady beep of a heart monitor. The whine of an overhead fluorescent light. Pings and clicks and hums of other medical equipment, all comforting in their familiarity. Cold comfort, but still, comfort,

Thoughts swam up, like curious fishes.

I'm not dead.

Where am I?

Why am I not dead?

A face appeared out of the shadows. Emily. Emily enraged, as he had last "seen" her. He cringed. And to avoid looking at that angry face any more, he opened his eyes.

And winced away from the light, that cold, pitiless fluorescence he had heard.

"Welcome back, Dr. Dufresne."

Marcus knew that voice. It filled him with an icy resolve. He let his eyes adjust to the light and looked around. There were the monitors, the IV drip, and next to his bed there was the man himself, Dr. Joseph Garvey.

"Where's Virtue?" Marcus said.

"I'm sorry, who?"

"Virtue," Marcus repeated. "Subject 0067."

"Oh, you need not worry about her anymore," Garvey said. "She's progressing nicely. No, Dr. Dufresne, I think our time would be better spent discussing *you*, and what a pleasant surprise you've turned out to be."

Marcus didn't respond, and instead tried to prop himself up on the bed. He felt some alarm as his arms refused to move. He strained to look down at himself, and snarled as something blocked his chin. Was he paralyzed? If this was paralysis, it wasn't like anything he would have imagined. For one thing, his senses seemed, if anything, ramped up. He could swear he felt slight eddies and shifts in the air around him. He thought he could taste a faint antiseptic perfume on Garvey, almost masking the metallic, oily aroma wafting off Garvey's metallic arm. Marcus felt alert, energized, *alive*. He tried to lift his head again, and caught a disturbing sight before he let his head fall back down again.

His body was in a full metal restraining suit.

"What have you done?" Marcus demanded, glaring up at Garvey, who smirked in return.

"I saved your life, you ungrateful twit," Garvey muttered. "And more. You, Dr. Dufresne, are the first successful test subject of the next stage of the *Icarus Project*. I suppose I should thank you. It seems being so close to death was an unforeseen exploit for portions of the process. Pity, if only we had known that before. So many test subjects lost to pointless, stubborn attempts by my witless team. As for you, virtually every bone in your body was broken. You had multiple internal ruptures and bleeding, and severe head trauma. As I told you at the time, I frankly had no expectation you would make it as far as the infirmary. In any case, it would seem that congratulations are in order. Believe me when I say I am *very* intrigued by what you are now capable of. We'll let you rest for a spell, of course. You will be very weak for a while. We will need to monitor you quite closely while you recover."

Garvey rested his metal hand gently on Marcus's chest, and smiled.

"But when you're ready, oh my boy ... you will be a wonder. The first of many. So believe me when I say, I *shiver* to think of the possibilities."

"You can't keep me here," Marcus seethed. "I did what you wanted. I got your results. A deal's a deal, Garvey."

"The situation has changed, dear boy," Garvey said. "You are now far more valuable to me than ever before. You can't think for a moment I would simply let my crowning achievement just ... *leave*."

"You can't keep me here," Marcus repeated.

"Of course I can," Garvey scoffed. "Like all my employees and subjects, you were vetted. There's no one to miss you. There's no one to come looking for you. You are mine, Dufresne, and the sooner you accept that, the easier your life will be. You are alone. Best you accept that."

"I'm not alone," Marcus said, struggling within his iron prison. "I'm not! I ..."

"You have no one," Garvey said. "You had ... what ... a sister? A sister who died years ago? I had you investigated quite thoroughly, you know. She was the only one, and from what I understand, you failed her. Spec-*tac*-ularly. You were supposedly a brilliant neurodegenerative specialist, Dufresne, but let's be blunt, hmmm? You were always a failure. And now, you are the first in a new, highly advanced line of prototypical meta-soldiers! You have me to thank for that."

Garvey leaned in closer and smiled again.

"Isn't it about time you did something *right*?"

Marcus didn't answer and continued to struggle against his restraints, for all the good it did him. He was stronger, much stronger, he could feel it, but it didn't seem to matter against the iron maiden that deadened any of his attempts to flex his muscles. He supposed he wasn't the first metahuman Garvey had had to restrain. The suit would be reinforced, of course. It had to be. Metahumans, especially newly minted ones, had a tendency for rage. Aside from the moment Emily announced her diagnosis, Marcus could not remember a time he had ever felt rage. Some people just didn't have the temperament for it. Instead, he felt what he always felt when on the defensive—an icy resolve to turn the tide, to find a weakness to exploit, to *win*.

He buzzed with energy. It was a strange sensation and so surreal—to be so confined and helpless, yet suffused with so much vigor and life. And it was growing. He exhaled, a faint and cold mist trailing off his lips. It felt odd and out of place. Under the harsh lights and encapsulated in a heavy metal prison, the room had felt so warm ...

"I asked you a question, Dufresne," Garvey said.

Marcus grunted, his breath steaming in the cold air.

"I asked you a question. Are you ready to finally do something *right*?"

Marcus glared at him and sneered.

Garvey sighed, and began to pull away. "A pity," he said. "Breaking your spirit will take time, and I was so hoping we could skip the dreary preliminaries and hit the ground running. Ah well. I suppose it was too much to ask for. I suppose it—" Garvey stopped, a puzzled expression on his face. He shook his arm, but it appeared to be stuck fast to the restraining suit, fused palm-down to Marcus's chest.

"What in the—"

Garvey's eyes widened as wispy ropes of vapor flowed from his metallic hand and a frosty rime traveled up the arm. Garvey couldn't move; he was pinned in place, immobilized as a sudden chill had fused them together, a chill that intensified in waves from Marcus's suit, from Marcus himself ...

Marcus felt the energy crescendo and let it flow over him, through him. In a sudden explosive burst he lashed out, shattering his now brittle prison into jagged pieces. Already he was moving, bounding from the confines of the bed, on his feet, his hand lashing out, gripping the astonished Garvey about the throat and ramming him back against the wall.

Garvey gurgled his surprise and tried to swing his arm. Nothing happened. The sound of the arm's hydraulics moaned and stopped. The arm shuddered in place and shattered, pieces falling to the floor, trailing wisps of vapor from the extreme cold, leaving nothing but a bloody stump that flailed wildly from his shoulder.

Marcus glanced at the stump, and back to Garvey.

"Oh dear," Marcus said. "I seem to have broken you."

He brought Garvey in close and scowled as he held the frightened man's eyes with his own.

"Now then. Where is *Virtue?*"

And this story is from just before the end of book six, Avalanche. *"People are going to want to know how Vix and Red got off that dying ship," I told Dennis. "And besides, Red needs something nice to happen to him for a change." So we wrote this. Makes me smile. Hope it does you, too.*

RUNNIN'

MERCEDES LACKEY AND DENNIS LEE

The process of getting from the disintegrating World-Ship to the deck of the aircraft carrier Vickie and Red were now on had been something of a blur for Vickie. She vaguely remembered Red picking her up ... somehow she had ended up in a kind of webby backpack between his shoulders ... and then it was all flashes of running, avoiding disaster by the skin of his teeth, and something that was so much beyond parkour that she didn't even have a word for it, ending in an impossible leap where he'd caught the skid of a hovering helicopter and pulled them both up onto it to cling there until they dropped off on the deck. She had been so emotionally and physically drained she couldn't even register more than a flicker of fear as he had pulled off impossible stunts to get them here. Only relief.

The webbing holding her like a papoose had dropped away, and she'd no sooner landed on the deck than people in white decontamination had suits swarmed them. Then they got separated, pushed into decontamination tents. As she stood there numbly, she was told to strip, her chainmail suit was taken aside to be dunked in a vat of something, while she got hosed down with salt water, fresh water, chemicals, and more fresh water. Then someone threw a towel at her, a T-shirt and sweatpants and flip-flops got shoved into her arms, along with a gym bag with her chainmail and belt in it, and they pushed her into another part of the tent where other women were donning the same basic outfits. *My sword and dagger are at the bottom of the ocean. I'm going to have to make a new pair.* It was a small, infinitesimally small price to pay for saving the world, really. Somehow she fumbled the clothing on, followed the other women out through tent flaps, and she found herself on the other side of the tents, looking around in dazed, utterly exhausted bewilderment.

And then, of course, she heard Red's voice ... raised. Evidently someone was preventing him from leaving his decontamination tent. That jarred her awake.

"There seems to be a problem," Eight said in her ear.

"It's Red," she sighed. "He attracts problems." She trudged

towards the tent and opened the flap. Presumably scrubbed men dressed in sweatpants and T-shirts like hers plodded past her as she aimed for the swirl of altercation.

"I'm sorry, who are you again?" asked someone in an ECHO Op1 suit with a pad in his hand.

"Red Djinni," Red repeated. It was amazing they had found a tee and sweatpants to fit him, but it looked even then like the fabric was strained to the breaking point. It was probably at least the third time he'd said his name, because he was beginning to look annoyed.

"Red Djinni's dead, and you look nothing like him."

Red favored the Op1 with a blank stare. "You know what my powers are, right? Saying I look nothing like him makes about as much sense as saying water doesn't look like ice."

The Op1 flushed, but didn't back down. "Well, yeah ... but c'mon man, you're twice his size. And you're all splotchy in places with rubbery treads, makes you look like you're changing into the Michelin Man."

"Bibendum," Red replied.

"What?"

"It's not the Michelin Man. It's Bibendum. Use his damn name, all right? And use mine. Red. Djinni. With a 'D', not a 'G.'"

"Eight, you'd better rescue him with some new records," Vickie muttered. "Look in your list," she called out. "Don't just assume you know something."

The Op1 turned to scowl at her, probably happy to deal with someone that wasn't able to loom over him. "And who the hell are you?" he asked.

She gave him the patented glare copied from her mother that had been cooling hotter jets than his since she was in high school. "Victoria Victrix. Overwatch, to you."

"New records inserted under 'Red Djinni II, Vickie," Eight said.

"FFS. Really?" Vickie muttered. "That's what you came up with?"

"*I'm rather handicapped by the fact he's been insisting he's Red Djinni, you know.*" Meanwhile, the Op1 had snapped his mouth shut, and was looking a bit ... sick. And hastily paging through the screens on his pad.

"It says here—" the Op1 stared at his screen, "—that you have chameleon powers." He glanced up at Red's massive body, his gaze running along the jagged and broken outcroppings of rubber that seemed to erupt from Red's skin. "Were you imitating a tire fire?"

"Something like that," Red muttered. "So, we done here, or do you need a demonstration of my powers? I've got some nifty claws. They can tear through flesh and bone. Wanna see?"

The sound of rotors nearby made her look aside for a moment. A chopper was setting down near the decontamination tents. Which seemed ... odd ... until Vickie recognized the lack-of-markings as being the hallmark of a Federal covert-ops bird. "*Vickie, your father has sent rescue of a sort ...*" Eight murmured, just as the pilot leaned out of the open door and shouted—with a bullhorn—"**Victrix and Djinni. On board now!**"

Vickie took advantage of everyone being startled and trotted wearily to Red's side, grabbing his elbow—which was all she could reach—and tugging. "Hurry up, our ride's here."

Red nodded with a grunt and elbowed his way past the Op1, knocking him roughly to the ground. "Don't have to tell me twice," he muttered. "Get me out of this freakshow."

After that, of course it was impossible to speak in the over-crowded chopper. The pilot didn't seem interested in saying anything more now that he'd made his pickup, and Vickie was happy just to curl into whatever space there was and half doze for the long trip back to land. Red took up most of the passenger compartment behind the pilot, and didn't even try to talk. Possibly he was getting his temper back under control. He should have been even more exhausted than she was, but his ability to bounce back now was off the charts ... so it probably wasn't that. Part of her wished she knew what he was thinking.

Most of her didn't care. They'd won, and they were together, at last, and that was all that mattered in the long or short run.

The chopper set down within a few yards of a sleek, white business jet. Vickie woke from her drowse as the skids touched the asphalt of the airport apron and recognized it immediately. "Eight, that's the Fibby jet, isn't it?" she asked, as Red sort of oozed his way out of the chopper.

"It is. Your father ... borrowed it."

"... oh boy ..."

By that point Red had cleared the chopper; she groaned as her muscles protested moving again, but hopped out beside his crouching figure and pointed at the jet. "That's our next ride!" she shouted, and left him no choice but to follow as she sprinted for it and jumped up the steps into the cabin. That was where she ran right into her father, who squeezed her tight enough to leave her breathless. He shoved her towards the back of the cabin, following her so Red could manage to wedge himself inside.

"Get strapped in quick, we're out of here in five minutes!" Alexander Nagy called over his shoulder, picking one of the conference chairs and making an example of himself. Vickie took the far end of the sofa, figuring Red could probably fit on that. The hatch had already been closed from outside and they were rolling.

"All this bulk is awkward, isn't it?" Red muttered, easing himself onto the sofa. "I've been looking for a place to shed all of this, but don't really feel like leaving bits of myself to rot in the hot sun."

"Not to mention leaving bits of yourself a sorcerer could use lying around is a bad idea." Alex stretched his hand out across the aisle as much as he could given he was strapped in. "Alexander Nagy, FBI Metahuman, Division 39."

"Djinni comma Red." Red took Alexander's hand gently and shook it. "Thanks for getting us out of there, didn't really feel like getting interrogated. Maybe after I lose about two hundred pounds and sleep for a week." Red paused, and gave Alexander a strange look. "What would a sorcerer want with rotting Djinni flesh?"

"Blessings and curses and ever-filled purses. More likely the curses than the blessings," Alex replied, before Vickie could say anything. "On you. Magicians are rightfully more than paranoid about leaving bits of themselves around for that reason. I'm Vickie's father, by the way."

"Oh, joy," Red replied, and looked down at himself. "Well, I wish I could say this is the worst first impression I've ever made, but I'd be lying."

"Pfft." Alex waved that away. "I gave my prospective in-laws Irish Water Dog fleas. Top that." He sucked on his lower lip a moment, and looked astonishingly like a male version of Vickie for an instant. "To be fair, I'd been staking out a property with a poorly-run kennel for a week and hadn't had time for a flea bath. And Moira thought surprising me with her parents was a good idea...."

As Red blinked for a moment at what seemed to be a non sequitur, Vickie added helpfully, "Dad's a werewolf. Division 39 is the only—" she yawned hugely "—magic based—division in the Feds ..."

Alex made a face, as Vickie felt herself fading out, her head resting against Red's side. "Class is having an FBI division of your own. Crass is when it's only three people," she heard him say, and then exhaustion took over, and that was that.

△

"Rockabye baby," Alex said fondly, with a glance at his daughter. "Give me a second, will you, Djinni? I need to file the paperwork for borrowing the jet before anyone notices I borrowed the jet." He turned and opened a laptop as the jet suddenly accelerated down the runway and shot up into the sky at what felt like an illegally steep angle.

"Uh, yeah, sure," Red said, watching Alex intently, and allowed himself to pat Vickie gently on her head once her father's back was turned. *Oh boy. Meet The Parents. So which version am I getting? "Break her heart and I'll break your spine?" "When are you popping the question?" "Get out of my baby's life, you hideous criminal bastard?"* He thought about that for a moment. The FBI probably had one helluva file on him. On the other hand, Alex had shown no sign of antagonism. And if Vickie was anything like him, Alex Nagy had to know that forcing his daughter to choose between Red and her parents would not end well.

This might not be a disaster. Did he dare to hope the incredible string of luck that had followed him since Vickie had discovered him back on the ship had not yet run out?

After a moment, Alex turned back, and Red had resumed his uneasy position of gently supporting Vickie while appearing aloof.

"Nice jet," Red offered, lamely.

Alex's eyes crinkled at the corners as he smiled slightly. "Usually gets used by the upper-ups. Don't believe everything you see on Criminal Minds; usually us working stiffs don't get this kind of treatment unless you can't get there in coach in time. But hey —it was sitting on the tarmac while all the VIPS were evaccing to bunkers, and by the time they decide it's safe to crawl back out of the bunkers, it'll be back in place in the hangar." The very blue eyes leveled on him got a steely glint. "So ... what are you to my daughter, and what's she to you? Inquiring minds want to know, so let's put our cards on the table, shall we?"

Red stared at Alex for a moment, and then smirked. "It turns out she's the love of my life," he said. "And I'm hers. You might want to keep that on the down-low, though. It's new to us, too."

Alex grinned, the smile reaching to his blue eyes and warming them. *"Fantasztikus,"* he said. "And if you're expecting the *you break her heart and I'll break your face* speech, forget it. You're both adults. Just, whatever shakes out, try to stay friends regardless. It's easier and more civilized that way—and a helluva lot safer when you're dealing with magicians." He paused for a moment. "Don't think I'm expecting you to be a prince or her to be a princess. I'm married to an Irish redhead, so screaming fights are par for the course. Just be glad my girl has my temper, not her mother's."

Red decided to be cautiously optimistic. *Seems like the man's a reasonable sort.*

"Wouldn't be right if we didn't fight," Red shrugged. "It's sort of our thing, you understand."

"Okay. You laid out your cards, so here's mine. I intercepted you in part because Division 39 has a proposition for you. You don't have to take it right now, but ... there's an asshat named Jensen with a bullet with your name on it, and you still have outstanding charges over your head. If he can connect the old you with the new you ..." Alex raised an eyebrow. "But if you're an FBI asset, he can't touch you. The problem is, being an asset comes with about a truckload of baggage. Still. We could certainly use someone who can look like anyone at all playing on our team. Especially someone that can survive the way you seem to be able to. You don't have to decide now. You don't have to decide ever, if things roll your way. But if they don't ... we're here. I'd rather the love of my baby's life didn't get hauled away to get turned into a one-man kamikaze squad."

Unexpected, this is. "Well, I do appreciate the offer," Red nodded. "Haven't had much chance to talk it over with the lady here, what with that whole fighting for all humanity thing we just wrapped up, but I think I might be leaning towards laying low for a while." He paused, his eyes weary as he met Alex's concerned look with one of exhaustion. "Bad things happen when I join organizations, man. It might be better if I just ... went away."

Alex made a wry face. "Good luck with that in the long run; I think you'll find the world doesn't let people like us do that. In the short run, though, well, we've got that going away part covered, I think. I hope you'll approve of what Moira arranged.

Vickie ever talk about her school? St. Rhiannon, not Merlin College. We're going to drop you two at the private airport where you'll be met by the school transport, and you two can lie as low there as you like for as long as you can stand it."

"You're sending us to a school."

"Yes."

"A magic school."

"Yes."

Red stifled the laugh that erupted from his chest. He didn't want to wake up Vickie.

"That's just perfect," he muttered. "I'm just starting to get comfortable around magic, so what happens? I get sent to a place that's just dripping with it ..."

"They have Netflix." Alex smirked.

"So do motels in the bowels of the Philippines ..."

"And they literally cannot be found. Magic version of what our space-Nazi buddies had." Alex put his hands behind his head, as if he was already confident Red was going to cave. "Put it this way. Where else are you going to find someone to teach you how to keep most of the magic cooties off of you?"

Red considered that and looked down at Vickie, who had begun to softly snore. "That place is like a home to her, isn't it?"

"We had to move a lot; comes with the job. It was the one stable thing in her life, besides her mom, Raven, and me." Alex sighed. "She's friends with a lot of the faculty and staff. So ... yeah. Home, comfort, protection, stability. After what Bela Nagy did to her, St. Rhia's was about the only place where she had friends until you folks in ECHO started to draw her out."

"I suppose I should make nice then," Red mused. "For Vickie."

"That would be a start," Alex chuckled. "Seems like both you kids could use some rest after all you've been through. I would start by trying to show a little respect to the Headmistresses, start soft and ease into their confidence. Sofia Knightly's a stiff-upper-lip Brit. Prudence Trevalen is a New Yawker, and pretty much exactly what you'd expect. Both of them will likely give you the hairy eyeball, given how attached they've become to Vickie. It won't just be about her, though. They're also going to be concerned about letting a giant magic monster inside their domain."

"Magic monster?"

Alex sighed. "Red, you are what we call in the arcane world something like a ..."

"Conundrum wrapped in a puzzle served on a bed of lettuce? International man of mystery?"

"... unidentified abomination," Alex finished. "It's not meant to be offensive, it's just that you're something of an enigma. Even if you put aside your metapowers, which seem to have taken on a whole new level of scary, what you and Vickie just pulled off did not go unnoticed by those of us who operate on a different plane of energy. You couldn't have known it, but some of them were lending Vickie their power through that whole ordeal, and to some extent they were connected to you as well, as Vickie's medium. From what I can tell, they've never come across anything like you, and while none of them will admit it, I think they're terrified of you. However you've managed to keep this secret over the years, that's over. A lot of newly interested parties are going to want a piece of you, and you're about to be targeted by a lot of new enemies that you couldn't even dream of. And the headmistresses are about to let you walk through their gates and grant you asylum. I think it's safe to say that even the staff are not all in agreement about this."

Red felt a tingle of alarm. "How do you know about all this already ...?"

"It's my job to stay on top of things," Alex said. "Why do you think I'm here? There is nothing I will not do for my daughter, but I'll admit my interest in you is something more than that. You just slammed into our world like a tactical nuke, and I think it's in everyone's best interest to get you squared away some-where that's safe, protected, and ..."

"... under observation?" Red offered, shaking his head.

"Yes," Alex admitted. "To have you roaming around in the open right now would be ... bad. At St. Rhia's you will be segregated, but also invisible. In four hundred years, no one has broken the shield around St. Rhia's or Merlin College, despite generations of magician-children running in and out of both places. This is where we keep the beings most precious to us until they can protect themselves."

"Out of one jail, and into another," Red muttered. He looked down again at Vickie and gently stroked her hair. "So much for touring the back alleys of Bangkok."

"We'll be landing soon," Alex said. "You can run as soon as the door of the plane is open. I can't stop you, you know I can't. Vickie won't hold it against you; might even agree with you." Alex shrugged. "Given you're in love, she'll probably run with you. It's a tough choice, but it is a choice. So is it really a jail? Or is it sanctuary? Or a little of both?"

"It's always a jail," Red muttered, cursing. "Always."

"So what's it going to be, Red?" Alex asked, quietly.

Red didn't answer.

△

Vickie woke up as the jet landed—it was a little spooky actually. One minute she was sound asleep. Then within the space of a few seconds she went from asleep to wide awake, without moving, without even opening her eyes. Red only knew she was awake because of his spatial awareness; there were tiny tells, muscles suddenly tensing, then relaxing, breathing changing ever so slightly. Then she opened her eyes and was completely there again, no yawning, no confusion.

The jet rolled to a quick stop, and Alex waved them out. Red went first, but he sensed Vickie stopping for a hug and a goodbye kiss with her father before following him out onto the tarmac. She gave him a little shove from behind, and he took the hint and trotted further off the runway, as the door to the jet closed, the jet pivoted in place, the engines screamed up in pitch, and the plane started rolling. It couldn't have been more than five minutes before it was disappearing into the sky. *Huh. I guess Nagy's not one for long goodbyes.*

He turned back to peer in the direction Vickie was looking. After a moment his vision sharpened as if he was looking through binoculars, and he made out a 1960s-era khaki-colored Land Rover approaching the unattended, deserted runway, just passing by a couple of lonely little Quonset-style hangers at the edge. The runway itself was surrounded by what looked like virgin forest.

Now would be the time to run. Now would be the time to grab her hand, say "We've got to get out of here," and take off. *They can't follow us into the woods in that thing. We could be miles away by nightfall.*

But he felt her small, calloused, slightly scarred hand reach for his; looked down to see her looking soberly up at him, and ... couldn't even suggest it. This was home to her. How could he take that from her?

Then she whispered something that made the tight bands around his heart ease, just a little. "If you hate this, we're leaving. Even if I have to hack our way out with a butterknife. No one is putting you in a cage again." There was steel in her voice, the same steel that had been there when she'd faced off against Doppelgänger.

So they waited as the Land Rover pulled up beside them, Vickie's bag of chain mail at their feet.

The first person to get out was the driver; by her gray hair she was elderly, but she was no granny—she was a full-on punk, with a Mohawk, half a dozen assorted piercings, a shoulder tattoo of some intricate design he couldn't quite puzzle out, black T-shirt, plaid pants held together with safety pins, heavy leather biker belt, and combat boots. The second was about the same age, but done up as if she was about to start a safari, complete with pith helmet and hair in a tight bun at the nape of her neck.

The punk-granny put her fists on her hips and looked him up and down. The safari-granny crossed her arms over her chest. The punk-granny spoke first.

"My word," she said, in a perfect, upper-class, BBC accent. "You're a bit of a monster, aren't you? How are we going to get you home? You won't fit in the Rover. Can you hold onto the roof rack?"

The safari-granny cackled. "Sure," came an accent that was pure Bronx. "Or we c'n strap 'im t'the hood like a dead deer." She pronounced it "dee-ah."

"Well, ducky," said the punk, tilting her head sideways for a moment. "The real problem is the children, don't you know. Seriously, now, is there ... something we can do about your appearance? I don't think you'd relish the notion of having three-hundred-odd teenagers and pre-teens trying to defend the place against you, and I'm not sure they'd listen to us before they attacked. I understand you don't care for having magic used on you, but would you object to an illusion just to get you in the door and out of sight? Or is there something you can do?"

Red gave both of them a long, speculative look. He opened his mouth a couple of times, and just as abruptly shut it, biting back a few choice words. Finally, he turned to Vickie, and grimaced.

"Your dad suggested I play nice, so here I am, playing nice. Guess we're about to field test something new. Hang on, don't really know how this is going to work out."

Vickie smiled at him and gave him an encouraging nod. Red reached down and pulled off his shirt, grasping it tightly in one hand as he closed his eyes and muttered a few choice oaths in concentration. He stood in place, his enormous chest heaving as he took a few long, exaggerated breaths. They all watched in fascination as the rubbery flesh covering his arms and legs followed his breathing, expanding with each fierce inhalation and collapsing with every forced exhalation, until he finally snarled and doubled over, crying out with pain.

"Red!" Vickie yelped, instinctively moving to help him, when she was stopped by his outstretched hand, motioning her away. She gasped and stepped back, astonishment painted on her face to see that the oversized rubber mitt she'd been holding onto was now ... a perfectly normal sized, flesh-and-blood hand, connected to a perfectly normal sized, flesh-and-blood Djinni.

Red knelt before them, gasping from the strain of absorbing that much mass back into himself. He took a moment to catch his breath and wearily wrapped the shirt around his face as a makeshift mask. He gingerly came to his feet, and motioned to the grannies.

"Anything else?" he asked.

"Holy crap!" said Bronx, her eyes wide. "That was a helluva show. Y'okay, buddy? Cramps? Nausea? Sofi's got ginger in the glove-box—"

"I'll be fine," Red answered. "About all I need right now is a bed. And a week in it."

"Don't embarrass the man, Pru," Sofi chided gently. "We haven't been properly introduced after all, so let me rectify this." She held out her hand for him to shake. "I'm Sofi. My partner is Pru. I can't say yet if we're all friends here as yet, but we're certainly all adults, so do feel free to use our nicknames."

"Name's Red," the Djinni offered, taking Sofi's hand and shaking it warmly. "I'm told I have you two to thank for offering us a bit of sanctuary."

Pru brayed a laugh. "Buddy, you just got done savin' the world. Least we c'n give ya is three hots an' a cot. Shorty there vouches for ya. That's good enough for us."

A look of utter relief passed over Vickie's face, and she took a couple steps forward, before Pru closed the distance and enveloped her in a warm hug. Sofi joined them in a three-way, enthusiastic embrace.

"No conditions?" Vickie asked, a little muffled.

Sofi rolled her eyes. "Really, ducky, don't you think we know you after all this? If we put conditions on his staying with us, you two would flee like deer. My only concern on seeing him—excuse me, Red, I shouldn't talk as if you aren't there—on seeing you, Red, was that the children would assume we had sprung one of our surprise defense drills on them. Someone might have gotten hurt." She let go of Pru and Vickie, and curtsied, taking the seams of her plaid pants between thumbs and forefingers. "*Mi casa es su casa.*"

"Much obliged," Red nodded. "Not sure I'm much on just bumming space on your couch. After I wrap my head around all this, maybe we can conjure up something I can do to help out."

"Parkour training," all three of the women chorused. They looked at each other and laughed.

"Flannery's laid up with a back sprain, and he's got nothin' on you in the first place, Red," said Pru. "Yer something of a legend, even here. Hell's Kitchen, right? Not that far from my ol' stompin' grounds."

Vickie rubbed her eyes tiredly. "Well, I'd already figured on tying you guys into the internet. I can make magic analogs to computers for those who can't use them, we can use the old shielded computer lab for kids that can handle tech without it exploding, and I can tie you all into Eight who can tie you into the Web."

Sofi's eyes glistened with a distinctly greedy look. "Done," she replied, and looked back at Red. "Provided you throw in the parkour training."

"My methods might be a bit ... strenuous," Red said with a grimace. "You sure your kids are up for it? I'm not known for coddling my recruits."

"I'll let you and the advanced students decide that for yourselves. They can drop out if they choose." Sofi held up a finger to stop him for a moment. "Bear in mind that our advanced students are doing live-steel and live-fire exercises. Like Vickie did. Vickie dear, this invitation is *come and go and look and know.*"

"Sure," Red nodded. "Listen, can you give me and Vix here a minute to talk?"

"Of course, ducks. Come along, Pru." Sofi gestured to her partner and they both walked back to the Rover, out of earshot.

"So ..." Red began. "Why do I get the feeling all that parkour stuff is just for my benefit? They'd be just as happy if we sat on our hands and did nothing, wouldn't they?"

"Probably, but if we did, we'd have ... restrictions. By freely offering we get the run of the place, *carte blanche*, and if you decide you actually do want some help with the magical aspects of your ..." she gestured a little helplessly at him. "... power enhancements? Well, you'll get that help, without anyone getting extra curious and snooping without your permission. *Come and go and look and know* is the key phrase for that sort of thing."

"Vickie, it's you ..." Red stumbled over his words, and started again. "I trust you more than anyone. I can believe you believe all this, but come on. No one offers that. You can't expect me to believe that I'm welcome to just come here and walk around freely, without somebody wanting something from me. That's just not how things work. What's their play? What's the sitch?"

She reached for his dangling hand and squeezed it. "I'm your parole, if you want it that way. If anything goes wrong with you, I answer for it. Of course they hope you'll let them poke and prod you. You're something extraordinary. But you don't have to let them. As for you walking around freely, frankly, love, short of you going psycho and trying to bash your way through a litera-ture class, they feel pretty secure about being able to stop you from doing anything to them or the school. Magically speaking, not only are you a toddler in a university, you're also outnum-bered about 400 to one."

"So this is just another jail ..."

"No," Vickie interrupted. "Listen to me, Red, and pay very close attention. You might not be used to the idea, but there are a few places in this world that are about helping others, about seeing what good can come from the most unexpected of people.

This is one of them. They want to help you. Now, it's not perfect. Not everybody gets along like it's a Quaker lovefest. It's a high school, when it comes down to it. There are cliques and jocks and mean girls and all the freaking draaaaamaaaa that comes with teenagers and hormones, there are teachers who don't care for each other or for Pru and Sofi, but everyone who works here buys wholly and completely into the mantra of *with great power comes great responsibility*. I think this is what we need right now, and if I had to guess, your real problem with this place is that you've never been anywhere like it."

"You mean a place of concentrated, terrifying magic?"

"No. I mean a place that's ready to accept you for ... you. No hidden agendas, no conditions. Just people ready to accept you as you are, their only agenda to help you find your place in this world."

Red stared at her, and began to look away when he felt her hand firmly grasp his chin. She pulled his head down and forced him to look her in the eyes.

"Give it a chance?" she whispered. "Just a chance. Trust me, I think this is right for us."

"I trust you," he said, immediately. "Of course I trust you." He glanced up, to see Pru and Sofi playing cat's cradle with a piece of string, making impossibly intricate figures, and chuckled. Reaching down, he took Vickie's hand and led her towards the waiting Headmistresses.

"For us," Red mused.

"Us. I like the sound of that," she sighed with content. "A lot."

ABOUT THE AUTHORS

Cody Martin has also written with Mercedes Lackey on the SERRAted Edge series as well as an original project, *Reboots* and *Reboots: Diabolical Streak*, for Phoenyx Press.

Dennis K. Lee enjoys putting his characters in extreme situations and making them fight each other, revealing the conflicts between reason and the demands of the heart. Dennis enjoys solving puzzles, whether deciphering crosswords, testing hypotheses, or weaving together the threads of an emerging storyline.

Veronica Giguere is a storyteller of the spoken and written word. She narrates across genres, but her favorites are science fiction and fantasy. Her passion for science and innovation shines in her roles as audiobook narrator, science fiction author, podcast producer, and forever-geeky mom. Her success with the Secret World Chronicle podcast novel series provided the initial experience to work with other authors.

Mercedes Lackey published her first book in 1985, and in 1990 she met artist Larry Dixon at a small science fiction convention in Meridian, Mississippi. She has written and published 135 books in many series, including the Secret World Chronicles, Hunter, Valdemar, Elemental Masters, SERRAted Edge, Elvenbane, and Obsidian Mountain series from Hyperion, DAW, Baen, Tor, and many others.

IF YOU LIKED ...

If you liked ECHO One, you might also enjoy:

Selected Stories: Science Fiction, Volume 1
by Kevin J. Anderson

X Marks the Spot
edited by Lisa Mangum

OTHER WORDFIRE PRESS TITLES

Lights in the Deep

by Brad Torgersen

Frank Herbert Unpublished Stories

by Frank Herbert

Our list of other WordFire Press authors and titles is always growing.
To find out more and to see our selection of titles, visit us at:

wordfirepress.com

ADDITIONAL COPYRIGHT INFORMATION